The Sean O'Rourke Series

Book 1

A Killer For The Common Good

by

Michael E. Cook

TELEMACHUS PRESS

Cover art and design by Tad Gallaugher

Published by Telemachus Press, LLC
http://www.telemachuspress.com

Contact the author at cookorourkeseries@gmail.com

ISBN: 978-1-941536-68-1 (eBook)
ISBN: 978-1-941536-69-8 (Paperback)

Version 2014.12.18

10 9 8 7 6 5 4 3 2 1

Table of Contents

INTRODUCTION

Sean O'Rourke, son of Irish immigrants, experiences the hardships of early pioneer life in the rapidly growing United States of America. Fortunately his father taught him several life skills at an early age—many of those help him out during his life.

Book 1 of the Sean O'Rourke series follows Sean through his early life. First, his young years in Tennessee before the Civil War. Then his life with the Cheyenne, after his small wagon train is massacred by white outlaws. It was a good life until the cholera came. Our young hero joins the Union Army and becomes a friend and aide to General William Tecumseh Sherman. His Irish friend, Michael, and he are always toasting, "to not getting killed", and plan to have a saloon after the war. Our hero learns the saloon business at one of the most prosperous saloons in St. Louis, and then becomes what he is really destined to be. A Federal Marshal, a killer of bad men, "A Killer for the Common Good."

A WORD FROM THE AUTHOR

This book is not based on any factual happenings whatsoever. It was written to be entertaining. If some words offend certain people, that was certainly not my intention. I tried to write it the way people actually might have talked. I may have made one mistake. I did not use the word "ain't." I do not use that word and I do not even like the sound of it. This is not Shakespeare. It's a Western. Do not judge this book as if it was written for an advanced composition class.

My goal was to write this book, which I have done.

I sincerely hope you enjoy reading this book. I greatly enjoyed writing it.

Thank you,
Mike Cook

The Sean O'Rourke Series

Book 1

A Killer For The Common Good

CHAPTER ONE

In 1854, Sean Michael O'Rourke was 11 years old. He was the son of Irish immigrants John and Margaret O'Rourke. They lived on a three hundred acre farm in central Tennessee near the small town of Higby, which was around one hundred miles north of Chattanooga. Here they raised mostly tobacco and corn, but his father's main business was that of blacksmith and horse trainer. John truly loved horses. He was always telling Sean, "Take care of your horses and they'll take care of you. Mistreat them, and one day you'll get what you deserve."

They had left Ireland before Sean was born. John had been a blacksmith at a coal mine, and the mine owner was some nasty English Lord, or at least thought he was. He treated all the Irish as though they were the lowest form of human possible. Most of the workers lived in a company town with the company store and they were charged too much for rent, and whatever they needed from the company store. Each little shack had a very small plot where they could have a small garden for a few vegetables.

John had it better than most of the workers since he didn't have to go into the mine, and he was such a good smithy, that he was able to earn extra money on the side. He did not like it at the mine and was always talking about going somewhere else and starting over.

One summer day, John came home from work and found Margaret crying hysterically. After a few minutes he finally got her calmed down enough to see what the problem was. "John, oh John," she cried, "I was out hanging the clothes when that despicable mine owner came riding by. He stopped and just sat there on his horse staring at me. I think he was drunk. When he didn't stop after a few minutes, I asked him what he wanted."

"I want you wench," he said, "I'm going to bed you and plant my seed in you. This may be Ireland, but I own this place, and I am your Lord. I intend to breed the Irish out one at a time starting with you."

Margaret was still crying, but she went on with her story. "Then he got off his horse and started after me. I ran into the front door and grabbed my heavy broom, came back out, and hit him upside the head and knocked him down. While he was down, I kicked him in his privates. Then I ran back inside and bolted the door. I kind of lost track of time, but when I looked back outside, he was gone. John, what are we going to do? I never have heard anyone talk like that. That pop and jay will say that I attacked him."

"Don't worry," John said, "I will take care of his mighty majesty. While I'm gone, you start packing. We don't have much so it won't take long. We'll be leaving when I get back."

"You're not going to kill him, are you John?" she asked.

"No," John said, "but when I get done with that poor excuse for a man, he will need plenty of time to heal, and he won't be able to talk very well for quite a while."

His Lordship lived in a huge mansion about a mile away. John took off at a gallop on a horse that he had brought home to be shod. When he got there, he ran up to the front door and kicked it in. As he started in the door he heard someone yell, "What the bloody hell was that?"

He spotted his Lordship sitting in a fancy chair smoking a pipe. He was a tall man, maybe thirty, of slender build, but had probably never worked a day in his life. John was just under six feet, twenty-four, maybe one hundred seventy pounds, but was strong as an ox. Being a blacksmith for the last eight years had made him that way.

Before the man could get a word out of his mouth, John ran over and threw him out of his chair. Before he could get up, John was on him. He started with his face, and beat him till it was a bloody mess. Then he went to work on his body. After he was done there, he stomped his right arm. When he was done, his Lordship had his jaw broken in two places, several busted ribs, and a broken right arm. Sometime during the beating, two servants had tried to pull John away from their boss, but they were knocked cold. During the beating, John had not said one word, or had allowed his Lordship to say a word.

When John decided the beating was done, he tried to think of something to say, but then decided that the beating had said enough. As he was nearing the door about to leave, he thought about giving him one more punch, but then decided his knuckles were banged up enough and he shouldn't risk breaking a hand when the job had been done.

When he arrived back home, he told Margaret, "Come on, we're going to America. Any country that has thrown out the British should be a good place to start a new life."

They were very lucky. When they got to the port, a ship was about to leave and was headed for America. They were short help and John agreed to help out on the ship where ever needed, so they only had to come up with the fare for Margaret. They were out of the country before any type of law knew they were gone.

Sean didn't know how his parents came to be in Tennessee, but he knew how his father had acquired his land. Their property was bordered on two sides by one of the largest plantations in the state. It was owned by a man named George Anderson. Sean didn't know how it came about, but there was a wager about a horse being trained and shod and some small tract of land.

George Anderson had this three-year-old stallion that no one could get near. The horse was chestnut, well over sixteen hands, and was half thoroughbred and half Tennessee Walker. He came from a great blood line, but something or someone had made him mean. All attempts to gentle him had failed, but George did not want to give up on him. When he heard that a new man had come to the area looking for work and a place to start his business, which was blacksmithing and horse training, he paid him a call. George like what he saw in John, and John was confident in his ability, so the wager was made. John had one week to break the stallion and get him shod. If he succeeded, he would acquire the three hundred acres tract that John now owns, plus the slave family that lives on, and works the farm. If John would lose, he would have to work on the Anderson plantation for two years.

Sean never knew how his father did it, but the stallion was broken in three days and shod in four. He kept the horse for the remaining time of the wager, and on the last day, he rode him over to the Anderson plantation. George was totally surprised. "How in the hell did you do that?" he asked. "No one has ever had any luck whatsoever. They have either been stomped, had the crap bitten out of them, or just couldn't even catch him."

John just sat there on the horse and said, "George, this is what I do for a living. I can't be telling people how I do things if I want to build my business." Then he got off the stallion and handed George the reins and said, "You will honor our wager, won't you sir?"

"Oh hell yes," George said. "I have very high hopes for this stallion. Really good horse flesh will bring in lots of money down the road."

"Well you need to know a few things before I leave," John said. First, stay out of his mouth and he doesn't need much bit. A straight bit will do. Second, do not ever use spurs on him. Third, don't ever use a whip on him. He's a good horse and he doesn't need to be beaten to get the job done. If you forget what I've said here and do what I've told you not to do, you will undo all that I have done. Now, before I leave, maybe you'd better take a ride and see how he feels to you. Rub his neck real gentle like and whisper something nice in his ear. Don't matter what, just so it's easy like."

George did as he was told, and mounted the big chestnut. He was amazed. The horse stood perfectly still. Then he gently nudged him with his legs and the horse took off at a slow walk.

Then John said, "Now just talk to him. Tell him what you want and he'll do it."

George was still in disbelief. He was giving the horse verbal commands and the horse was obeying. If he used his legs, the horse obeyed.

"Mr. O'Rourke," he said. "You have my sincere gratitude. I will tell everyone I know about your great skill and I wish you a good first crop on your new land."

~~~~

The slave who lived on the property was a big man, tall, and had scars on his back where he had been whipped by one of his masters before he came here. The name given him by his first master was Jim. His wife's name was Betsy and they had a two-year-old son they called Little Jim. Later on, Sean and Little Jim would become best friends.

When the O'Rourke's first arrived at the new place, John went directly to Jim's shack and introduced himself and Margaret. "Hello, we're the O'Rourke's. I'm John, and this is Margaret." He offered Jim his hand.

Jim wasn't sure what to do since slaves didn't shake hands, but he offered his hand and gave as good a handshake as he knew how.

"How do," said Jim. "They call me Jim, and this here's Betsy, and the young'un we call Little Jim. So you the new Massuh?"

"Jim," John started. "I am not a Massuh. I do not believe in slavery. I will never be owned, nor will I ever own another human being. We were not much more than slaves ourselves in Ireland. That's one of the reasons we left there. As of right now, you and your family are free. I will get any necessary papers."

Jim had no idea what to think. He had been born a slave and knew nothing else. "So what this freedom mean, Massuh?" he asked.

"Stop right there Jim," John said. "My name is John, it's not *Massuh*. Freedom means you can leave here any time, go anywhere, and do whatever you want. Although I doubt it'll be that easy for you, so I have a proposition for you."

"A propo-what?" asked Jim.

"A proposition, Jim," John said. "It's like making a deal. This is what I would like. You and your family stay here and work the farm. You teach me all you know about tobacco and corn and such, and I'll teach you about blacksmithing and horse training. When we get to where we're making money, I'll pay you a decent wage. This may take some time, but I believe we'll make it. Do we have a deal, Jim?"

"Yes suh, mas—, I mean John. We does." Then he wasn't sure, but it seemed like a good idea to offer his hand to John. It was accepted.

"Alright Jim," John said. "Now would you please help us unload the wagon so we can get set for the night. Tomorrow I'll go into town and start getting some lumber so we can get started building the house. When we get done with the house, we can fix up your shack."

They had the new house livable the first month they were there. All that was left to finish was the inside walls. Before this month was half over, people were stopping by asking John when he could start training a horse or do some smithing. Apparently, George Anderson had put the word out about John's skills.

One day right before the house was finished, George stopped by riding his stallion. "I see things are moving along John. I hope your first crop will do as well," he said.

"Thanks," John said. "I see that stallion of yours still looks mighty good."

"Yes, he's as gentle as a lamb for me," George said. "I let that bull-headed son of mine ride him last week. Told 'em up front what not to do, so what's the first thing he does? He puts on his spurs, then gives him a kick. I've never seen anyone thrown that far into the air before in my life. After he gets up, he took after him with a whip. Well that was a bad mistake, cause that's when Charlie took after him. Oh, I guess I never told you I named him Charlie. Anyway, if I hadn't been there, Charlie would have busted him up something awful, or even killed him. He wanted to shoot him right then and there, but I told him if he did, he would never have the plantation when I'm gone. Told him it was his fault for not listening to me in the first place. Course he didn't want to hear that. We've grown apart ever since my wife died about ten years ago. We're always too busy for each other. He likes being the overseer and I'm always tied up with the business stuff. I think he's too harsh with the darkies, but I stay out of his way unless I see a bad problem. Sorry, I didn't mean to ramble on about my problems."

"Well George," John said. "I'm sorry to hear about your son getting thrown, but I've got something to tell you that I don't know if you or folks here will like."

"O.K. John, what is it?" George asked.

"I gave Jim and his family their freedom," John said. "They're working on the place for wages."

"John," George started, "I was born right here on this planta-tion. My family has always had slaves. I have never known any other way of life. Over the years we have fought off the British, the Shawnee, and the Cherokee. The slaves we had fought right along with us. We have always treated our slaves well and never broken apart their families. But I have learned over the years that sooner or later, slavery will be less and less profitable. Good slaves are expensive. If you have a bumper crop, you need more slaves to get it harvested. If you have drought, sometimes you sell slaves so you can keep your head above water. Business keeps changing, always more and more and more. I always thought that one day I would free my slaves, but now I'm old and my son can't wait to take over. I'm glad you freed Jim. He was a good worker before, but I'm sure he'll be even better now that he's getting wages. But John, you mark my word. There's a war coming. It might not happen in my lifetime, but I believe you will be right in the thick of it. There are' a lot of radicals down South, especially over in South Carolina, always complaining about state's rights and such. Plus there's that new abolitionist movement started up North. Like I said, this war won't be in my lifetime, but some of these expansion people are trying to start a war with Mexico. Why, I don't know. The Texans took Texas from the Mexicans. The Mexicans took it from the Spanish, and the Spanish took if from the Indians. I guess some people want Texas to be part of the United States, plus they want to grab California and whatever else they can grab. Some of those people down in Texas already have slaves, so that'll be one more state to yell about state's rights. Hey, I'm sorry John, I got to rambling again. I hate politics— always did."

"That's O.K. George," said John, "A man needs to let out some steam once in a while. I know two things though. I have nothing against Mexico, so if that war comes, I will not be in it. If we get into a war right here, I'll be heading west. Where, I won't care. Just so my family is away from it."

CHAPTER TWO

Sean Michael O'Rourke was born almost exactly nine months after the house was finished. Betsy helped with the birth and there were no problems, so Sean was a good healthy boy. The first few years were just typical years for a young boy, but by the time Sean was six years old, he was already helping John with the horses. By the time he was ten, he could shoe about any horse around, except for a team of huge Percherons that was owned by a freight company in town. They were good workers, but they were lazy when it came to getting shod. Once you picked up a hoof, it belonged to you. They would not hold it up for you. Sean could get it done, but it took him way too long, so his father usually took care of them when they were there. The freight company was always in a hurry anyway.

John started teaching Sean how to fight when he was only five years old. He told him that he wanted him to be able to protect himself before he started school. The instructions were not on a regular schedule because of the work on the farm and the smithing, but whenever they had time, they had a lesson.

John always said, "There is no such thing as a fair fight. That's for those fools who beat each other senseless in the ring. If a man wants to fight you, he wants to hurt you, so you need to hurt him first. And when you get a man down, keep him down. There's other weapons on your body besides your fists. You have elbows, knees, feet, and your head. I don't mean just using your head to fight smart. I mean using it for a good head butt if the need would arise. A good head butt can break a nose easily." So over the years, Sean learned to be a very good fighter.

Sean didn't have many friends his age. Probably because of where they lived, and because he was always helping with the work. Although almost three years older, He and Little Jim became best friends. They did everything together, working in the fields, working with the horses. Sometimes they could sneak off and go fishing or squirrel hunting. But there was one thing they could not do together. Little Jim was not allowed to go to school.

School didn't start out being a bad place. They had a good schoolmarm and she really enjoyed the children. But after four years, she got herself married and left the area. The next teacher was a bitter man, maybe forty years old, and was more concerned about how many switches he could wear out in a day, than he was about teaching anything. The least little infraction, and out came the switches. It didn't matter if it was a boy or a girl.

Sean's first experience with the switches happened when he ten years old. All the children were outside for a recess when Sean saw this older boy punching the heck out of some girl. He went over and grabbed the older and bigger boy off the girl and asked him to leave her alone. Sean didn't know it at the time, but the boy was George Anderson III, and the girl was his younger sister Sarah.

"Just who do you think you are, you little bastard?" George asked.

"Name's Sean O'Rourke," Sean said, "and I asked you real nice like to leave the girl alone, and now I'm asking you nicely not to bad mouth me."

"Why you little shit," George said. "I'm gonna beat the hell outta you."

Before George could say or do anything, Sean was on him. First a left to the belly that doubled him over, and then an uppercut that caught his chin and put him flat on his back. Sean stood over him ready to inflict more pain, when the teacher came running out and grabbed him. He took Sean inside and wore out two switches on his backside. "You little trouble maker," he said. "I'll teach you to make trouble at my school. Now you go over to that corner and stand there the rest of the day." Sean was glad he didn't have to sit the rest of the day.

Finally, the school day was over. On the way out the door, George got up beside Sean and said, "Hope it hurts like hell. I will get even with you one day, you bastard."

"Wrong thing to say," Sean said, and he tore into George again. First a right to the jaw, then a left to the gut. Then when he was bent over, a knee came up and blood from his nose was going everywhere. About that time, the teacher came running after Sean. Sean turned to face him and when he was close enough, Sean kicked him square in the privates. The teacher went down hard. When Sean saw that the teacher wasn't getting up anytime soon, he went back over to George and said. "Look you stupid fool. You'd better learn how to fight or just plain leave me alone, and if I ever see you hitting that girl again, I'll teach you some more manners."

Sean didn't know it at the time, but he had made an enemy for life. He had also made a good friend out of Sarah. It seems that her brother was always giving her a hard time.

Sean and all the children went home leaving the teacher still there lying on the ground.

When Sean came home, John could see that he wasn't moving too well, and asked him what had happened. Sean gave him the whole story, and then he showed John the welts on his backside. John was plainly upset. "I'll be going to school early in the morning and have some words with that teacher," he said.

After dinner that evening, they had a visitor. It was George Anderson II. Sean wasn't sure he wanted to hear this conversation, so he stayed in the house while his father and George talked.

George dismounted and walked up to John offering his hand. John offered his back. "Names' Anderson, George Anderson. You know my father. I understand that your boy gave my boy a whoop'n today," he said.

"I'm John O'Rourke, and yes, my son told me about what happened today," John said.

"Well," George said, "I'm not here to give you trouble because your boy whooped mine. I was ticked at first, but I got the full story from his sister Sarah. Seems he got what he deserved. As I said, you'll have no trouble from me."

"That's good to know," John said. "There's something else I want you to know before you get it second hand. "I'm going to that school tomorrow and have some words with that teacher. Besides whipping my boy, I hear he's wearing out switches on anyone for just about anything. I can't abide beating children. A little spanking never hurt anyone, but what he did to my son is not tolerable. If I can't straighten him out, I'll throw him out. Just thought you should know since you're a prominent person in this area, and I don't know how you all go about handling a teacher's behavior, or hiring a new teacher."

"John, you have my support," George said. "I heard he was wearing out switches, but I never believed it. I just thought the kids were telling stories. I've been so busy at the plantation, I guess I haven't paid attention to anything else."

"Why not set for a spell, have a drink, relax, and talk some? John asked.

"What have you got to offer?" asked George.

"How about some good Kentucky bourbon?" John asked.

"Bring it on," George said. "That's the nectar of the gods."

They talked till almost dark. John told him about Ireland and how it was over there for him and his family before him. George talked about his family and the plantation. He even told John the story about riding, or trying to ride Charlie. He said at the time he was ticked, but after a few days, he realized that he hadn't listened to his father. "That stallion's gonna bring in a lot of money when we start using him for stud. I hope his offspring look half as good as him," George said. The subject of slavery did not come up.

~~~~

The next morning, John went to the school early as planned. He found the teacher setting at his desk and checking out his switches.

"Name's O'Rourke," John said. "I understand you whipped the daylights outta my boy yesterday. You got a name?"

"Yes, Mr. O'Rourke, my name is Wilson, Brad Wilson, and your son is a trouble maker. I whipped him once yesterday for starting a fight. Then I was going to whip him again when he started another one, but he kicked me in my privates. Mr. O'Rourke, your son will grow up to be a menace to society if he is not controlled now. I fully intend to whip him again today soon as class begins."

"Mr. Wilson," John started, "You're lucky my son only kicked you in your privates. If I had been anywhere near here and knew what was going on, I would have beaten you till you couldn't stand. You sir, are no teacher. You haven't taught a single thing since you've been here but fear. I don't know how you ever got to be a teacher, but if you don't change your ways, your days here are numbered. You have two choices. You can either straighten up and be a real teacher, or you can stay as you are. If you stay as you are, I will physically haul your ass out of here. Do you understand?"

"Now see here, Mr. O'Rourke," Wilson said. "I will not be intimidated by the likes of you. If you think—"

Before he could finish, John had ahold of him and was dragging him out of the door. "Now, Mr. Wilson," John said, "You will get whatever personal property you have, and you will get out of this area as of right now. If I see you around here any time after today. I will hurt you." Mr. Wilson probably never knew he could move that fast, but he was out of John's sight in no time. John waited around the school for awhile for the children to arrive. When they had all arrived, John made an announcement. "Mr. Wilson has decided to move on to bigger and better things. There will be no school until next week. There will be a replacement by then, we hope. Thank you for your attention." The children didn't waste anytime leaving. John was sure their parents would want to know what had happened.

Sean stood there looking at his father. "Well Pa," he said, "I guess you better go to town and find out who's in charge of finding us a teacher."

"Yeh, I reckon I should," John said. "I already have a temporary replacement in mind if no one objects."

"Who might that be, Pa?" Sean asked.

"Well your mother, of course," John answered, "I'm sure she could handle things till a replacement is found. She's good with numbers, reads and writes as well as anyone I know. She doesn't know much about American history, but if it's in a book, she can find out about it. You go on home now and tell your mother what's happened, and I'm going into town and find out who's in charge of this stuff."

John started asking around, and found out that this town actually had a mayor and a city council. He guessed he'd been too busy working to find out about such things. The mayor seemed to be a nice older man, and told John he would round up the council and they would have a meeting the next night. John thanked him and went home.

When he got home, he figured Margaret would be waiting on him with fire in her eyes, but that was not the case. She ran up to him, gave him a very passionate kiss, and said. "I would be very happy to help at the school. I always fancied myself a teacher. Now I will be, if no one objects. There are so many children that can't read or write. They don't know what they're missing. I would even teach some of the parents that want to learn. It'll probably take them who knows how long to find that replacement, so John, if you are serious, and won't miss me during the day, I'm all for it."

"That's great you gorgeous hunk of womanhood," George said, "I have to attend a council meeting tomorrow. You should come also."

"Of course I'll be there," she said, "They need to see who they are getting."

The time came for the meeting. John and Margaret arrived at the General Store which was where the city meetings were held. The Mayor was there with three other men. He introduced himself and the others to John and Margaret. "Glad to meet you," he said, "I'm the Mayor, name's Bill Hanson. The other three are Tom Harper, Sam Jones, and Luke Tilton. Tom runs the General Store. Sam owns a local tavern, and Luke is our town doctor."

"It's nice to finally meet you all," John said. "I'm John O'Rourke and this is my wife Margaret. We haven't been here but a short while, but we like it here and plan to stay as long as we're welcome."

The Mayor started speaking first. "John, we've heard stories about Mr. Wilson, but like most parents, we thought most of the stories were exaggerated. From what you told me, and I've now heard from other children, we needed to get him out of here. How do you councilmen feel about this?"

Luke Tilton, the doctor, spoke first. "I reckon we needed to get rid of that man, but I'd like to see some of Mrs. O'Rourke's skills. Mrs. O'Rourke, would you show us some of your writing, and some work with numbers?"

"I'd be glad to," she said. "Now if you don't mind, I'll do some numbers and some writing on that board where some of the prices are marked down." Margaret proceeded to do several number problems for them, addition, subtraction, and division. Then she started writing several quotes from some Shakespeare plays.

They were amazed. Even John didn't know that Margaret knew Shakespeare.

The Mayor then spoke. "Margaret, do you mind if I call you Margaret?"

"No sir," she said. "That's my name."

"Well Margaret, I believe you have impressed all of us. If it is possible, could you start next week?" he asked.

"Yes Mayor," she said. "I will be glad to start next Monday."

"Wonderful," he said, "We'll pay you fifteen dollars a month till a replacement can be found. I have only one request though. Would it be possible to tone down your Irish accent a little? Most of these kids around here speak with a southern drawl because that's the way most folks talk around here. If you slow down your talking a little, I'm sure they'll understand you all right."

"I will do my best, Mayor," she said. "Anytime a child cannot understand anything at all, I will do whatever it takes so they will understand. Whether it's a lesson, or how I talk."

"John, Margaret," the Mayor said, "Thank you for being here. I hope things work out for the best."

~~~~

Margaret started teaching the next Monday as planned. There were twenty children in the class, from six to twelve years of age. She started out by finding out who in the class could already read. She had the one's who could read, help the one's who couldn't. It worked out very well. It made the more advanced students feel important, like they were actually contributing. There were no discipline problems at all. The children were probably overjoyed to not worry about a good switching every time they did not perform perfectly, but Margaret did let them know that they were there to learn and not play during class time. At first, she was a little worried about having Sean in the class. She didn't want to be accused of playing favorites, or him being the teacher's pet. But that was not the case. Even George Anderson III behaved.

A month came and went, and no replacement was found, so Margaret stayed. Summer vacation was coming in another month, so the Mayor had asked Margaret to stay on until that time. That would give them three months to find a replacement before the next year started.

Summer came and went. John's businesses were booming. His reputation with the horses and smithing had spread. He even had people bringing him horses from as far away as Chattanooga. The corn and tobacco were doing great, thanks to Jim and his family. Sean was getting better and better with the horses too.

September came and there was still no replacement teacher, so Margaret was asked if she would take the position on a permanent basis. She was glad to accept. Sean was now eleven and would be twelve before the end of the term, so after this term, he would be finished with all the schooling he could get in this area. The nearest school for children over twelve years of age was in Chattanooga, so Sean wouldn't be going there. He would be home full time and could spend more time with the horses, smithing, and the crops.

The school year started out well. There were a few new students and they were eager to learn. George Anderson was no longer there, but his sister Sarah had this last year to complete. Now that George wasn't there, she and Sean became very good friends. Sean even put up with a little teasing from the other children about having a girl friend. He didn't mind. He did have a girl friend. She was at an age where she was starting to develop, and Sean wasn't the only one to notice. The other boys noticed, but they knew better than to say anything out of line around Sean, as he would probably beat them senseless. Margaret noticed too, and she was worried that Sean would be distracted from his studies, but this was not the case. He and Sarah both did very well.

Sean spent more and more time with Sarah whenever he could. He was always in a hurry to get his work done so he could be with her. John didn't mind, as long as the work was done. Whenever they were together, taking walks, or even fishing, they made sure they avoided brother George. Sean was not afraid of him at all, but it just kept things uncomplicated if he weren't around.

One evening, in late October, right after Sean had turned twelve, he got his first kiss. He wasn't sure if he did it right, but it sure felt good. He had never had any feeling like that. He couldn't describe it. All he knew then was that he wanted to do it again. Sarah must have felt the same way because she pulled him to her again, and again, and again. "Sean," she said after the fourth kiss, "I don't know how you feel right now, but my body feels like it's on fire. I've never felt anything like this before. How do you feel?"

"I can't really describe it," Sean said. "All I know is that I have never felt anything like this, and I would like to feel like this as much as possible." Then he pulled her to him and kissed her again.

"Do you suppose that after people have been married for a long time," she asked, "that their kisses still feel like that?"

"I sure do hope so." Sean said. "I know I can't wait to find out."

"Well let's kiss a little more, then we better get ourselves home before our parents start worrying." she said.

Letting her go after the last kiss, seemed like one of the hardest things Sean had ever had to do. His mind was going crazy. He made up his mind that when he got home, he was going to set down with his folks, and have a talk about feelings and such.

When Sean got home, John and Margaret didn't need to ask where he'd been. They already knew, but they were quite surprised when Sean wanted to sit down and have a talk with them. "Pa," Sean started, "When you kiss Ma, do you feel strange all over, a really good strange. Something hard to describe—but really good. And do you feel the same way Ma?"

First thing John said was, "Did you get your first kiss today, son?"

"Yes, I did Pa, and it was wonderful." he answered, "And Sarah and I were wondering that after someone has been married for a long time, does it still feel that good?"

John was trying to keep a straight face, as was Margaret. Then he answered.

"Son, your mother and I have been married for fourteen years, and every time I kiss her, I feel like I'm on a cloud and floating through the air and she's there with me and we just can't get enough of each other," John said. "When you truly love someone, that special feeling never goes away."

"Is it the same for you, Ma?" Sean asked.

"Yes it is Sean," she answered. "Your father lights a fire in me that seems to never go out, but you need to understand a lot more about this. You're getting to be a young man now, and you may have several girlfriends before you find the one you want to spend your life with. We are not like most animals. They mate by instinct. Certain times of the year, after the male becomes mature, and the females hit their cycles, the males do what nature

intended them to do. Then they move on to another one and forget about the first one. You know, you've seen what it's like when
we have a stallion here and someone brings over a mare in heat. I
hope you know what I'm trying to say. Loving someone on a full
time basis is more than just moments of passion."

"Yes Ma, I do. I know about sex and what can happen when
things get out of hand. I really was just curious about that special
feeling," Sean said.

"So, young man, are you going to tell me how you know about
sex?" She asked.

"No Ma, I'm not, but don't worry, I haven't done anything
wrong or been anywhere bad," he answered.

"John," she said, "Have you got anything to say here?"

"No, my love. You're doing fine," he answered.

John figured he'd be in the doghouse that night after their
speaking with Sean, but not so. After some very passionate love
making, Margaret looked at him and said, "Our son is growing up.
He is going to be a good man, a good provider, and with his looks,
the women will all love him. He's as good looking as his father."
With that kind of encouragement, they were soon making love
again.

The next morning while Margaret was still fixing breakfast,
John asked Sean to go out to the barn with him. He said he
wanted to show him what needed to be done when he got home
from school that day. When they got out to the barn, John asked
him. "O.K. son, where did you learn about sex? Don't worry, I
won't tell your mother, I promise."

"Well Pa, he said. You know how boys talk. I'm sure you did
when you were a boy. Anyway, I was in town one day when you
sent me in for supplies and I ran into one of the guys from school.

He said, hey come here, got something to show you. We went back behind one of the taverns and we could hear some carryin' on before we got back there. To make this story short, they run a whorehouse behind that tavern, and that one lady likes to leave her windows and her curtains open. Now you promised you wouldn't tell Ma, didn't you?"

"Yeh, I promised." John said. "One day I'll tell you how I learned about sex, but not when you mother is around."

CHAPTER THREE

A change was starting to take place. All anyone ever talked about anymore was slavery. Kansas was already being called "Bloody Kansas" because of all the border raiding that was going on between the gangs from Missouri and Kansas. South Carolina was always banging the drum about state's rights. The abolitionists were always giving fiery speeches. Even the school children wouldn't quit talking about it. It was nigger this, nigger that, or my pa says that nigger so and so, or damn Yankees this or that.

Margaret knew she had her hands full. Most of the children in the area were from families who had never owned a slave, but they had learned from parents and most of the adults they knew, that negroes were an inferior race, and should be treated accordingly. So she tried as best she could, to keep teaching the basics, reading, writing, and arithmetic. Once, she tried to spend a day telling the children about the other races of the world. Most of them already knew about American Indians and were convinced that they hated them, even though they had never known one. Some of them had heard about the Chinese, but who cared about them. They were thousands of miles away. Then she asked them why they thought that some white people hate other white people. She kept trying to make the point that some people are convinced that they hate other people, not because they really hate them, but because they are afraid of them because they are different.

About mid November, Betsy caught pneumonia. Doc Tilton spent a lot of time out there trying to save her. She died before the end of the month. Several people in the area were very upset because their doctor had even treated a darky. They threatened to throw him out of town and find another doctor, but he wouldn't be intimidated. He told them, "I may be a doctor, and I've taken the Hippocratic Oath, but I keep a shotgun in my office and another one at the house, and I know how to use them. Anyone messes with me or one of my patients, will become a patient himself."

John's business started to suffer some about this same time. He knew that some folks didn't like the fact that he had a free Negro working for him, but he didn't care. Jim was a good worker. He took Betsy's death very well, and he and Little Jim worked even harder. Besides, if they ever did decide to move, they had done very well over the years, and money would not be a problem.

Sean spent a little more time with Little Jim after Betsy died just to make sure his friend kept in good spirits, but whenever he got a chance, he was with Sarah. He figured he'd try to be with her as much as possible, because he knew that sooner of later, they would be moving. Of course every time he would mention moving, Sarah would start crying and beg him not to leave. Then she would always ask him if he would come back some day. He always assured her that he would.

One day in early December, John had to go into town and pick up some steel that he had ordered for making horseshoes. There was a good amount and it would be heavy work, so he took

Jim with him. They got the steel loaded, and were on their way out of town, when they were approached by four men who had apparently been in a local tavern.

"Get that nigger of yours outta town, you stupid Mick," he said.

John stopped the wagon right then. He got down from the wagon and got right into the man's face. "You've just given out three insults. First you called Jim a nigger. Second, you said he was my nigger, which means I own him. I do not own him. He's a free man. Third, you called me a stupid Mick. Now does anyone know if Doc Tilton is in town?"

"Why do you want the Doc you stupid Mick?" the man asked.

"Cause I'm going to beat you till you can't stand," John said. Then before the man could open his mouth or do anything, John was on him. A right cross knocked him sideways, then a left hook to the ribs. Then another right and blood came pouring out of his nose. About this time, the other three decided to get involved. John turned and kicked one of them square in his privates. When he went down to his knees, John caught him square on the jaw with a right and he went down and didn't move. Another one tried to grab John from the back, but John put his right elbow into the man's right eye and he fell back. Jim decided it was time for him to get involved. He rushed over to the last man, picked him up clear over his head, and threw him to the ground. All the man could do was lay there and moan. The other two were still standing, so John and Jim were on them. John took the one he started with, and Jim the other one. The man was standing there trying to get his nose to quit bleeding when John put a solid left right into his gut. He doubled over, then went down on his knees. When he was down, another right to the jaw put him down. Jim had ahold of the last man by the front of his shirt and had him up in the air and was shaking him. Then he threw him to the ground and kicked him in the ribs.

About that time, the mayor came running out into the street. "What the hell is goin' on here? This is bad, this is bad," he said. "We don't have a constable in this town, so I reckon it's up to me to find out what the hell is going on."

"We were just teaching some of your citizens some manners," John said, "And if there are any more who would like learn their manners, we'd be glad to help them."

"John," the mayor started, "I reckon I already know what went on here. I think it's best that you stay out of town for a while and let these hot heads cool off. You stay vigilant out there, John. You never know what some of these folks might try, especially after too much whiskey. Sometimes all it takes is one loud mouth to get them stirred up."

"Well Bill," John said, "I don't figure those four are going to cool off. They took a beating today, in their town, and a black man helped beat them. They will not forget it. I'm letting you know Bill, that I'm not a man looking for trouble, but if anyone threatens my family, or my friends, it will cost them dearly. I've never killed anything I wasn't going to eat, but I will protect my family. You understand me, don't you Bill?"

"I surely do John, and I hope it never comes to that, but you're probably right," Bill said, "When Jim got involved, that was just too much for that white trash. You take care out there. If I hear of anything stirring, I'll do my best to get word to you if I can."

"Thanks Bill," John said, "You look out for yourself too. Some of your concerned citizens might not like it that you didn't have

Jim and I lynched on the spot, because you saw a black man beat a white man and let him get away with it. Might not set too well with some folks."

"That's probably true, John," Bill said. "No one knows this, but I keep a derringer in my vest pocket. If need be, I'll use it."

"Do you know these men Bill?" John asked.

"I don't know them by name, but I have seen them from time to time. They come in town about once a month or so, get drunk, and get a woman," Bill said.

"That's good," John said. "It's better that I don't know their names in case I have to shoot them later. Jim, you keep an eye on them while I go to the General Store for a few minutes. If they even look at you cross-eyed, give a yell. I'll be right out."

John found Tom Harper in the store in the back room. "Have you got any shotguns?" John asked.

"Yeh John," he said, "I have two double barrel 10 gauges, and I have something else here that may come in handy. Got it in just yesterday."

"My oh my," John said. "That looks like one piece of killing machine. What is it?"

"This is a Colt Walker," Tom said. ".44 caliber, six shot, and it's the biggest revolver ever made by anyone. Uses half agin as much powder as Colt's other revolvers. Fella was in here yesterday traded it for something smaller. Said it was too much gun for him. Think you can handle this thing?"

"Well, I've never been around hand guns too much, but I know how to handle one," John said. I'll take the Walker, both the shotguns, some 00 buck, pistol balls, and some powder and caps for both."

"Reckon you're gonna be ready for whatever comes up, aren't you John." said Tom.

"Yes I will be, but I hope it doesn't come to that," said John.

Before leaving town, John walked over to the men still lying on the ground and said, "If you come out to my place causing trouble, I'll send you straight to hell where you belong."

~~~~

On the way back to the farm, John and Jim didn't say much. Then John said, "I've got this extra shotgun that I want you to keep near you at all times. Even when you're in the field. Don't be too far from it. Make sure you let Little Jim know what could happen. I don't figure anyone will try anything in the daylight, but you never know."

"I'll be ready as best I can," Jim said. "I've got an old shotgun at the house that George Anderson gave me years ago so I could shoot critters and such when they got into the corn. Ran outta powder and caps years ago, but it looks like you got plenty. This way, Little Jim and me both will be armed."

When they got home, John told Margaret and Sean what had happened in town. Then they all went out side for some shooting lessons. The shotguns were not a problem, but the Walker was a bit much for Margaret, but she did hit what she shot at. Sean was a natural with the Walker, but he needed two hands to hold it up.

"Do you think there will be more trouble, John?" Margaret asked.

"I hope not," he answered, "but I figure there will be. Jim and I gave those boys a good beating. Black folks are not held in high esteem around here. If we do have trouble, I don't know when it will be or how many of them there will be. Could be as early as tonight if those boys can drink up the courage."

Two days came and went with no sign of trouble. Then on the third day, about an hour before sunset, the Mayor came riding out to John's place. "Well John," he started, "they finally got enough whiskey to get their courage up. There's six of them now and they'll pay you a visit around midnight or so from what I overheard. Don't know for sure what guns they all have, but I did see some shotguns. They were mostly saying that they were gonna burn you and Jim out, and then hang both of you. I can stay and help, or I can ride to the county seat and see if I can get the sheriff."

"You go on and see if you can get the sheriff," John said. "If there's only six of them, and they've been drinking, I think we can handle them."

"O.K.," said Bill. "I'll be back as soon as I can." Then he rode off at a gallop.

"Sean," John began, "Go get Jim and Little Jim and bring them to the house. We've got to make plans."

When they arrived back at the house, John told them that tonight was going to be "THE NIGHT." "Now," he started, "We have a few things in our favor. It's a full moon tonight so we should be able to see well. They've been drinking, so they'll be overconfident. This is our place. We know our way around and all the good hiding places. They don't."

"Ya know John," Jim said, "That full moon gonna help them see good too."

"That's true Jim," John answered, "but hopefully, they'll come in on horseback and stand out better. Now, I want everyone to get dressed in some dark clothing. Nothing light that can show in the moon light. We won't be in houses when they get here. We'll be out behind stuff in the shadows."

"Excuse me there John," Jim said, "Won't we be better inside with them house walls for protection?"

"We might be," John answered, "But if they set the houses on fire, we might get burned alive. Jim, this will be my first gun battle. I'm not sure what's best, but I know I'd rather get shot than burned alive. We also want to get the animals out of the barns so we don't have to worry about them. If they get out of the pens, we can round them up later. Now Jim, you and Little Jim go on back to your house and get ready. Get yourself plenty of powder, caps, and buckshot, and any other weapons you have, axes, picks, knives. Just remember, these men will be trying to kill us. You cannot hesitate. When the time comes, make sure the lamps are off in the house, and pick a good spot in the shadows. Know each other's positions. Shoot and move, but move in the shadows. Remember, we're using shotguns. They've got to be close. Who knows, maybe if they come in close together, you can knock down two with one shot. Don't talk and give away your position. And yes, we're all scared. Now go get ready."

Then John sat down with Margaret and Sean and began giving them more instructions. "Sean," he started, "You'll be using the Walker. You got six shots. Don't waste any. They'll need to be close. Aim dead center, right at the breastbone. Get your skinning knife and if you have to use it, go for the gut. You don't want it getting stuck in someone's ribs. Margaret, you and I will both have shotguns. Get your good butcher knife and keep it on you. I'll have an axe and a hatchet with me. Let's all make sure we got plenty of powder, caps, and lead. Hopefully this will be over quickly and we won't need to reload much. Also, if they come in carrying torches, don't look at them. You'll lose your night vision for a few seconds. Sean, you'll be behind that woodpile out front. Margaret, you will be behind the forge, and I will be out front behind the oak trees with the bushes around them."

"John," cried Margaret, "Why has it come to this? I'm afraid for us. I'm not sure I can kill someone."

"Margaret," he started, "I don't want to kill anyone either, but we must do this if we wish to stay alive. I don't know what makes people this way, but people have been killing each other since the beginning. I don't reckon it's going to stop in our lifetime. Now let's get ready. When the time gets closer, we'll make sure the lamps are out, and we'll smear some ash on our faces so they won't shine in the moon light."

About 11:30, John had everyone go out and take their positions. "Remember," he said, "Don't hesitate. These men are trying to kill us. Shoot, and move, and stay in the shadows when you move. I still say they'll be on horseback, so we shouldn't accidentally shoot each other. They'll be easy targets against the moonlight. I figure they'll expect us to be holed up in the houses, and when we open up on them from outside, maybe they'll get scared and run off. Maybe not, might depend on the whiskey. I'll shoot first. Stay low and pick your target. Remember, they gotta be close."

They had all been in their positions for just a short time, when they could hear them coming. Through the trees, they could see the torches they were carrying. John started counting, "Two, three, four, five, six, more than six. There's eight of them," he said to himself. He didn't want to risk being seen in the moon light so he stayed put and waited on them to start down his lane toward the house. He heard one of them yell. "You go fire up the barn, and you go fire up the house. I'm goin' back and get that nigger,"

John stayed low and when they were about twenty feet away, he cut loose with the shotgun. First one barrel, and the other. Two men hit the ground dead. The rest of them were totally surprised, but did not run off. They took out shotguns and started firing blindly. Then they got out their pistols and started firing. Two of them charged the house. They were about fifteen feet from Sean when they neared the woodpile where he was hiding. He took aim and squeezed. One of the men went flying backwards out of the saddle. The other one started firing into the woodpile. Sean stayed down, took aim, squeezed, and another man flew out of the saddle. Another man tried to take cover behind the forge, but when he got closer to it, Margaret opened up with her shotgun, catching him right in the face. The remaining three took off towards Jim's house. John could hear Jim's shotgun going off and some pistol fire. Then it got quiet. A lone rider came galloping back toward the main house firing his pistol. Sean moved in the shadows and over behind the house and lay flat on the ground taking aim. When the rider was about fifty feet away, Sean squeezed the trigger again, and again, another rider flew backwards out of the saddle. Then it was quiet again.

After what seemed like an eternity, John spoke. "Margaret, Sean, are you all right?

"Yes Pa, I'm good, and I see Ma. She's good too." Sean said.

"Is it over John?" Margaret asked.

"I don't know yet," he answered. "Gotta check on Jim and Little Jim."

They waited a few more minutes, then headed towards Jim house. When they got closer, John yelled out. "Jim, Little Jim, are you all right?

Little Jim answered, "We're both hit. Me in my left shoulder, and Pa's bad off. He's bleeding from his mouth."

Jim had been hit in the chest and blood was pouring out of his mouth. Beside him were two of the riders, dead. Jim was still alive, but just barely. "John, you a good man, none better. Look after my boy." Then he died. Margaret started crying, but then snapped out of it.

"John," she said, "I'll take Little Jim to the house and patch him up as best I can. The bullet passed through and he's not bleeding too badly. I should be able to clean him up good till we can get Doc Tilton here."

"O.K.," John said, "Sean and I will see if any of these night riders are still alive." They were all dead where they went down. The two that John had shot with the shotgun at the start, were ripped to pieces. The one Margaret shot didn't have a face. The three Sean had shot with the Walker had been hit square in the chest. There were huge holes in their backs where the pistol balls had ripped through their spines. The other two beside Jim had taken shotgun blasts in the chest.

"Well son," John started, "You just killed three men. How does that make you feel?"

"I reckon I'm supposed to feel bad taking someone's life, but Pa, those men wanted us dead. I don't feel bad at all," Sean said. "Better them than us."

"I feel that way too. I just hope your mother will be all right," John said. "Let's get to the house and see how Little Jim is doing, then we'll start digging Jim a proper grave."

Little Jim was doing fine. Margaret had gotten the bleeding stopped and he was bandaged up and was asleep on Sean's bed. John was about to ask Margaret how she was doing when they heard some riders outside. John looked out the window. It was Bill and the County Sheriff.

"Looks like we didn't get here in time," said Bill. "This is Sheriff Wade, John. You've probably never met him because this part of the county is usually quiet."

"Sheriff," John said, "Name's John O'Rourke. That's the wife Margaret, and my son Sean. Little Jim is in the bedroom. Been hit in the shoulder. Jim's dead. All of them, all eight, are dead."

"You mean to tell me that you all killed eight of them. Damn, if I ever get into a scrap like this, I hope you're on my side," the Sheriff said. "Sorry your man got killed."

"He wasn't my man," said John. "He was a free man."

"Sorry," said the Sheriff, "I didn't mean it that way. Bill, you go into town and come morning, bring out a wagon so we can get these corpses out of here and see if anyone will claim them. I sure hope they don't have much kin. We don't want to get a big feud going. Mr. O'Rourke, there won't be no hearing or anything. Bill told me what was going on. As far as I'm concerned, this was self-defense. Bill, don't forget the Doc. I'm gonna snoop around the area and make sure nothing else is gonna happen tonight. Then I'll slip into town and see if I can pick up any gossip. Some folks talk an awful lot when they get to drinkin'. Hopefully when folks hear what happened here, they'll think more about living than dying. This bullshit of hatin' someone for the color of their skin is just what I said, bull shit! This may cost me the election next time, but this needs to stop sometime, but we know it won't happen in our lifetime." Then he and Bill left.

Finally, John was able to speak with Margaret. "How do you feel about all this?" he asked. "We killed eight men today. That's something that will stay with us forever."

"John, we were raised to be good Catholics," she said, "but since we've been in America, we haven't been to mass or confession one time. I doubt there's a priest within a hundred miles of here. In my heart though, I still believe we are good Christians, but I also believe that we cannot turn the other cheek. We killed those men, and we will always have to live with that, but live with it, we will. I'd rather see them dead than you or Sean. But, I believe it might be wise for us to move on. There is a war coming, sooner or later, and I don't want any of us to have to kill someone else because of the color of someone's skin. Maybe we should go west. I've never heard or read anything about trouble in Oregon."

"Margaret, you are my own personal angel. God was looking out for me when I found you," John said. "We'll get Little Jim healed up, make sure no more trouble is brewing for us, and we'll find out what we can about Oregon."

The next day, Bill showed up with the wagon and they loaded up the bodies. "I haven't heard of any more goin' ons," Bill said, "If anybody else knew what was to happen last night, they didn't leak it to me. I saw the Sheriff too, and he hadn't seen or heard anything either. I'll leave the bodies behind the General Store and put the word out so anyone can claim a body if they're a relative or something. If I hear or see anything, I'll get ahold of you as best I can. Doc'll be out shortly."

"Thanks Bill," John said. "We'll give Jim a good burial today. Don't know of any relatives or anyone, so we'll get it done ourselves."

Later that morning, they had a small service for Jim. They sang a few hymns, said a few prayers, and each of them gave a few good words about Jim. When they were all through, Little Jim had some other words to say. "As soon as I get healed enough," he started, "I think I'll go up North somewhere. I'm almost fifteen now and I can do the work most men can do. Pa saved darn near all the money, so I'll be O.K. for a good while. There's more work up there besides workin' in the fields. I want to see how folks up there treat folks like me. I heard about this thing called the underground railroad. They help escaped slaves get up North. Well I'm no slave, but maybe they can help me get somewhere where I can find work. I do have something to ask. Mr. John, would you help me get up North? If I take off by myself, papers or not, someone we'll grab me as a runaway, sure as standin' right here."

"Little Jim," he said, "It's about time we quit calling you Little Jim. How about just plain Jim or James? Whenever you're ready, I'll take you. Most white folks have a last name too. If you ever think you'd like to have one, you can use ours. You've been part of our family for twelve years now."

A little while later, Doc Tilton arrived. "Margaret, did you tend this wound? Why am I asking, I know you did. You should have been a nurse. I couldn't have done better myself. Young man, you were very lucky. That ball went straight through and didn't take anything important with it, no bones chipped, or main blood vessels cut. You'll be in good shape in no time. All we need to do is keep it clean so no infection starts, but with Margaret here, I doubt that would happen. I'll make you a sling and you keep it on, even when you're sleeping, at least for the first two weeks. We don't want to stretch it out just yet and open it back up. Now you rest and do whatever Margaret tells you. I'll check back in a couple of weeks. I gotta get goin' now. Got a baby due on the other side of town."

Two bodies were claimed the first day, and three more the second day. No one seemed to know the other three, so the county buried them. There wasn't much talk in town about what happened. Everyone seemed to know. Some people were glad that one more nigger was dead, and some were glad that some white trash was dead. It seemed too quiet, but nothing happened.

Doc checked on Little Jim after two weeks and he was healing fine. After a month Jim said he was ready to head north, but John told him he wanted him to be completely healed before they left. After three more weeks, they decided it was time to go. They would catch a train out of Chattanooga, and go to Cincinnati. John assured Margaret that it wouldn't take that long. "Those trains can run up to twenty five miles an hour, or even faster on a good straight stretch. I'll be back before you know it."

Then he had a good long talk with Jim and tried to explain how things could be up North as best he could. "Jim," he started, "Just because there's no slavery up North doesn't mean it will be all that nice. Some people don't like black folks period. Up there, they have the rich white folks, the ones between the rich and the poor, then the poor white folks, and then the black folks and the really poor black folks. You might be treated worse than we Irish were treated by the British. I just don't know. I'm not trying to scare you. Just letting you know it may not be what you expect. Be careful with your money. Don't let anyone know you're carrying much. There are people who would kill someone for five dollars. There are professional pickpockets everywhere in big cities. I would tell you that if it doesn't work out, you could come back, but we're going west. We'll probably leave in the spring sometime."

"I knows that it might not be the land of milk and honey," Jim said, "but I gotsta see for myself."

CHAPTER FOUR

F inally it came time for them to go. There hadn't been any trouble at all, but John told Sean before leaving, that he wanted him to keep the Colt Walker near or on him the whole time he was gone. He also told Margaret to keep both shotguns loaded and have one of them near wherever she went.

John and Jim really enjoyed the train ride. It was the first train ride for both of them. When they got to the depot, John noticed a big sign. "Frederick Douglas Speaks at the Second Street Theatre Today at 3PM." John had heard of Frederick Douglas and figured it would be a good idea to attend. They got directions from a man at the depot and easily found the theatre. It was early yet and they needed to eat. The first restaurant they entered had a sign, "Whites Only." They tried another one. This one had a sign that said, "No Negroes Allowed." John went on into the second one, ordered some sandwiches and took them outside. Then he and Jim found a small park, sat on a bench and ate. Jim did not seem discouraged by all this.

Three o'clock came and they were in the theatre. There was a good mix of people attending. There were several black folks, but most of them were white. John figured that some of these people must be those abolitionists he'd heard about. When they started with their speeches, he was sure they were. There were several white men to speak first, then Frederick Douglas came to the podium. He got right to the point. He wanted freedom for the slaves, and he wanted it right now.

When the speaking was over, John mingled with some of the speakers and introduced Jim. They said they would be glad to help him find some work. One of them assured Jim that he could find him work with a local blacksmith right there in Cincinnati. In fact, he said he would be working as early as tomorrow. He would even find Jim a place to stay until he got settled. Thanks were given, and then it was time to tell Jim goodbye. "You and your family have been part of my family for twelve years, Jim," John said, "We will miss you and we hope the best for you. Who knows, maybe we will see each other again someday."

"I sure do hope so, Mr. John," he said, "I hopes the best fo you and yo famly."

They shook hands and John left to get back to the depot. The next train heading south wasn't leaving for a few hours, so John went downtown shopping. He was just window shopping, when he spotted a gunsmith shop. In the front window, on display was something he'd never seen before, so he decided to have a look. "What's that brand new rifle you have in the front window?" asked John.

"That, my good man, is a Sharp's rifle, made by Christian Sharps. It's a lever action, breech loader, .52 caliber, and accurate out to five hundred yards. Would you like to handle it, sir?"

"Yes I would," John answered. "My family is heading west and we can probably use something like this." John placed the Sharps in his shoulder and looked down the sights. "Oh my," he said, "This rifle feels like it becomes part of your body when you look down the sights. Do you have two of them?"

"Yes sir, I do," he answered, "You'll be needing caps and ammunition too? We have these paper cartridges already made up."

"I'll take two hundred rounds, caps, extra powder, lead, and a bullet mold if you have one," John said. "Also, I have a Colt Walker back home. Would you happen to have an extra cylinder for it?"

"I have all that you need, sir," he said, "We'll wrap this stuff up so it won't look like you're a walking armory while going down the street."

"Do me a favor, will you?" John asked, "Quit calling me sir. Name's O'Rourke, John O'Rourke."

"Sorry John," he answered, "I usually call the customers sir to be respectful. My name is David, David Holmes, and I wish you well on your trip west. I hope you only need to use those Sharps on animals and not people."

"Thanks David," John said, "And I hope the same as you. I don't want to shoot anything I'm not going to eat."

~~~~

John again enjoyed the train ride. He spent a lot of time on the trip thinking about the trip west. He'd heard that it would take four to six months by wagon train. They would need to get the place sold, decide what they need to take, and then get out to Westport Missouri. They could probably get out to Missouri by train, and then get outfitted once they got there. They would need to leave early enough so they could get through the rough country before winter. Everyone had heard of the Donner party by this time. Would it be worth it to go? Is there really a war coming? As soon as he asked himself that, he knew the answer. There is a war coming, and it will be fought down South. All the manufacturing facilities are up North. What's the South got, cotton and tobacco?

When John got home, Margaret kissed him over and over like he'd been gone for years. Sean had missed his father too, and gave him a firm handshake. Then John showed Sean the new Sharps rifles he'd bought. Sean was excited and couldn't wait to try them out. "We'll go out tomorrow and try them out," John said, "And then we have a lot of planning to do before we make this trip. It's getting to be late winter, so we don't have much longer to get started. It takes four to six months to make this trip once we get to Missouri, so we'll have to leave sometime in the spring to make it out there before winter hits. I'll go over to Anderson's tomorrow and see if he'd like to buy the place. He might not, since he already owned it once and might not want to pay for it again. Anyway, I'm sure we'll be able to sell the place."

That night, after John and Margaret made love a couple of times, they talked about the trip. "It won't be hard for me to decide what to take with us," Margaret said. "We started with nothing in Ireland. We had nothing when we came to America, and we didn't have much more when we came to this place. As long as I have you and Sean, I do not need anything else."

"You are still my girl," John said, and soon they were making love again.

The next morning after taking care of the animals, John and Sean got out the Sharps. "These rifles are supposed to be accurate up to five hundred yards," said John. "Tell you what we'll do. We'll pace off one hundred, two hundred, and three hundred yards, put up some targets, and see what we can do. There's no wind today, so we won't have to worry about that. Get some old boards and we'll draw about a ten inch circle on each one. We'll get down and shoot in the prone position so we can be more accurate. These rifles probably have a good kick, so hold it tight. Down in the prone, there won't be much give in your body when the round is fired."

The targets were set and they were ready. "Do you want to go first, son?" John asked.

"No Pa, you go ahead," Sean answered.

John got down in position, loaded a cartridge, placed a cap, and took aim. He squeezed the trigger and the Sharps let out a tremendous roar. Sean could see that this rifle had a tremendous recoil by the way it moved his father. "Not quite dead center," John said, "I'll fire one more and compare."

The second round struck almost dead center. "All right son," John said, "Now you fire a couple. Remember, hold tight and squeeze that trigger, don't pull."

Sean got into position, loaded up, and fired. The first round struck about one inch above dead center. The second round about a half inch lower. "Good shooting son," John said. "How's that recoil feel to you?"

"It has a good kick, Pa," Sean answered. "But I like the feel of it."

"O.K.," John said, "Let's try two hundred yards. Let's raise up the rear sight maybe two notches."

John fired first and was amazed. Both rounds were almost dead center. Sean fired with the same results.

At three hundred yards, they raised the rear sight another two notches. The results were the same. Both of them had hit almost dead center with their rounds. "This is one fine piece of weaponry, son," John said, "And it sure beats ramming a ball down with a ramrod each shot. I think these rifles will serve us well."

Then John remembered something. "Sean, I forgot to tell you. I got another cylinder for the Walker. That'll cut down on reloading if needed. Twelve shots can be a pretty good edge if needed,"

Later that morning, John went over to the Anderson plantation. George senior and George II were both there. "Good morning to both of you," John said, "Just stopped by to let you know that we're heading west and we're selling the place. I thought I'd let you know first since you used to own it. We'll be leaving in the spring."

George II was the first to speak. "Dad," he started, "I don't think we should pay for land that we have previously owned. It doesn't seem right to me"

"Son," he answered, "You're forgetting. John built a nice house and some barns and buildings on the place. The old slave shanty is now a decent house. It's worth a lot more now than when we owned it. They've kept the fields in good shape and they've had good crops ever since they've been here. If we don't buy it, someone else surely will. Those houses can be rented if we don't put our own people in there. Now what do you think now, son?"

"O.K., dad, "he answered, "I guess I wasn't thinking about the houses and buildings. Yes, we'd better get it before someone else does."

"John," the senior George said, "Let's meet at the bank tomorrow morning, say ten o'clock, and get this settled. Do you have time for a little brandy?"

"Thanks for the drink offer, George," John said, "But I have so many things to get done before we leave. I'll see you at the bank tomorrow at ten."

John went back home and gave the good news to Margaret and Sean. "I'll be meeting George at the bank tomorrow," he said, "I'll ask George to make the purchase effective the middle of March. That way, we'll have time to get to Missouri and be ready to leave early spring. That should give us plenty of time to get provisioned. We each need to figure out what is important and needs to go, and what we can live without. I'm figuring on taking two wagons. I want to make sure we are well provisioned. Some people use oxen, but I'd rather use mules if we can get them. We all know how to handle a team. We'll need extra feed for them. I guess we'll find out more once we get to Missouri. Don't have any doubts. This is going to be a long hard trip. There could be disease, outlaws, Indians, and Mother Nature, but we're a tough bunch."

Everything went O.K. at the bank the next morning. The effective date of the sale was March 15, so John had plenty of time to get everything done before they would catch the train to Missouri. There were only four horses that needed to be shod, and after that, just packing, and selling everything else that wasn't going.

The day before they were to leave, Sean went over to the Anderson's to tell Sarah goodbye. She cried a little and Sean was about to give her a last kiss when brother George showed up. "So you're finally leaving. Good riddance you stupid bastard," he said, "If I ever see you again, I might just shoot your ass."

"George," Sean said, "Since you've been so nice, I'm going to give you a going away present." Then Sean got right in his face and punched his left eye. "You can think about me the whole time you're sporting that black eye you're going to have. Now back off, or you'll get some more."

George stayed back as ordered. Then Sean gave Sarah a good-bye kiss. "We will see each other again Sarah, I promise. I don't know when, but we will see each other." Then Sean went back home.

CHAPTER FIVE

T he day of departure finally arrived. They would be able to take the train all the way to Kansas City, Missouri. As this was Margaret and Sean's first train ride, they really enjoyed it. There were no complaints about how long it took, or how many times they had to change trains along the way. It was easy to find Westport and where the wagon trains were formed. They found out right away that there would be a lot of price gouging. Supplies were about half again what they expected to pay, but John managed to get two wagons, mules, grain and feed for the mules, and most of the food supplies they would need. They would hunt some along the way to get fresh meat at times. John had heard that there were times on the trail, when you could go all day, and see buffalo by the thousands. There had even been wagons trampled by stampeding buffalo. Antelope were plentiful also. John managed to make a deal and get a better price for the mules. Some of them were not even broke to harness, so John helped out, and got a good price in return. They were also told that the Indians were mostly peaceful, but still liked to steal horses and mules.

Now that they were ready to go, there was a problem. The last train left five days ago, and the next train wouldn't leave for another month and a half to two months. Did they want to afford to stay there and wait that long? John discovered that there were two other families there who were ready to go and didn't want to wait for the next train. If they would leave the next day, they could catch that last train in a week and a half or less. They were told that most of the wagons were using oxen and would only make about twelve miles a day. John and the others were using mules and could make twenty miles on a good day. Following the trail wouldn't be a problem as it had been used for years and was well worn. If they stuck close together, stayed well armed, and kept watches both day and night, they should be all right. Then when they caught up to the train, they would pay the wagon master his fee.

John also bought two good saddle horses. They would come in handy for hunting and such.

So it was decided that they would leave the next day. They all got up before daylight, ate breakfast, made sure their guns were loaded and ready, and started the trip. John's wagon took the lead. Then Margaret driving the second wagon, and the other two following. Anyone not driving was to keep a sharp lookout for anything and everything. Sean would mount one of the saddle horses bare back whenever they approached a rolling hill that they couldn't see over to make sure nothing was on the other side. He was to take the Walker with him and fire a warning shot if needed. It was beautiful country, but it was the plains, mostly flat with some rolling hills, and hardly any brush or trees. They did bring a little firewood, but mostly, they would be using buffalo chips for the cook fires.

They did well the first day, just stopping at times to rest and water the mules, and no problems. John figured they had made over twenty miles this day. That night, they made a little circle with the wagons, let the mules graze for a while, then placed them in the center in a rope corral with their legs hobbled. They had their meals and got the guard posted. Each man or boy over sixteen would take a two-hour watch. It worked out well because the other two families each had a boy over sixteen. John and Margaret let Sean take a turn because they knew his abilities.

The first night was quiet. Everyone slept well probably because they were worn out from the long day yesterday. They were up at sunrise, had their morning meal, and started off again. This day there seemed to be buffalo everywhere. There were times when they had to stop the wagons to let them pass. None of them really knew anything about buffalo, except that they were huge, so whenever Sean was out on the saddle horse seeing if anything was over the next rise, he kept his distance from them. They seemed peaceful, but maybe they were like cattle. Sometimes the least little thing can spook them. There were also plenty of antelope and some white-tailed deer. Maybe tomorrow or the next day, he would take the Sharps and get some fresh meat.

John figured they made less than twenty miles this day, probably because they had to stop for the buffalo, but everyone was in good spirits. That evening, when they stopped and made camp, they actually had some conversation. All the families told about where they were from, and why they were going, and what they expected when they got there. "Nice folks," John thought to himself, "should make the trip a lot nicer."

That night was again peaceful. They all got up at sunrise, had their meal, and took off again. Today was different. After seeing thousands of buffalo yesterday, there were none anywhere in sight today. There were a few antelope, but few and far in between. They crossed a small stream today, so they refilled the water barrels, even though they hadn't used much yet. They also let the mules have a good drink and graze a little. Then they were on their way again. The rest of the day was the same. Still no buffalo, but there were plenty of chips.

The third night was again uneventful. The next morning started out the same. Have the morning meal, hitch up, and take off again. After two hours on the trail, they started seeing buffalo again, thousands of them. How could it be that one day you see thousands of them, none the next day, then thousands again the next day. They seemed too vast and huge to just disappear like that. There were plenty of antelope and deer also.

John decided that it would be all right for Sean to do some hunting today. He was to see if he could get a deer or an antelope. He wasn't to shoot any buffalo. That would be too much meat, and they weren't going to stop and dry it. A deer or an antelope would be fine. That would give each family some fresh meat for a day or two.

Sean was eager to go. While he was saddling one of the horses, John told him, "Now you take twenty rounds for the Sharps with you. Take the Walker and the extra cylinder with you also. We try our best, but we can't see what's on the other side of every rise. Once you fire a shot, with this open plain, it will be heard for miles. Don't go too far out and always be aware of what's going on around you. Watch the birds and animals. If some birds flush and you know you didn't cause it, be on the look out. If you're watching some deer or antelope, and they're watching something and it's not you, be on the look out. If you drop a deer or antelope, get it gutted quickly as you can, and get back to us. Keep alert while you're gutting the animal. Besides Indians, there could be wolves out here too. Stay on the north side of the trail. That way if we would see someone coming on the south side, we would know it wasn't you. That may seem like a lot to remember, son, but you've got a good head on your shoulders. You'll be fine."

"Yes Pa," Sean said, I'll do my best, and we'll have some fresh meat before you know it."

Sean finished rounding up his gear, grabbed a canteen of water, and started the horse at a nice walk on the north side of the trail. He would try to ride parallel about five hundred yards out from the wagons and stay off the tops of any rises so as to not stand out on the skyline. After about only half an hour, he spotted a small herd of antelope. They were maybe five hundred yards out, grazing, and slowly headed his way. He decided he would wait on them to get closer instead of him moving towards them. He found a small scrubby bush and tied the horse. Then he moved about ten yards from the horse and lied down in the high grass to wait. "What if the antelope spotted the horse," he thought? "Maybe antelopes don't mind horses, especially if there's no one on the horse. I reckon I'll find out," he said to himself.

When they were about two hundred yards out, they stopped. They were all looking his way. "Have they spotted me, or are they looking at the horse?" he thought. In just a few minutes, they started moving again. "They must not be concerned about the horse, so I'll just wait till they get about one hundred yards out, and drop one," he said to himself with confidence.

Sean had his target picked out, and was already starting his squeeze on the trigger, when he heard a shot, then more shots, dozens of them. Most of them sounded like pistol shots, but he heard shotgun blasts too. Then he heard what he knew was his father's Sharps. Then there were more pistol shots. The Sharps fired again. More pistol shots were fired, then quiet. Sean had gotten up and was headed towards the rise that was overlooking the wagons. Before he reached the top, the firing had quit. When he got to the top, his worst fears were realized. There were dead people all over the place, and there were five men starting to rummage through the wagons. He couldn't see his parents, but Sean knew that wasn't them going through the wagons.

He decided right then that he had to kill these men if he could. He estimated the range to be around four hundred yards, and he didn't want to risk being seen by trying to get closer. He crawled back to the horse and got all his ammunition and the extra Walker cylinder. He crawled back to the top of the rise and took a position just below the top. He set his sights on the notch that he had used when his father and him first fired the Sharps. "Let's see," he said to himself, "sights set on three hundred, so I'll just aim a little high." He picked out a target and took careful aim. "Remember, squeeze," he said. Hopefully, they wouldn't be able to pick him out of the tall grass after he fired.

The Sharps roared, and in a split second, the man's head exploded. "Holy shit!" one of the men said, "Where in the hell did that come from?"

"Shooting just a little high," Sean thought. Then he took aim again. The Sharps roared again, and another man fell dead.

"That's gotta be that kid out there," one of the men said, "I know one of these family's had a young boy that I don't see here."

Another man answered him. "I don't care who he is. That son of a bitch can shoot. I'm gettin' the hell outta here."

"You'll stay right here, or I'll shoot you myself. We gotta kill him. He's seen us. He's gotta be up on that rise in the high grass. You and Sam get your horses and try to come in on him from two sides. I'll stay down here, and if he moves this way, I'll get him," the other man said.

Sean noticed right away that this man must be giving the orders. He looked familiar, but Sean couldn't place him. Sean saw what the other two were trying to do, so he figured while they were trying to get beside him on both sides, he'd go ahead and take another shot. The boss man was trying to stay concealed behind one of the wagons. He wasn't too smart about it. Sean knew right where he was, so he took a shot right through the wagon. He saw the man fall backwards.

Now he had to get ready for these other two. He figured they would arrive about the same time. He could get one at maybe a hundred yards with the Sharps, then get the other one with the Walker when he got closer. They would be charging in on their horses and wouldn't be shooting accurately anyway.

He guessed right. He adjusted his sights, stayed low, and waited. Sean took aim on the one to his right and fired. The man went flying out of the saddle, having been hit dead center in the chest. Then Sean set the Sharps aside, grabbed the Walker, turned on the ground staying low, and took aim on the last man. He was coming at a full gallop, firing his pistol, dirt flying all around. Sean fired when the man was about fifty yards away. The shot hit him, but only grazed his left side. He kept coming and kept firing. Sean fired again when he was twenty yards away. This shot caught him square between the eyes and he went backwards out of the saddle. The back of the man's head went flying to his left side.

"What had just happened?" Sean thought. "Did I just kill all these men? Are my parents and the others all dead?" He knew the answers already. All the thoughts and wishes going around in his head wouldn't change things. Slowly, he went back to his horse, then headed down to the wagons. Yes, he was right. They were all dead. His father had been hit three times in the chest and his mother twice. The others had been hit more than once. Sean wondered if some of the shots weren't just taken out of meanness or to make sure they were dead. There were also seven dead outlaws there, and two more up on the rise, but where was the one he'd shot as he was hiding behind the wagon? Sean checked where the man had fallen and there was a good bit of blood and a trail leading away. He looked some more, but the trail stopped. It looked like the wounded man had managed to slip away on his horse. Sean figured that this must have happened when he was busy with the other two on the rise. So there must have been ten of them. He himself had killed four, wounded one, and his father and the others had killed the other five. Now was the time for burying.

The prairie ground was not hard, so the digging went easily. He buried his parents first, said a few words, then started digging more graves. He had two more of them buried when he saw riders coming from the south. He couldn't tell who or what they were, but there were four of them. He knew they had seen him, but still decided it would be a good idea to take cover. As they got closer, he could tell that three of them were Indians, and the other was a white man. They had him tied. His hands were tied in the front, but there was a big stick across his back, and the stick was between his back and his arms. He had been bleeding from his left shoulder.

When they got closer, one of the Indians spoke. "White man, we are not here to fight. We heard shooting in the distance and headed this way. We came across this white man on the way. When he saw us, he tried to shoot us, but his gun wouldn't shoot. We ran him down and brought him with us to see what happened here."

Sean was amazed. This Indian spoke English. He had heard about them wearing war paint, but none of them had been painted. Sean stepped out from behind the wagon. He could tell that the Indians were amazed that he was a young boy. "This man here and all these others, ambushed our wagons and killed everyone. I was on that rise over there hunting antelope when the shooting started," he said. "I shot two of them from the rise, and when two more came after me, I killed them too. I shot that one while he was hiding behind a wagon. My Pa and the others killed the rest of them." Then Sean walked over to the wounded man, pulled the Walker, and without saying a word, shot the man through the head.

"Thanks for catching him for me," Sean said. "Save me the trouble of chasing him down. If you all are not in a hurry, could you help me bury these folks? I mean just the folks from the wagons. We'll leave the others for the coyotes or whatever gets them. If you help me, you can have everything here you want, except what goes with my wagon."

"We could take whatever we want, white boy," the Indian said.

"You could try, but I'll kill two of you before you kill me," Sean said. "Now wouldn't it just be better to help out. There's rifles and pistols, horses, mules, food, and whatever else those people had. Like I said, you can have everything that doesn't go with my wagon. My Pa's rifle and shotguns go with the wagon."

"We'll help you, white boy," the Indian said, "If you killed all these men, you are a brave warrior and we respect brave warriors, even if they are enemies. When we are done here, we will take you to our camp. It is only a half day's ride to the north. Maybe a little longer if you bring that wagon."

"I'll bring the wagon, and after we get there, I'll sort through it and anything I don't want, you may have," Sean said. "There may be some of my mother's things in there that some of your women may like."

CHAPTER SIX

T hey finished, and Sean said a few words. Then they were on their way. Sean and the one who could speak English, talked a good bit. "How is it that you can speak English?" Sean asked.

"We are Cheyenne. My father was killed in a raid by the Pawnee when I was very small," he answered. "My mother took up with a white man the next year. The tribe likes him and he has stayed with us the whole time. He used to be what you call a mountain man. He taught English to my mother and me. I have a sister too. She must be about your age. How old are you?"

"I'm twelve," answered Sean.

"Only twelve to have killed so many today?" he said.

"I killed three men back in Tennessee not long before we left there," Sean said.

"What is your given name?" the Indian asked.

"I am Sean Michael O'Rourke," Sean answered.

"I am called Black Wolf. The other two are Running Fox, and Swimming Otter," the Indian said. "We shall have to come up with a good Cheyenne name for you since you have killed so many at so young an age. You are not just a shooter, you are a killer. You did not flinch one bit when you shot that white man in the head."

"That man needed to die," Sean said. "I remember seeing him in Missouri when we were getting provisioned. He knew there would only be us three families out there, and he brought out his gang to kill us and steal everything. I didn't mind killing him at all."

Black Wolf didn't speak again till they got close to the village. "Our village is just over the next rise," he said. "If you didn't know where it was, you could look in all directions for miles, and not see it." He was right. It was down in a small valley beside a small stream. The pony herd was grazing on the side opposite the village. It would be hard to find out on the open plain. It was a small village. Sean could see maybe twenty-five or thirty teepees.

"We are a small band," said black Wolf. "The larger bands are just a little north of here. Our main Chief is Black Kettle. The Chief of our band here is Standing Bear. I will take you to meet him, and then I will take you to my mother's lodge where you will be welcome. When we go to meet Standing Bear, leave your weapons in the wagon. They will be safe. No one will touch them."

Standing Bear was an older man, but looked to be in good shape. He did not speak English, so black Wolf was their translator. Black Wolf spent several minutes telling the Chief about Sean's family being killed and how Sean had killed his family's killers, and about the gifts he had given them for helping to bury the wagon train people.

The Chief thought for a moment, then he spoke. "It is good that you have killed the men who killed your family," he said. "That is what a warrior should do. You are very brave for such a young one. You are welcome in our village." Then he gave a nod and asked to see some of the gifts. He seemed pleased with what he saw, especially the guns. When they first entered the village,

Sean noticed that very few of the men had any type of rifle. Most of them had bows and arrows, or carried a lance, or both. He remembered that when he first met Black Wolf and the others, they were armed with bows and arrows. All of the Indians, even the young ones and the women, all had some type of knife on them.

Then they went to Black Wolf's mother's lodge. She was waiting for them. Sean thought she was an attractive woman. "I am called Blue Swan," she said, "You are welcome in my lodge. I heard all about you from others while you were meeting our Chief. This is my daughter Katie. My husband is a white man and that's what he wanted to call her. He's out hunting now, but you will meet him shortly. His name is John Braddock, and he likes to be called just Braddock."

"I thank you for your kindness Blue Swan," Sean said. "I hope I will be a good guest. I do not know anything of your customs, but I would like to learn. When I sort through the wagon tomorrow, maybe there will be something of my mother's in there that you would like."

"You sound very wise for a young boy," she said. "Your parents must have taught you good manners."

"They taught me well," Sean said. "I will miss them probably more than I can say." then he was quiet for a while. "Does Black Wolf live in your lodge too?" Sean asked.

"No," she answered, "he may look young and he is only eighteen, but he has his own lodge, a wife, and a baby on the way. Only Braddock, Katie, and I live in this lodge. There will be plenty of room for you. My Braddock is a good man. I know he will like you right away. You must be hungry. We will eat shortly and then you can rest."

"Yes, I am hungry," said Sean. "I haven't eaten since just before daylight this morning, and it wouldn't take much for me to fall asleep right now."

"After we eat," she said, "you can sleep all you want. If my Braddock doesn't get back before you sleep, you will meet him in the morning."

Sean wasn't sure what he was eating, but whatever it was, Blue Swan was a good cook. He stuffed himself, thanked her, grabbed a blanket from the wagon, and was asleep in no time.

Next morning, when he awoke, there was a bearded, rough looking man, dressed in buckskins, staring at him. "Mornin' there, young fella," he said, "I'm Braddock, and you must be that white boy I been hearin' about ever since I got back. They tell me yer not just a shooter, but a killer."

"I've killed some," Sean answered, "Name's O'Rourke, Sean O'Rourke, and I want to thank you for the hospitality of your lodge."

"Damn," Braddock said, "Blue Swan was right about you. You do have manners. That goes a long way with these Cheyenne. What's that rifle you carry? I've never seen anything like that before. Looks to be fine piece of weaponry."

"It's a Sharps," said Sean, "lever action, breech-loading, .52 caliber, and accurate out to five hundred yards, and it is a fine weapon. I killed two men yesterday at four hundred yards with it, and hit another one. I shot another man at one hundred yards."

"I've been using this .50 caliber Hawken for mebbe twenty years," said Braddock, "and it's a good rifle, but that breech loader makes it a might faster loadin', I 'spect. Now what's that big pistol you got?"

"It's a Colt Walker," answered Sean. "I hear it's about the biggest revolver ever made. Six shot, .44 caliber, and uses half again as much powder as Colt's other revolvers."

"I've seen a few of them revolvers over the years," said Braddock, "but never one this big. I seen some of those Colt Patterson's they give the Rangers down in Texas. I think they was only .36 caliber, or something like that. They had a foldin' trigger. Surprised the heck outta the Comanche first time they used 'em on 'em. Anyway, never could get my hands on one. This Hawken'll drop a buffalo or a grizzly bear, but on a grizzly, you better make a good shot, or he'll kill ya sure. Let's see what Blue Swan's got fer breakfast?"

They all sat and ate together, Sean, Blue Swan, Braddock, and Katie. Sean still didn't know what it was, but it was good. He got to looking at Katie. He could tell that she was going to grow into a very good-looking woman, and that wasn't going to be too far down the road. Her skin was lighter than Blue Swan's, and she had light brown hair like Braddock, and blue eyes.

After the meal, Sean thanked Blue Swan, and told them he was going to go out and sort through the wagon. Food was the main thing on the wagon. There were hams, salt pork, beans, jerky, flour, salt, dried apples, coffee, and more. Sean gave all this to Blue Swan and Braddock, and they could share with the rest of the band. There was some clothing for Sean, his father, and mother. He gave his mother's dresses to Blue Swan, plus some under garment items he thought she might like. He kept his and his father's clothes. He figured it wouldn't be long before he could wear his father's clothes. Blue Swan and Katie really liked the brushes and combs and the mirror. The rest was ammunition, powder, and such. While sorting through the ammunition, Sean discovered some loose boards on the floor of the wagon. He removed them and found his father had built a false bottom in the wagon. In the opening were several leather bags. He pulled one out and opened it. It was all gold coin. If each bag was gold, there must be $2,000 or more. Sean wondered why his father had never told him where the money was hidden, but then decided it was most likely for the best. If he didn't know, he couldn't tell, if someone tried to force it out of him. Then he found something he thought Braddock might really like, several bottles of Kentucky Bourbon. The sorting was finally done. He gave the four mules to Blue Swan. One of the saddle horses, and one of the shotguns and extra powder, lead, and caps, he gave to Braddock. He set out the feed they had brought for the mules, for anyone who wanted it. If anyone had use for the wagon, they could take it. If not, it would probably be busted up for firewood.

Sean asked Blue Swan and Braddock if it was all right to store his belongings in their lodge. "You were told already by the Chief that you are welcome in our village," Blue Swan said, "and I'm telling you that you are welcome in our lodge for as long as you want to stay."

"You heard the woman," said Braddock. "What she says, goes around here, and I do appreciate a good drink of whiskey once in a while. I don't abuse it and get drunk, but I do like it. Mebbe afore too long, you and I will sit down and have a drink."

Sean thanked them all again. The rest of that day, Katie took him around and introduced him to the other members of the band. They were all very nice and couldn't quit thanking Sean for everything he had given the village.

That evening, after the meal, Braddock told Sean that they would go out hunting in the morning. "Just cause we have all this food you give us," he said, "don't mean we need to slack off any. Indians is just like white folks in some respects. We gotta spend a good part of the warm months gettin' ready for the winter. You're gonna learn how to track, how to use the wind, and whatever it takes to stay alive out here. Just cause you can shoot, don't mean you know when to. You need to know how to tell when a storm's brewin', so you can be ready for it, or git outta it. We'll talk more tomorrow." Then he pulled Blue Swan under the buffalo robes to him. Katie said goodnight too.

The next morning after breakfast, Sean and Braddock saddled up and got ready to head out. Sean offered Braddock the use of the other Sharps, but Braddock said he'd stick with the Hawken for now. "Bring along that big pistol of yours," Braddock said. "You just never know what you might run into out there. Make sure you got some water, and we'll take some jerky."

When they were ready, they took off at a slow walk headed northwest. Sean was the first to speak. "What are we after today?" he asked.

"We won't shoot no buffalo today," answered Braddock. "We'll take some deer or antelope. Tribe's gonna have a big buffalo hunt shortly and you're gonna see how they do it. With these long guns, we don't hafta hunt that way, but it's a tradition with them and it'll last as long as the buffalo last."

"What do you mean as long as the buffalo lasts?" asked Sean. "There's thousands and thousands of them."

"Yep, young fella, there are thousands of them," he answered, "but there are more and more white folks coming all the time. A few of them will shoot a buffalo for meat, but a good many want to shoot them and call it sport. Some sport. When our buffalo hunt starts, I'll show you something about buffalo. They're big and they can be mean, but they are pretty darn dumb sometimes. All a man has gotta do is get down wind of them at a decent range, and start shootin'. There can be buffalo droppin' dead all over the place, but if the herd can't smell you, they'll just keep right on grazin'. If the wind stays right, a man could shoot darn near all day, or till he runs outta ammunition. Once more white folks learn this, the slaughter will commence. It'll take years, but you mark my word. It'll happen. They'll end up starvin' the Indians out here, or force them on one of those reservations like they have over East where they call it the Nations. Most of the tribes out here will fight before that happens. Damn, I haven't spoke that much in years. Let's go find some antelope and deer."

They had gone just a little farther, when Braddock stopped. "Look down there young fella, and tell me what you see," he said.

"Looks like deer droppings to me," Sean said.

"Yep, sure is," Braddock said, "now git down, look at it up close, smell it, feel it if ya hafta, and tell me how old it is, and see if you can find the tracks."

"It smells fresh, and feels really warm yet," Sean said, "I'd say it's not a half hour old. The tracks head north."

"Not bad, young fella," Braddock said, "now if yer right, they'll be just on the other side of this next rise. Let's tie our horses and ease up on that rise. When we git near the top, we'll crawl a bit. Wind's in our faces so they won't smell us. No talkin'.'"

When they finished crawling to the top, there they were, twenty or more deer, about one hundred yards out. Sean and Braddock both took aim and fired. Two deer fell. The rest took off at a dead run. Sean quickly reloaded and took aim again. "Don't waste your shot," Braddock said. "I never seen anyone hit a deer in a dead run that far away."

The deer were about two hundred yards out now, running straight away. Sean was still on target and waiting patiently. Finally the lead deer changed direction and turned to the right offering a broad side shot at around two hundred fifty yards. Sean fired, and the deer rolled over and over.

"Jesus Christ, boy," Braddock said, "who taught you to shoot anyway? We get into a scrape sometime, I sure hope yer on my side."

"My Pa basically taught me how to shoot," answered Sean, "but it's just something that I seem to be really good at."

"Well let's git these critters gutted and git back," Braddock said. "We should git back well before dark so I can tell everyone that you are one hell of a shot."

They went back and got the horses and went to work on the deer. They had two of them done, when Sean thought he saw some movement out of the corner of his right eye. He didn't turn to look, but put his right hand on the Walker. He then turned and it was just in time. A wolf was making it's charge and was about to leap for his throat when he fired the Walker. Without knowing if he hit the wolf or not, he turned to check on Braddock. Another wolf had charged Braddock and he was standing there getting ready to use his rifle like a club when Sean fired the Walker again. Sean then looked back to his right, and another wolf had started a charge. The Walker fired again. There were two more wolves, but they decided to get out of there.

"Hot damn, boy," said Braddock, "Yer as good with that pistol as you are with that Sharps. I wouldn't believe what just happened if I wasn't here. Did you just learn anything?"

"You mean about keeping yourself aware at all times?" answered Sean.

"No," said Braddock, "I mean about me not reloading my rifle right after I shot. I was too excited about that shot you made on that last deer, and I plum forgot to reload. I feel like a real greenhorn. Did you reload your rifle?"

"No," Sean answered, "I guess we both got stupid for a short time. Glad I brought the pistol along. Better get it reloaded too!"

"There's one more thing you should have noticed," Braddock said, "Them wolves came in from down wind. The horses didn't even see or smell them till they were about on us. Anyway, remember that. A grizzly bear can get up on you like that too, and that pistol won't stop a grizz unless you'd be lucky enough to hit it in the head. Not too many of them out here on the plains, but ever once in a while, one'll show up. Now if a critter can slip up on you like that, so can a Comanche or a Pawnee. They can put an arrow in you, and you won't know where it came from. Don't ever forget this."

"Yessiree," Braddock said, "Two deer and three wolves. Yer gonna be what white folks would call a celebrity when I get done tellin' 'em all about yer shootin' today. Now let's skin them wolves. They're not prime this time of year, but we'll get some use out of 'em.

When they got back to the village, Braddock spread the word about Sean's marksmanship. He became even more of a celebrity than he already was. At the evening meal, Braddock told Sean that the next time they went hunting, he would take him up on his offer to use the Sharps. Katie said that starting tomorrow, she would start teaching Sean the Cheyenne language, and sign. If he was going to be there, he may as well learn the language. Sign would come in handy when they were around other tribes. Plus she would let him know about other tribes and who got along with who, and who hated who.

The next day, Katie started the lessons right away. They started out simple, just giving the Cheyenne words for different things. Cheyenne women were always busy doing chores. They were always collecting firewood, or chips if there was no wood. Food gathering never ended, roots, berries, nuts, or whatever was in their area. They did most of the butchering after a hunt, worked the hides and bones, and all of the cooking. Sean went with her and helped her during her chores, and she gave him the Cheyenne words for everything they were doing. They did this for a few days, then she told him it was time for the big buffalo hunt.

The morning of the hunt, Sean and Braddock went out before the main hunt started. They weren't going to go out with the men during the hunt. They would watch it from the highest rise. But before the hunt was to start, Sean and Braddock would go out and shoot some buffalo for his family. That's how it worked. What each warrior killed was for his family, but if someone came up short, they always shared.

The herd was not far from the village, and when they spotted them, they got down wind of them, and picked a good firing position less than two hundred yards from the herd. They tied the horses a few yards back on some scrub bushes.

"Now I'll show you what I was talkin' about when I said buffalo were pretty dumb," Braddock said, "The meat's better on the smaller cows, so that's what I always shoot. Now go ahead and pick a target. Aim just behind the shoulder and such just like you was shootin' a deer or something."

Sean took aim on a cow and fired. Down she went. Not the least bit of concern came from the rest of them. He was amazed.

"Now take another one," Braddock said. Same thing as last time. He fired, the cow dropped, and the others kept grazing. "Now take one more," said Braddock again. Nothing changed. He fired, the cow went down, and the others kept on grazing. "Now I'll take a couple and that will be enough for us." said Braddock.

It was still the same. Braddock fired twice. Two cows went down, and the others kept grazing.

"I never would have believed that," said Sean, "I see what you mean about them being pretty dumb. You are right though. If too many white folks figure this out, it could be a slaughter."

"Let's get back to the village now," Braddock said, "those we shot'll be all right till the hunt's over."

They got back to the village and it was a sight. The warriors had painted themselves and their ponies all kinds of different ways and colors. Everyone was anxious to start. After they let the women know they were back, Braddock and Sean went up on the highest rise so they could watch the hunt.

The hunt was something to behold. The warriors got into small groups, rode right into the buffalo, shooting arrows into them and throwing lances, and at the same time trying to keep the herd somewhat circling. Most of the ones hit, did not die right away. They had to run till they bled to death. Some of them had three or four arrows in them. The hunt didn't last a full hour. Sean just couldn't believe how fast a warrior could accurately shoot his bow, while at a full gallop at times in the thick of this huge herd.

When they had killed enough, the rest of the tribe came out and went to work on the carcasses. Each person knew what buffalo was killed by their family by the markings on the arrows and lances. Nothing was wasted. Sean went down and helped Katie and Blue swan. Braddock was about the best Sean had ever seen with a skinning knife.

After a long day of butchering and such, there was feasting that night. The next day would be spent working the hides and getting meat ready to be cured. Certain organs were cleaned up to be used for water jugs. Sinew was collected to be cured for bowstrings and such. Bones were used to make needles for sewing, clubs, and all kinds of tools. Everything that they did, Katie was giving him the Cheyenne words for it. He was learning fast.

After the meat was cured, and the hides worked, it would be time to move the village again. Sean learned that this was how they existed. They weren't like white folks who built a house and lived there forever. The Cheyenne's home was wherever he was at that time. They would go somewhere, following the buffalo and antelope and deer, and when the herds moved, so did they. They always tried to honor the lands of other tribes in their movements.

They were going to move in a few days when Katie started her lessons on the tribes. First she began by telling him who were the friends of the Cheyenne, and where their territory was. They were the Lakota, or Sioux, and the Arapaho. Then she told him about their two main enemies, which were the Comanche and the Pawnee. "The Comanche are mainly down in what is called Texas, but they roam wherever they please. They raid just to be raiding. They love to get captives and trade or sell them to the Mexicans. Most tribes fear them, and they believe that their warriors can do things on a horse that no one else can do. The Comanche get along well with the Kiowa, but we have never been raided by the Kiowa."

"The Pawnee do not get along with any tribe that I know of. They are fierce fighters, and they raid us a lot. That was how my mother's first husband got killed. The Pawnee raided after a big hunt. We drove them off, but many Cheyenne were killed, including him. They have raided us many times since I was young. Sometimes, just to steal horses, sometimes food. We raid them too. I guess it's been going on for years. I have also heard that the Pawnee like to scout for the white soldiers."

"If you stay with us long enough, you will learn about the Comanche and the Pawnee," Katie said. "I hope that big pistol of yours is loaded when you find out."

"There are many more tribes that I have heard about, but never seen," said Katie. "The Crow and the Blackfeet have been killing each other for years, and the Crow hate the Lakota. I don't know if the Blackfeet do or not. Then there is the Shoshone. I don't think they get along with anyone. The Utes don't get along with the Lakota either. The Nez Perce live way up to the northwest and get along with about everyone. I know there are a more tribes out there, but these are the main ones. There's many more tribes on that reservation they call the Nations. I've heard of the Choctaw, the Osage, and the Fox, and I know the Cherokee are there. I know they were forced there on the 'Trail of Tears.' I do know that the Cheyenne will fight before they get forced on any reservation."

CHAPTER SEVEN

T he day for the move came. Sean was amazed at how efficient everything was done. It was no time at all and they were moving. When they got to the new village site, Sean noticed right off that it was almost identical to the last spot. It was down in a small valley beside a small stream and as before, if a person was out on the plain, he could look for miles in all direction, and not see it. Setting up the village was something to see. It was set up in no time at all, and then everyone starting doing their chores, gathering wood or chips, gathering food, and such.

Sean was becoming very good at learning the Cheyenne language and sign. During the move, they had met some Arapaho scouts. Sean didn't know how, but they had heard of this young white boy who could shoot so well, and were eager to meet him. He communicated with them without too much help from Katie. As a show of politeness, they were invited for a meal in their lodge. During the meal, Braddock asked them if there had been any trouble with the Pawnee or Comanche. They said it had been quiet for some time. They did say that they were seeing more white men all the time and were concerned about it. After the meal, they were invited to spend the night, and they accepted.

After a morning meal, they gave their thanks and were on their way.

Life at this site was the same as the other site. They hunted for fresh meat when needed, and had a big buffalo hunt, and when the time came, they moved again. This went on several times, and then it came time to move to the winter site.

The winter site was similar to the other sites, in that it was hard to find if you didn't know it was there, but it was more protected from the wind. There were more trees, and the hills around the village were higher. They would be here till spring.

Game was not as plentiful as in the warmer months, but Sean and Braddock had no trouble keeping the family supplied, and even helped anyone who came up short. Katie had made Sean a good coat from buffalo hide and kept him supplied with moccasins as his boots had worn out some time back, and he had grown a lot this last year. He was nearly six feet tall now. He could wear his father's clothes, but his boots were too small. Katie helped him keep his dark hair trimmed. He kept it long in the back, but shorter around his ears. He thought hair that hung over the ears would restrict his hearing just slightly and decided he needed all the help he could get. Some of the Cheyenne men braided their hair, others did not, and they were not concerned about their hearing being obstructed, but Sean still didn't want his ears covered. The hair on his face was starting to grow, but Sean didn't want to scrape his face just yet.

It was a mild winter, but everyone still wanted spring to come. When it finally came, they moved the village. Whichever way the herds moved, they moved that way also. The site was found, and the village set as always. The women and everyone got busy on their daily chores, and the men went hunting.

Braddock had taken to using the Sharps more and more, but still used his old Hawken from time to time. "I wanna make sure she stays in shape," he would always say. He still had some of the Kentucky bourbon and every once in a while, Sean and he would have a drink. At first Sean couldn't understand why anyone would drink something that tasted like that and burned going down to boot, but before too long, he acquired a taste for it. One time, they had one too many, Sean found out what it was like to be sick, and have a hangover the next day.

Sometimes, there would be white traders in the village. Braddock always liked to be there during the trading to make sure everyone got a square deal. Sometimes they had rifles, but they were usually old and worn out and couldn't be expected to shoot accurately, so Braddock made sure none of the Cheyenne wasted their goods on them. They always had powder, paper, caps, and lead, so Sean and Braddock always traded for these items. Sometimes the traders would try to sell whiskey in the village. Standing Bear did not want any of his people to have any whiskey and at times, he ran off these people. He didn't care if Braddock took a drink on occasion, but he knew that his people couldn't handle the white man's whiskey. Most of the time, the whiskey was some rot gut that came from who knows where, but every once in a while, a trader would show up with some real stuff, and Braddock would trade for it.

Sean decided that he really loved this life. He could speak Cheyenne fluently, and communicate with other tribes very well. This summer, he met some Lakota. They were fierce looking men, but they were polite, and they had heard of this young white boy who could shoot so well. Only this white boy had grown a good bit since the stories about him had circulated. They said that they had had a little trouble with the Crow sometime back, but things had been peaceful for a while. As with the Arapaho Sean had met last year, they were concerned about seeing more white men from time to time. Were they just passing through, or were they intending to stay?

Sean and Katie grew more attached to each other every day. Whenever Sean wasn't hunting, he was always with Katie, and helped her with her chores. Some of the men and the young boys thought Sean was silly for doing woman's work, but most of them wouldn't say anything to his face. They knew he could be a rough customer and wanted no part of tangling with him.

Fall came, and Sean and Katie were now fourteen. Sean had grown a little more, and was now over six foot tall. He also decided to scrape the hair from his face, but he did keep his moustache. Katie was a fully developed woman and some other girls her age had already taken husbands. Sean thought hard about this almost all the time. White folks just didn't get married this young unless there was a baby involved. He'd heard of girls back in Tennessee getting married at fifteen, but they were usually marrying a guy who was at least a little older. He decided that next time they went out hunting, he would have a long talk with Braddock about this.

~~~~

Two days later, He and Braddock were out after antelope. When they were out of sight of the village, Sean turned to Braddock, and said, "You and I need to have a talk."

"Yeah, what about?" Braddock said. "Is it about Katie? Heck the whole world knows you two are gonna end up together. So are you asking me for her hand?"

"I am asking you for her hand," answered Sean, "But it doesn't seem right since we're both so young. White folks don't get married this young unless there's a baby involved, and I assure you, this is not the case."

"Most white folks don't get married this young because they don't have to." said Braddock. "At your age, most white boys don't know a thing about how the world even works. They haven't been out in the real world where they gotta supply food for a family, or a home, or anything. They want something, they get money from their Ma or Pa, and go to the store and get it. There's no stores out here. Ya gotta know how to survive. These Injuns know how to survive. They grow up learnin' it. Another thing, Injuns, most of the time, don't live as long as white folks. You've been lucky here so far. You haven't seen a hard winter, or a Comanche or a Pawnee raiding party. People die or get killed. We haven't lost a man the last two years on a buffalo hunt, but there were times that we had several men trampled or gored. One more thing. Injuns don't have the diseases that white folks carry around. I've seen lots of them die from a simple case of the measles. Do you understand me, young man?"

"Yes, I do," Sean answered, "so if it's all right with you and Blue Swan, I'd like to make Katie my wife in the next Fall."

"That's O.K. by me," Braddock answered, "And I don't s'pect Blue Swan will have any objections. There is a tradition that we should discuss before then."

"All right, what is it?" asked Sean.

"Among these Plains Injuns, the man is s'posed to give gifts to the family of the woman." He said. "If the family accepts the gifts, then they can get married. If they don't, he needs to come up with something better."

"Well just for starters, you can keep that Sharps," Sean said, "I was gonna give that to you anyway."

"I'm not concerned about gifts, Sean," Braddock said, "I was just seeing if I could get a rise out of you. You know when we get back today, after you tell Katie and Blue Swan, we're gonna have to have a shot of that bourbon. I still got a little of it left."

"Sounds good to me," said Sean.

When they got back to the village, Sean kept tripping all over himself trying to get to Katie to tell her the news. Before he got to her, he thought to himself, "You know, I haven't actually asked Katie to marry me. I reckon I better do that first before I tell her that Braddock said it was O.K." He found Katie. She was out gathering berries. She knew what he was going to say before he even said it and she ran to him, threw her arms around him, and kissed him over and over. Then she said, "Yes, I will be your wife." Then she kissed him until they were both out of breath.

That evening, Blue Swan made a very fancy meal to celebrate. Sean sure hoped that Katie could cook like her mother. After the meal, Braddock pulled out the bourbon and the men had a drink, and then another one. But that was it. The bourbon had finally run out. "We'll make sure we get some good whiskey before you two get hitched," Braddock said. "I'll be needin' to really celebrate. My little girl will be gettin' herself one hell of a man."

Fall gave way to winter and the winter was a little harder than last winter, but Sean and Braddock did not have any trouble keeping the fresh meat supplied. Sean and Katie were still staying in the same lodge with Braddock and Blue swan. Sean hoped that he didn't make strange noises or talk in his sleep, because he constantly thought of being with Katie.

Spring came and then the summer. The village moved several times while they followed the herds. During one of the moves, they ran into some scouts from another one of the Cheyenne bands. They told them that they had heard from the Arapaho, that the Comanche had been raiding towards the north. This is not what anyone wanted to hear. Standing Bear decided to keep scouts out at all times in all directions.

Another week went by and all was quiet, then one evening, a scout came riding hard into the village. He said that there was a war party of maybe thirty Comanche warriors about a half days ride to the south and they were headed this way. Standing Bear told everyone to gather their weapons, and be ready to fight in the morning.

Sean had an idea. He went to Standing Bear and spoke. "Braddock and I can take our long guns, and with the scout who found them, we can find their camp, and when it gets daylight, we can kill several of them at a long range. Maybe they will get discouraged and leave. If not, there will be less of them to fight if they get past us. Then Standing Bear spoke. "That is a good plan, Shooter. Besides the scout, you will take Black Wolf with you. After the Comanche camp is spotted and the shooting starts, the scout and Black Wolf will make sure some of them don't get behind you. Go whenever you are ready."

"Thanks for volunteering me for this," said Braddock, "But ya know, it is a good plan. If we can cut 'em down some, mebbe they will get discouraged, but one thing ya need to know about these Comanche. They hold a grudge longer than anyone alive. Once they know who we are, They'll be after us, even if it takes years. Another thing too, once they get on a horse, they are slicker than greased lightnin'. They can hang on one side of a horse and shoot arrows under it's belly or neck. If they get to doin' that, don't hesitate to shoot the horse. Most Injuns don't wanna shoot a horse cause they're too valuable, but if you bring down a horse with a Comanche brave hangin' on the other side of it, mebbe it'll fall on him and hurt him bad or kill him. These Sharps might put a slug through a horse's neck and hit a Comanche on the other side. We can hope. Now we better go tell the women goodbye."

Sean got out the shotguns and made sure they were loaded and the women knew how to use them. Then they left. Neither Black Swan nor Katie shed a tear. They knew their men would be back.

The Comanche camp was found. They must be very confident thought Sean when he saw that they didn't have a scout out. He wouldn't dare do that in someone else's territory. They were down in a small valley beside a small stream and there was a grove of trees for cover. Their ponies were tied not far away. Sean and Braddock took positions about two hundred yards apart and around four hundred yards from the camp and waited.

Daylight came and the Comanche began waking up. Some of them were standing, relieving themselves, when Sean and Braddock fired almost at the same time. Two Comanche fell dead. They started running to their horses when Sean and Braddock fired again. Two more Comanche fell. By now, they knew where the firing was coming from, mounted their horses, and came charging. They were still over three hundred yards away when Sean and Braddock fired again. Two Comanche were thrown backwards off their horses, but the others kept coming. Sean and Braddock reloaded as fast as they could and fired again. Two more Comanche fell. It didn't look like these Comanche were going to leave any time soon. At around two hundred yards, both Sharps barked again, and two more Comanche fell. They had dropped ten of them, and the others were still coming.

The Comanche changed tactics now. Instead of a head long charge, they split up and were trying to get around them. As they got closer, they would hang on the opposite side of their horses. Sean dropped a horse. He heard the Comanche let out a groan and he didn't move. Braddock had shot a horse, but the rider got right up and was charging him. He reloaded the Sharps and dropped the Comanche at around fifty yards. Black Wolf was laying low in the grass. When another Comanche slipped up behind Sean and was about fifty yards away, Black Wolf let out a battle cry, leapt up and hit the Comanche on the left side of his head with a war club.

The Comanche were close now. Sean reloaded the Sharps, but pulled out the Walker. Just in time too. Two Comanche came charging straight at Sean shooting arrows. The scout who had spotted the Comanche loosed an arrow and hit the one on the left, but he didn't fall. Sean stayed low, took careful aim, and fired once, and then again. Both Comanche were thrown backwards off their horses. Sean hadn't heard Braddock fire for a while and looked over to make sure he was all right. He was. Apparently, the Comanche had finally decided that they had enough.

Black Wolf and the scout started shouting victory cries at the retreating Comanche. Even Braddock let out a few. Sean was just glad it was over. He didn't feel like yelling. Then he felt something rip into his left side. He looked down and there was an arrow sticking in him. It had caught him just below the ribs, just about two inches in. He could see the head of it sticking out the other side. Sean heard Black Wolf let out a yell, and then he saw him run over and club a Comanche who was laying on the ground This apparently was the Comanche that was hanging on the horse that

Sean had dropped. He hadn't been killed when the horse fell on him. He was dead now. Black Wolf saw to that.

Braddock came running over to Sean. "Let's see what we got here," he said, "No vitals hit. You'll be fine. We'll just break off one end, and pull it out the other side. This'll hurt a might as he pulled the arrow through." Then he told Black Wolf and the scout to check the Comanche gear that got left behind. Maybe they had a little whiskey.

They were lucky. There was a little whiskey in a pouch on one of the Comanche horses. Braddock poured it on Sean's wound. "Damn," he said, "That hurt worse than getting shot." Then Braddock made a bandage and wrapped it around Sean's waist. "You'll be O.K. to ride," Braddock told him. "We don't have that far to get to the village. If you get to hurtin' too much, just give a yell, and I'll build a travois. Black Wolf and that scout can round up them Comanche ponies and take whatever prizes they want, but we're gonna go ahead and start back."

~~~~

They got back to the village in a few hours. Sean had made the ride O.K., but was starting to hurt. Braddock took him straight to their lodge. Katie began right away cleaning his wound and making a poultice for each side. Blue Swan gave Braddock a big hug and then started helping Katie.

Braddock then went to Standing Bear and told everything that had happened. "Braddock," he started, "I want to thank you and the others for our great victory. There will be feasting and dancing tonight. I pray that Shooter will heal well from his wound."

The dancing went on well into the night. There had never been such a lopsided victory over any of the Cheyenne enemies. Blue Swan and Braddock stayed out dancing most of the night. Katie stayed in the lodge looking after Sean. They talked well into the night. "I feel foolish," Sean said, "I should have known better than to assume that Comanche was dead. At least now I know that I can bleed just like anyone else."

"Yes, you can bleed like anyone else," Katie said, "And you are a great warrior, but you can be killed just like anyone else. Word of what happened today will spread. The Comanche will be after you, even if it takes years. They can hold a grudge for years. I have heard of them waiting as long as five or more years to kill someone who has humiliated them. You have a reputation now. You are the white man who kills with the long gun and the big pistol. Even the Pawnee might consider you a prize if they were to kill you. But first, we must get you healed up. You were very lucky today. There were no pieces of wood or arrowhead in your side, so you should heal quickly. It is not long before we will be married, and I want you in perfect condition for our wedding night."

"I will make sure I heal fast," Sean said, "I intend to make love to you all night long on our wedding night, and then start over again the next day."

"We better talk about something else," Katie said, "I am like you. I can't wait until we can be together. It's taking all my will power right now to keep from mounting you."

They didn't have to worry about things getting out of hand, because just as Katie finished talking, Blue Swan and Braddock came back to the lodge. "Time for you two to be asleep," Blue Swan said. Then Braddock pulled her under their blanket, and soon he and Blue Swan were making love. This didn't help Katie's and Sean's frame of mind.

CHAPTER EIGHT

With Katie's superb care, Sean was completely healed and ready for anything in only a month. He and Katie took several rides together; before he went out hunting to make sure that the motion of the horse would not bother him or re-injure his wound.

The first time he and Braddock went hunting, Sean thought himself to be overly cautious. He suspected a Comanche behind every rise and every bush. "Take it easy there, son," said Braddock. "What are ya afraid of anyway?"

"Gettin' killed," said Sean.

"It'll be all right, son," said Braddock, "Ya only been out of the saddle for a month. Ya haven't lost yer touch. Ya know that we could get killed any time out here. That's just the way it is, so don't dote on it. I don't think them Comanche will be back for a spell, but who knows for sure. We whipped them for fair and they won't forget it. Now let's do like we always do and pay attention to what sign we see and smell, not what we imagine. I'd sure hate to run into a grizz cause we're too busy worryin' 'bout them Comanche that aren't there."

Sean calmed down a bit, and after a short time he felt comfortable again. About an hour later, they found some sign and were working their way toward a small herd of antelope. "They should be just on the other side of this rise," said Braddock, "We'll tie the horses here. You ease around the left side and I'll ease to the right. Wind's in our favor."

Sean was almost around the rise, so he got down and crawled the rest of the way. The small herd came into view about two hundred yards out. He could not see Braddock, but the herd was watching something, and it wasn't him. Were they watching Braddock? Finally Braddock came into view, but it wasn't him they were watching either. Whatever it was, it was more to the right. "I better ease that way and be ready," Sean thought to himself. He hadn't crawled twenty yards when the antelope herd took off. Just as they bolted, Sean noticed movement about fifty yards in front of Braddock. "Just what in the hell? Pawnee?"

Three Pawnee warriors were running straight at Braddock. Sean took aim and fired, and one of the Pawnee fell. Braddock fired and another Pawnee flew backwards. The third one kept coming at Braddock. He stopped and loosed an arrow at Braddock, but missed. The Pawnee nocked another arrow and took off running toward Braddock again, but by now, Sean had the Walker out and was on target and squeezing. The Walker barked, and the Pawnee flew to his left, having been hit just above his right ear. He fell about twenty feet from Braddock

"Damn," said Braddock, "See, I told ya. Ya haven't lost it, and yer still a hell of a shot with that Sharps and that big pistol. Must've hit that Pawnee at fifty, sixty yards with that pistol. Shit, like I said before. My daughter's getting one hell of a man."

"I don't understand it," Sean said, "Why in the hell would they stand up and run straight at you? They got to know we have rifles. Don't they know we're gonna kill them?"

"Looks to me like these are just some young bucks tryin' to make a name fer themselves," Braddock said, "If they woulda stayed down and stuck arrows in us, there would be no glory in it. They mighta figured that if they went chargin' at us, we would just panic, and shoot wild. That would show how brave they were. That's important if a young brave is tryin' to make a name for his-self. But, it could be, they didn't know you was there."

"Well that's a possibility," said Sean, "But they sure learned the hard way. Now let's get back to huntin'. We still have a few hours."

"Yep," Braddock said, "And we best keep a good lookout in case them Pawnee got some friends around. You want any of them Pawnee ponies?"

"No, I don't," said Sean, "This horse I'm on is all I need. Some-thin' happens to him, then I'll get another. Now let's hunt."

They lucked out. They were all set to head back when they found some deer sign. They were able to drop two deer without any trouble from any Pawnee or other critters.

When they got back to the village, Sean asked Braddock not to tell the women about what had happened today. Braddock ex-plained to him that they should be told. It was their right to know because this is just the way things are, and trying to hide it, won't make it go away. Sean was surprised. Katie was not upset in the least. She told him that she knew she was getting a good man and he could take care of himself, and her too, and their children when they came.

~~~~

The next few months moved along without any trouble from the Pawnee or the Comanche. The women of the village were making Katie and Sean a new lodge that would be ready for the wedding night, and Blue Swan was making Katie a new wedding dress. She had also made Sean a new set of buckskin clothing for the wedding. There would be a buffalo hunt, and after the meat was cured and everything else done, the village would move. The wedding would take place at the new village after everything was properly set up.

The day of the wedding finally came. The morning of the wedding, Sean had a talk with Braddock. "Do you remember that talk we had sometime back about that custom of the man giving gifts to the family of the woman he wanted to marry?" asked Sean.

"Yeh, I recollect that talk," Braddock answered, "But I told ya I said that stuff just to get a rise out of ya. Ya already gave me that Sharps, and we're not wanting for anything."

"Well I've got something I've wanted you and Blue Swan to have for a long time. Now will you accept my gift?" Sean asked.

"I reckon I will," Braddock answered, "I wouldn't want to insult ya. So what is it?"

"Let's go into the lodge," Sean said. "I don't want the world to see this."

"Ya got my curiosity a goin' now, son," Braddock said.

They went into the lodge, and Sean started going through all the things he had kept from the wagon back when he first came to be with the Cheyenne. He took one of the leather bags that he had found in the false bottom of the wagon and handed it to Braddock.

"Holy shit," said Braddock. "That's gold. Where in the hell did you get this? There must be $500 here."

"There is $500 there, and it was my family's," said Sean. "And I want you to have it. This is some of the money they were going to use to start a new life in Oregon. I don't need all of it. I still have some left. Besides, I started my new life with you and the Cheyenne."

"I never knew that much gold even existed," said Braddock. "I don't think I've had any type of coin in my pocket for the last ten years. Been trading for anything we ever needed. One thing fer sure. If either of us go to spendin' this gold, we best be careful, and not flash too much around at once. If word would get out that we got gold coin to spend, some nasty white folks might like to find out where it is, and how much of it there is. Most Injuns don't have much use fer any type of money, but it won't be long till they learn what they can get with it, namely guns and such. Anyway, mebbe we can slip away from the village sometime and get ourselves to one of them new towns the white folks keep buildin'. Mebbe we can get somethin' nice for our women, and mebbe I can get some good whiskey. I got a little bit left that I'm gonna drink after the ceremony to celebrate a bit. You won't need any. That girl of mine intends to wear you out."

"Well, I want to thank you for allowing me to marry your daughter, and allowing me to live in your lodge for these last few years," said Sean, "And a man couldn't ask for a better father-in-law."

"Damn, son," Braddock said, "Ya still got them manners."

~~~~

It was finally time for the wedding. Sean just could not believe how beautiful Katie looked in her wedding dress. There were fancy beads all over it. Blue Swan must have worked very hard making it. The whole tribe stood and listened as the Holy Man said the words. Then the last words he said were, "Take her inside, she' s now your wife." Sean gave her a kiss that must have lasted at least a few minutes, then picked her up and carried her into the lodge. That was the last that anyone saw of them for three days. Even after three days, when someone saw them, they didn't see them for long.

After about a week, Blue Swan and Braddock were having an evening meal, when she said, "Braddock, if those two keep this up, you will be a grandfather this coming summer."

"Well don't you forget," Braddock said, "Yer gonna be a grandmother yerself, that is, unless them two keep this up and screw theirselves to death. I never heard of anybody doin' that, but these two might just be the first. He'll have to come out before too much longer. We got to git to huntin'. That love stuff is great, but ya gotta have somethin' to eat, so ya can keep up yer strength. Their gonna need all the strength they can get if they are gonna keep this up."

After about another week, Sean finally decided it was time to do some hunting. As they were leaving the village, Braddock asked Sean. "Are ya goin' for a record, son? We were startin' to worry. We thought maybe you was in there dead."

"I bet that when you were first with Blue Swan, folks were wondering about you too," Sean said. "She's a beautiful woman."

"Yeh, that's prob'ly true," Braddock said, "Sometimes I think about them days. It seems like ya just can't get enough of each other. We still have our moments, but not as often as we used to."

"I remember when I got my first kiss back in Tennessee," Sean said, "I was twelve. That feeling I got then was like nothing I'd ever felt before, and I don't just mean that feeling you get in your pants. I asked my Ma and Pa if those feelings stay with you even after you've been married a long time. Pa said it was like he was floating on a cloud and Ma was with him and they just couldn't get enough of each other., and it never went away. Ma said that Pa lit a fire in her that never seemed to go out. That's a pretty fair description of how I feel when I'm with Katie, and even when I'm not, like now. I believe Katie feels the same as me."

"That's good," Braddock said. "But we best quit talking about romance and such and pay attention to what we're out here for. I'd hate to get an arrow stuck in me cause I was daydreamin' bout the finer things in life instead of lookin' fer sign."

"Yep," said Sean, "Let's find some deer and get back. The women'll be there when we get back."

"Damn, son," Braddock said, "All this talk's gettin' me worked up. Blue Swan and me's gonna get down to business tonight."

It wasn't long before they found sign and made their stalk. They had their deer tied to the horses and were heading back well before dark. When they got back, Blue Swan could tell by just looking at Braddock what he wanted, but she knew she wanted it too. "Did you men have a nice hunt today?" She asked.

"Yeh," he answered, "But we did a good buncha talkin' too. Did you talk with Katie any today?"

"Yes I did," Blue Swan answered, "And from what I can see by the look in your eyes, we talked about the same things. Now let's go inside, we can have a meal later."

It was the same for Sean. As soon as he got to the lodge, Katie grabbed him and they went inside. They weren't seen till the next morning.

This is how it was until they went to the winter camp. But still, the only difference was that game was not as plentiful in the winter, and Sean was out a little longer, but when he got back each time, they were all over each other. They were getting quite a reputation. Some of the people thought that maybe white people had some strange power that made them so virile.

Everyone was surprised when spring arrived because Katie was not pregnant yet. Some of them were telling her that she should see the Medicine Man, and he would give her some special herbs that would help her get pregnant, but Katie and Sean were not worried about it. They knew that it would happen sooner or later, but for now, they didn't mind that it was just the two of them.

Spring gave way to summer, and summer to fall. The buffalo were plentiful, and there had been no trouble with the Pawnee or Comanche, but some of the other tribes had been having trouble with white men. The main Cheyenne Chief, Black Kettle, always tried to avoid trouble when he could, but he would fight if necessary. They had also heard that several of the tribes, especially the Comanche and the Pawnee, had been acquiring rifles from white traders.

Most of the rifles that the white traders brought to Standing Bears' band, were old and wore out. Some were even flintlock. But who knows, if the Comanche or the Pawnee came up with the right price, maybe they did have good rifles, maybe even breech loaders. Sean surely hoped they didn't.

Standing Bear and the elders believed that winter would come early this year, so they went to the winter camp a little earlier that usual. They were right. The first snow fell one week after the move. Ever since Sean had been with the Cheyenne, he never worried about keeping track of the days or the months. All he knew now were the seasons, but now he wondered about it some. Katie was finally pregnant. She would have the baby in the summer, but what month would it be? Would it be June or July? Was this month October? "Oh well," he said to himself, "It doesn't really matter. The baby will come out when it's ready, and it will be in the warm months. I hope my Katie won't get too uncomfortable in the heat."

"I suppose you expect me to give you a son," Katie said soon after she discovered she was pregnant.

"Katie darlin'," answered Sean, "If you don't mind, I'd like to have a little girl. It seems like everyone thinks they need to have a son, but if everyone did, sooner or later, there wouldn't be any girls. And with no girls, there couldn't be any more boys. But, my beautiful woman, I'll settle for strong and healthy, no matter the gender."

"You're a good man, my husband and lover," Katie said, "I will love you forever."

~~~~

Winter was very hard and lasted longer than usual, but even though the hunting was much harder, the clan still had plenty of food. They had done very well on the buffalo hunts, so there was plenty of dried meat and warm robes. With their long guns, Sean and Braddock were able to take a deer now and then, and sometimes, even an elk. Everyone enjoyed it when an elk was taken. There was plenty of fresh meat to go around, and the hides were highly prized.

When spring finally came, the camp was moved as usual, but this time, it was more to the west. Sean had heard a white trader say that they were now in Colorado. Sean had known that he'd been in Kansas, Nebraska, and the Dakotas, but this was the first time in Colorado. The buffalo herds were huge and the village was located next to some high hills that were covered with aspen, and the hills higher up were covered with pine. Sean wondered if this was part of the Rocky Mountains he'd heard about, or at least the foothills.

Katie was getting bigger all the time, but she still kept up with her normal duties. Sean always helped when he was not out hunting. Even though she was five or six months pregnant, Katie still had the urges of a young woman. Sometimes they would be out gathering wood, and she would grab Sean, and hurry him back to the lodge. "I need you now, my lover," Katie would always say, and Sean would always say, "Is it all right to do this, we won't hurt the baby, will we?" Then she always had to tell him how Blue Swan and Braddock kept it up until the day before she was born. "You must enter me from behind and be gentle. The baby will be fine," she would always say.

Every time Sean and Braddock went hunting up into the hills, Braddock was always telling Sean to watch for bear sign. They had seen, and had taken a few black bears in the hills, but Braddock knew that sooner or later, someone from the band would have a run in with a grizz. It was spring, and a sow with cubs was one of the most dangerous things around. Braddock always told Sean, "When a grizz comes chargin' at you, it won't be standin' on it's hind legs like some folks think. It'll come barrelin' in on all fours faster'n a horse and go to bitin' at your head and neck. And they can be so quiet. It just don't seem possible that somethin' that big can be so quiet. Plus they can smell as well as any critter I know. I think they can smell blood a mile off. I've seem them run down a buffalo calf too. Any time we shoot some game, we need to reload quick, and one of us watch while the other goes to work. A big boar just loves to take food from some other critter who's done all the work. Keep that big pistol handy too. Don't mean to sound overly concerned, but I've seen what a grizz can do."

"We'll be as ready as ready can be," said Sean, "Now I saw some movement over to the right. Let's slip over that way. I'm hopin' it was an elk."

It was an elk, and Sean closed in and dropped it at two hundred yards. Sean went to work on it while Braddock kept watch. It was a smaller cow, and Sean got it quartered and tied to the horses in no time. "Let's get down outta these hills now where we can see better just in case a grizz would try to slip up on us." Braddock said. "This wind is startin' to whip around too. That makes me a little edgy. I must be gettin' spooky in my old age."

"It doesn't sound like you're over doin' it when it comes to a grizzly," Sean said, "If what you tell me is even half true, we can't ever be too cautious. If we ever do have a run in with one, I just hope we see him before he knows we're even around. And you're not gettin' old. At least that's not what Katie hears from Blue Swan."

"Now let's not get started talkin' bout them things," Braddock said, "I don't wanna think myself into gettin' worked up till we get back."

When they got back to the village, Katie was anxiously waiting. As soon as the meat and the horses were taken care of, she pulled Sean into the lodge. "We can eat later," she said.

After the evening meal, Sean asked Katie if she could make something for him.

"What is it I can make for you?" She asked.

"I need a new holster for this big pistol," Sean answered. "This thing I've been using for over four years now is just worn out. I never did like that flap. It'll need to be fairly hard so the pistol will slide out easily when I pull it, and long enough so the front sight won't stick out and get caught at the bottom. The top must be low enough so I can grab the handle easily, and I need a small strap so I can strap it in so it won't slide out. Make the strap easy to undo so I can flip it off with my thumb in a hurry if the need arises. Then I'll need a belt and the holster can slide over the belt so I can wear it on my left side and pull the pistol with my right hand. This will make it more comfortable when I'm riding too. If I did have an accidental discharge, it would miss my leg. The only thing I would get would be maybe a powder burn."

"We have plenty of hides already cured, thanks to your hunting skill," she said, "I should have this made before you hunt again. Since you brought in the elk today, you won't need to go out real soon. I can get this done, and still have time for you."

Katie had the belt and holster done in two days. She had used the old flap holster as a model to get started, then finished it the way Sean wanted. Sean was totally impressed. The pistol fit in it perfectly, not too tight. The strap was made to be flipped off with his thumb, and was positioned so it wouldn't catch the hammer when the pistol was drawn. She had also greased the inside of the holster to help with speed in drawing the pistol. If there was a better woman than Katie anywhere in the world, Sean wouldn't believe it. They wouldn't get much sleep tonight.

CHAPTER NINE

Two days later, Sean and Braddock went hunting up in the hills. They had found some elk droppings and figured they were less than an hour old. "Let's get up near the top of this next hill," Braddock said, "They could be grazing down the other side in that small clearing we spotted last time out." As they neared the top, Braddock stopped and told Sean to stop too. "Look up that tree straight ahead about nine, ten feet off the ground," Braddock said, "You see that?"

"I sure do," said Sean, "Is that where some big boar grizzly marked his territory?"

"It surely is," answered Braddock, "And by the look of that sap runnin' outta that tree, it wasn't done too long ago. We best be on the look out. This wind is whippin'. If he's near, he could come at us from any direction."

Before anything else was said by either of them, the horses started prancing and bucking, and both of them were thrown. The horses then ran off back down the hill. "Damn," said Braddock, "Our rifles are with them horses. That grizz must be close. We better—" He couldn't finish.

Sean had just got back up and was getting his wits back when he saw the bear charging straight at him. He wasn't one hundred feet away. Sean drew the Walker and fired three shots so quickly, they sounded like one. The bear was still coming and slammed right into Sean. He went down with the bear right on top of him. "Do I know any good prayers?" thought Sean, "I better get a good one and real quick like." The bear didn't move.

"Son of a bitch," shouted Braddock, "You killed that son of a bitch. Just how in the hell? Shit, there's three holes in his damn head. Just how could anyone do that? Are you still with me there son?"

"Yes, I'm still with you," answered Sean, "I don't why I'm not dead, but let's get this big boy offa me."

It took some doing to get the bear off of Sean. He was huge. Braddock had to go round up the horses and tie ropes to the bear's legs and then to the saddles to get it pulled off Sean. The horses were not happy. They could smell this bear and didn't like it. They didn't care if it was dead or not. When the bear was off of Sean, Braddock checked him out to make sure there were no broken bones and if maybe something inside got hurt. He was fine.

"I never ate grizz before, but I s'pect we'll be eatin' some now," said Braddock, "That big boy'll make you a fine rug too. Damn, son, just how in the hell can you shoot like that. It just don't seem possible. If someone told me what just happened, I wouldn't believe it. Damn!"

"I probably wouldn't believe it if someone told me either," said Sean, "But that bear's dead and I'm not, so it must've happened. Now let's get this thing skinned and cut up. We'll need to build some travoises to haul stuff. These horses won't tolerate a fresh bear skin on their back."

When they got back to the village, it was much later that usual, and the women had been worried. Sean ran up to Katie, grabbed her up and kissed her till he was out of breath. "Katie darlin'," Sean said, "I want to thank you for saving my life today."

"How did I do that?" Katie asked.

"That holster you made me, darlin'," Sean said, "I was able to get my pistol out and kill that bear before he killed me."

The rest of spring went by and was uneventful. Nothing happened that could compare to the grizzly incident. Summer came and it became much warmer. Katie looked very uncomfortable at times, but she still kept up with her duties. One day she was out gathering firewood when her water broke. Sean was with her at the time and he picked her up and carried her back to the lodge. Blue Swan and some of the other women stayed with her. There were no problems, and a few hours later, a beautiful baby girl was born. Sean was so proud. The women cleaned up the baby and handed her to Sean for a look, then gave her back to Katie. It wasn't long, and she had the baby pressed to her breast and the milk was flowing.

"What should we name our daughter, my husband and lover?" Katie asked.

"I've thought and thought about this," Sean answered, "But I'm still not sure. What would you like to name her, Katie darlin'?"

"Well, you are white, and I am half white, so our daughter is three fourths white," Katie said. "I think we should give her a white name. I have one. What was you mother's name?"

"It was Margaret," answered Sean, "Some people call women named Margaret, Maggie for short. We could call her Maggie if it's all right with you?"

"Maggie," she said, "That sounds good. We will call her Maggie, Maggie O'Rourke."

Little Maggie was a good healthy baby and grew like a weed. Katie was anxious to have another baby, so as soon as she was ready, they got busy trying. Blue Swan didn't mind keeping little Maggie at times when Sean and Katie felt romantically inclined. It had been a long time since she had taken care of a young one. She also liked to take Maggie out and show her off.

~~~~

It was fall now. There would be one more buffalo hunt, then they would go to the winter camp. Sean and Braddock got their buffalo as usual, but this hunt, several of the warriors had been hurt. Several horses had been killed too. Sean and Braddock went back out after the braves had finished their hunt, and took several more buffalo to help out the families of the injured braves. The braves later recovered from their injuries, but some of them would walk with a limp the rest of their lives. One of them was Black Wolf, Sean's brother-in-law.

The move to the winter camp went without any problems at all. It was a good spot, good water, plenty of trees, and well protected from the wind. Katie became pregnant again, and if Sean had figured it right, the baby would be born about late summer. He hoped the heat would not bother Katie. Even though this was their second child, Katie still showed no signs of losing interest in being with Sean. Sean felt the same way. They didn't like the winter because of the cold, but they did like it because the days were shorter and they would spend more time in the lodge.

Braddock and Sean did a good job supplying the fresh meat as usual. On one of their hunts, they ran into some Pawnee. These Pawnee were carrying rifles, but Sean and Braddock could see that they were old muzzle loaders. At first, it looked like there might be a fight, but when the Pawnee got closer, they just turned and rode away. "I bet them Pawnee know who you are and saw these long guns of ours, and decided it best to leave us alone," Braddock said.

"I hope you're right," said Sean, "And I hope that if we run into any Comanche this winter, they act the same."

There were no Pawnee or Comanche seen the rest of the winter. They did run into a small party of Arapaho on a hunt one day and invited them back to the village for a meal and to spend the night. They accepted. Sean asked them if they were well supplied for winter and could he help if anything was needed.

"Damn, son," Braddock said, "After all this time, ya still got them manners."

The Arapaho said that they were well supplied and thanked Sean for the offer, but then they said they were having more problems with the white men. The white men were everywhere trying to find the yellow stone. Sean knew they were talking about gold, and he had heard that it makes most men crazy. He remembered Braddock telling him to be careful not to flash around the gold coins too much if they went to a town sometime.

Next morning, the Arapaho thanked them, and then were on their way. "I sure hope there's no gold in our territory," said Braddock, "I heard all kindsa stories about killin' and such out in California when the rush was on out there. Sure a few got rich, but the one's that made the money, were the one's sellin' the liquor and the women. Weren't no law out in them gold fields. Lotta claim jumpin' goin' on."

"I hope you're right," Sean said, "If they did find gold out here, then all them folks would expect the soldiers to come out here and protect them. It'd end up being a big mess. There's more of them than there is us. We may kill some of them, but they'd get us in the end."

"You sound just like Black Kettle," Braddock said, "He always keeps out of a fight if he can, but he'll get right in it, if there's no other way. He knows in the end, we couldn't win. There just too many of them."

~~~~

Spring came and the village was moved. Little Maggie was walking now, but she still needed to be carried on the move. Sean had her on his horse a good bit of the time. Katie wasn't too big and was able ride her pony with no problems. Sean wasn't sure, but he figured they were somewhere in Nebraska. The countryside was mostly open plains with rolling hills, very little brush, and there were small groves of trees next to the small streams. They had seen plenty of buffalo, deer, and antelope during the move, so they would be well supplied with meat.

Sean and Braddock were out hunting one day, had gotten their game, and were on their way back to the village, when Braddock said to Sean. "I heard tell of a town not too far from here. S'posed to be fair sized. Bet they got some good stores. How bout us goin' there soon and get somethin' nice for the women. If it's where I think it is, we won't be gone even fer a week."

"Sounds good to me," Sean said, "If Katie and Blue Swan don't mind, we could go after our next hunt. Make sure they got plenty before we go."

That evening, Sean told Katie about proposed trip. At first she didn't seem too happy. She and Sean had never spent even one night apart after they had been married. She thought about it for a while, and then decided it was a good idea. "You know what I want you to bring us?" she said, "I want some of that ham like you had from your wagon when you first came to be with us. I had never had it before and it was very good. I know Braddock will want to get some whiskey. You can keep an eye on him and make sure he doesn't get drunk and get into trouble before you get back. Other than that, I do not need anything. Of course if you see something pretty, and think I might like it, that would be O.K. too."

CHAPTER TEN

A few days later, the men had their hunt. There would be plenty of meat during their absence.

The day before they were to leave, Sean asked Standing Bear if there was anything he could get him from this town. Standing Bear told him he wanted this thing you could look through, and it would make stuff far away, look closer. Sean explained to him that this was called a telescope, or a spyglass, which was what most people called it.

The next morning, they kissed the women goodbye, little Maggie too, and were on their way. They each had a packhorse. Braddock insisted on this. "You never know what we might be bringin' back," he said. "Might be too much fer us to carry on our ridin' horses." They had made sure they had plenty of ammunition, food, water, and money too. "Remember what I said about not flashing too mucha this gold coin around," Braddock said, "Someone might try to take it from us, and then we'd hafta kill 'em. White folks can be funny about killins in a town. Some crap bout law and order and such. Let's just be careful as best we can."

The ride to town took three days, but they had no problems. When they did get there, Braddock was amazed. It must have been a heck of a long time since he'd been to a town by the way he was acting. "Looky there son," Braddock said, "This town's got two saloons. There's the general store over there. They even got a Marshal's office. We wanna make sure we don't end up in there."

"O.K., where we going first?" asked Sean.

"Well let's get a drink at this first saloon, then a drink at the other, then we'll do our shoppin'," said Braddock. "We'll keep our guns with us."

"What'll ya have?" the bartender asked as they stepped up to the bar.

"Got any bourbon?" Braddock asked.

"Yes sir we do, just come in last week," he answered.

"Get us both one," said Braddock.

"Comin' right up," the bartender said, "Where you fellers from? Haven't seen ya in here before. Don't get too many men wearing buckskins any more either."

"We're from southa here, just passin' through," answered Braddock.

"Did ya have any Injun trouble on yer way here?" the bartender asked.

"No, we don't bother them, and they don't bother us," said Braddock.

"They don't bother you cause you smell just like an Injun," came a voice from across the room.

Sean turned around to see a big man standing with his back to the far wall, and rolling up his sleeves like he was getting ready for a fight. Sean could see that the man wasn't armed, so he handed Braddock his gun belt and Sharps, and went over to the man and got right in his face. Without saying a word, Sean gave him a left in the gut, then a right upper cut, knocking him backwards. He didn't go down, and came back and took a swing at Sean with his right, but missed. Sean had side stepped, and then came back with another right to his gut. He buckled over and then Sean grabbed the back of his head and slammed his face into his right knee. Blood went flying from his nose. He went down, but didn't stay down. He took another swing with his right and missed again. Sean put a left hook to his right jaw and sent him sideways. As he was falling, Sean gave him another left hook to the jaw again. This time he stayed down.

"Holy shit, son," said Braddock, "Yer not just a shooter. You can fight too."

"Yes, I can," said Sean. "I don't mind being told I smell like an Indian, I just didn't like the way he said it. Hey bartender, is that fella someone of any importance around here?"

"No, he's just a local loud mouth," the bartender answered, "but he's got a couple brothers that are worse than him. Don't know if they're in town or not. I'd keep my eyes peeled if I was you."

"Thanks, appreciate it," Sean said. "There wasn't any chairs or anything broken, so you don't have to worry about any damages. Only thing hurt was that fella. Hey Braddock, let's finish this drink, then try that other place."

"Sounds good," Braddock said. "Yer not gonna whip anybody in that place are ya?

"Only if they need it," Sean said.

This saloon wasn't too much different from the other one, but there were a couple of women there. Sean didn't know if they were whores, or if they were there just to get the men to buy more drinks. It didn't matter. One drink, and then they'd go shopping.

"I think I'll try a beer this time," he told Braddock. "I've never had beer before. May as well give it a try. Got any beer there, bartender?" asked Sean.

"Sorry son," said the bartender, "my shipment hasn't made it yet this week."

"Well I reckon we'll have bourbon if you have it, if not, your best whiskey will do," said Sean.

The drinks arrived, and they were about to take a sip, when they heard a voice from behind. "You fellas intend to be in town very long?"

They turned around and the first thing they saw was the tin star. "You must be the Marshal," said Braddock.

"Yes I am, name's Luke Wilson. Now would you mind answering my question?" he said.

"No we don't mind answering your question," said Sean. "We intend to finish this drink, go to the general store, then be on our way. Does that suit you, Marshal?"

"Yes sir, it surely does," answered the Marshal. "That asshole you just whooped over there's got two brothers. They all could use a good whoopin', but I'd rather it happened out of town."

"Well, if they don't bother us, we won't bother them," said Sean, "and I thank you for your kindness. Now we'll finish them drinks. Two bottles to go, bartender."

The general store had about anything anyone could want. After spending some time looking, they made their purchases. Braddock bought Blue Swan a whole new set of cooking pots, and a coffee pot, with some coffee too. Sean bought several hams and a nice necklace that he thought Katie would like, plus some more ammunition for the Sharps. Then he remembered the spyglass for Standing Bear. They paid, went out the door, and were putting their gifts on the packhorses, when the brothers showed up, all three of them.

They were all armed. Two were packing pistols, and the other one, on the far left, had a shotgun, a double barrel. "We don't like Injuns," said the one who had taken the beating. "We kill 'em when we see 'em." Sean looked across the street. The Marshal was watching.

"Are you gonna talk us to death?" asked Sean.

As soon as Sean finished speaking, the one with the shotgun, started lowering the barrel to fire. Before he got it lowered, Sean had drawn the Walker and put a round in his chest. Before the other two could get their pistols clear of their holsters, they were falling backwards with holes in their chests. They were dead before they hit the ground.

The Marshal came running out in the street. "Jesus H. Christ," he said, "How in the hell did you just do that? They never even got their guns pulled. I never. I just never. I never even heard of something like this. How would you like a job? Town's growing. Sure could use a deputy."

"Thanks, but no thanks," said Sean, "We got to be on our way. At least you won't have to worry about those three anymore."

On the way back, Braddock was unusually quiet. Then he said, "Damn, son, I didn't even get a shot off back there. I feel embarrassed, but I sure am glad you know how to use that pistol. I'd say it's a good thing nobody knows us around here. Shootin' like that draws attention. White folks are kinda like Injuns in some ways. A young brave's gotta prove he's better than someone else. Could be some white fella thinks he'd be better than you and hafta find out."

They got back to the village in less than a week as Braddock had expected, but when they came to where they would be able to see the village, it wasn't there. "Just what in the hell," said Braddock. "Why'd they move? I don't see any bad sign. Get out that spyglass and take a look, son."

Sean took out the spyglass, looked all around, and didn't see anything. Then he saw them. "Look in the trees," he told Braddock, "Look in the trees."

Braddock looked and then he cursed. "Damn it, damn it to hell," he said. There must have been twenty or more bodies up in the trees. "We best go down there and see what we can see."

When they got to the village, Sean's worst fears were confirmed. He found Katie's body and little Maggie's was with her. Why? What had happened? Braddock looked at the other bodies. He didn't see Blue Swan. Standing Bear and several of the elders had died too. What or who did this? Sean cried for the first time since he was a little kid back in Tennessee. "We best get moving and find the village. Can't be more'n a days ride from here," said Braddock.

They found the village the next day. They heard it before they got there. A lot of the women were still wailing. They found Blue Swan. She began telling them what had happened. "Right after you had left, a few people started getting sick. No one thought too much about it. The next day a few more got sick, and the next day a few more. The next day, the first ones who got sick, died. The next day, more got sick, and more died. Then the next day, more died.

Katie and little Maggie were the first ones to die. Standing Bear said there was something in this place that was making us sick and we had to move. He died before we got moved. I think it was the cholera that was killing us. I have heard other tribes talk about the cholera and how fast it can kill. They died so fast, there was nothing we could do. We placed the bodies in the trees because we didn't want to stay any longer building the burial platforms. No one has been sick since we have come to this place. Black Wolf is now our Chief. His wife and children died also. Every lodge has lost someone. Black Wolf thinks it would be best if we joined another band since we are so small now. I think he is right."

Sean was hurting. He didn't know what he wanted to do. He thought to himself, "First my parents, and now my own family. Why? Just why in the hell? It would have been bad enough if they had been killed by Pawnee or Comanche, but this? Something you can't see. You don't know how to fight back." He couldn't sleep, and he couldn't eat.

Blue Swan tried to comfort him, but it was hard for her too. She had lost a daughter, three grandchildren, and many friends. "You must try to eat," she told Sean. "You must keep up your strength so you do not become sick. What has happened will be very hard to live with, but we must live with it. Life is not always fair, no matter where you are."

"I'm going to take off and be by myself for a while," said Sean, "I need time to think. I don't know how long I will be gone. I will be back some day, and I want you to know that I have loved you, Braddock, and all the Cheyenne. You were my new family, and I needed you."

~~~~

The next day, Sean loaded up his belongings, and went to tell everyone goodbye. First he went to Black Wolf and told him he was thankful because Black Wolf had brought him to the

Cheyenne and to his mother's lodge. Then, he went to every lodge, and said his goodbyes. Then he went back to Blue Swan's lodge. Braddock and she were waiting for him. Sean reached into his saddlebags and pulled out a small package and handed it to Blue Swan. "This is the necklace I bought for Katie," Sean said, "I want you to have it. Braddock, do you have plenty of ammunition for the Sharps? I have extra that I bought in that town if you need any?"

"I'm good son," Braddock said, "Ya got any idea where yer goin'?"

"No, not really," Sean answered, "I'm just going. I do believe I'll head south for a while though."

"Well, if yer agoin' that way, keep an eye out fer them Comanche," Braddock said, "I figure they still remember back when we whipped 'em. Don't forget us, son. You'll always be in our hearts. Take care of that mare you got yer belongins on. She's young yet, and a little high strung, but she can run like the wind."

When Sean saddled up, Blue swan ran over to him. "Bend down so I can kiss my son-in-law goodbye," she said. Sean bent down and when she kissed his cheek, he gave her a good hug, and then was on his way.

The first day, he just rode and rode, stopping only to rest and water the horses. He drank some water, but he did not eat. He never saw a living soul or even a buffalo, or an antelope. At night, he camped, but he still did not eat. He couldn't sleep either. He hobbled the horses, but not tightly, so they could graze a little if they wanted.

The next morning, he drank a little water, watered the horses, and took off headed south again. He cried a little that morning and was glad there was no one around to see him. In the afternoon, he finally decided he was hungry and needed to eat. "Should I have a fire out here on this open plain for the whole world to see?" he thought to himself, "Or should I just eat some of this jerky? I'm havin' a fire. Gonna make some coffee, and heat up some of that ham Katie liked so well."

He slept well that night. He had dreams of Katie and all the good times they had. Everything they ever did together was in his dreams. Little Maggie was there too. Then he woke up. He looked all around. Where were they? Then he realized that he was just dreaming. He cried a little, then went back to sleep.

A week went by, and he still did not see anyone. He had seen unshod pony tracks, but no people. Buffalo seemed plentiful now. There were also antelope and deer herds. He figured with this much game around, sooner or later, he would see some Pawnee, or maybe even another band of Cheyenne.

The next day, he came to a big rise and decided to get to the top and get a good look, but kept himself off the skyline. When he neared the top, he tied the horses to a scrub bush, got out the spyglass that he had bought for Standing Bear, and crawled to the top. Down below was a big village. He could tell right away that it was Pawnee. "I best get down from here and swing out to the west and try to get around them without getting spotted," Sean said to himself. He crawled back down to his horses.

Sean kept a few miles back from the village while heading west. Then after several miles, he turned back south. "I might as well go to Texas," Sean said to himself. "I've never been there. I might as well go down there and see why the Comanche like it down there. Maybe I'll go see the Alamo. Might be interesting to see. I hear there's plenty of Mexicans in Texas too. Never have seen one of them either. Maybe I could learn to speak Mexican too, or is it called Spanish?"

A few days later, Sean decided it was time to get some fresh meat, so when he got the chance, he dropped an antelope. He was just about to start working on it when he noticed three riders coming from the south. Sean got out the spyglass to have a look. They were Indians, and they were not wearing paint and they looked tired and worn out. When they got closer, Sean used some sign language to let them know he was peaceful, and welcomed them. They signed back. They were Kiowa. They had come up from Texas to get away from the Rangers who were always after them. Then Sean spoke some Cheyenne to see if any of them understood, and one of them did. "I am called Dark Horse," he said. "Are you the young white man who lives with the Cheyenne and kills with the long gun and the big pistol?"

"Yes, I am," answered Sean. "My name is O'Rourke, Sean O'Rourke."

"Why are you out here and not with your people?" asked Dark Horse.

"The cholera took my family and many of our band," answered Sean. "I am out here trying to figure out what to do."

"I have heard of the cholera. It is not a good way to die. We have heard about you from our friends the Comanche," the Kiowa said. "They talked about you for a long time. and how they were going to kill you. But their band was almost wiped out by the white man's sickness. I think you call it the smallpox."

"I always heard that the Comanche would keep a grudge forever," Sean said, "So it must be true. You look tired and hungry. I will gladly share this antelope with you."

"Yes, we are tired and hungry," the Kiowas said. "We are a small band, and we have no rifles. We have been hunting, but with no luck. There are just too many white people here now. It seems they kill off the game just to be killing. Let us go to our village. You will be welcome."

On the way to the village, Sean spotted some deer a good way off. A small herd of twelve or so. "You stay here," he told the Kiowa. I will see if I can get a deer or two for you."

"They are too far, white man," said the Kiowa, "No one can shoot that far."

"Don't be too sure of that," Sean said. "Now you just stay put and let me get to work."

The deer were well over six hundred yards away and were upwind. If they knew Sean was there, they didn't seem to care. They just kept grazing. Sean crawled another fifty yards toward them, then got ready to fire. He squeezed the trigger and the Sharps barked. Before the bullet struck its target, Sean had reloaded. Before the deer reacted, he fired again. Two deer lay dead.

"You are the shooter, aren't you white man?" the Kiowa said. "No wonder you killed so many Comanche, and no wonder they wanted to kill you."

They picked up the deer and headed for the Kiowa village. When they arrived, Sean could see that they were a poor band. When Dark Horse introduced Sean to everyone and told what he had done, several of the women ran up to him and hugged him. It apparently had been a long time since they had a good meal. The Chief's name was Flying Eagle, and he began telling Sean about all the troubles they were having in Texas. Sooner or later he said, they were going to band together with the Comanche and have a big war against the whites. The Rangers had been especially hard on them. Even if it wasn't the Kiowa that caused any trouble, it didn't matter. An Indian was an Indian.

"How much farther is it till I get to Texas?" Sean asked the Chief.

"Why do you want to go to Texas?" asked the Chief.

"Because I've never been there," said Sean. "After I see it, I might go somewhere else."

"When is the last time you talked with any other white men?" the Chief asked.

"It hasn't been too long ago," answered Sean. "I was up in Nebraska. Why do you ask?"

"We have heard from white traders, that sooner or later, there will be a big war back east, a war about the black men. We are hoping it will come and the Rangers and the blue soldiers will leave and go to be in it. I have never seen a black man. What are they like?" he asked.

"They are people just like anyone else," answered Sean. "Their skin is dark, much darker than yours. Years ago, they were taken by force, from a place called Africa to be used as slaves on big farms called plantations. The slaves can be bought and sold like cattle. The plantations are in the southern part of the country. After all these years, some people up North have decided that slavery should not be allowed. The southern part of the country thinks they should be able to do whatever they want. If the North doesn't like it, they will form their own country. The North will fight to keep the country from breaking apart."

"My family left the South five years ago because we knew that sooner or later, a war was coming. They will not be alive to see it. They were killed by bad white men when we were on our way to

Oregon. That is how I came to be with the Cheyenne. They found me right after my parents were killed."

"You have told us much," the Chief said. "I sort of understand about the slaves, and I hope the war comes and the Rangers and blue soldiers go back to be in it. We will talk more tomorrow. Let's eat now. Then I'm going to rest. I'm old now and I need more rest than I used to. Dark Horse has asked that you spend the night in his lodge."

The next morning, Sean was up at daybreak, thanked everyone for their hospitality, and was on his way. "You are a good man, Sean O'Rourke," Flying Eagle said as Sean was leaving. "You will always be welcome in our village."

CHAPTER ELEVEN

As he was moving along, Sean spent a lot of time thinking about what he would do if a war did come. Would he go back and join the North? He knew there was no way he would join the South just because he was from Tennessee. His family had come West to avoid the war they knew would come. Most of the people in the South didn't have slaves. Only the rich people, the bankers, lawyers, plantation owners, and whoever else had money were the slave owners. Would the common people help fight a war because the people in power in their state want to keep slaves? That wouldn't make sense. That war with Mexico a few years back didn't make any sense either, but the country went along with it. "I guess I'll worry about it when it happens," he said to himself. "I surely hope it doesn't." Then he said to himself, "I better quit thinking so hard and talking to myself and pay attention to where I am and what's goin' on around me. I didn't come down here to get another arrow stuck in me."

Just about the time Sean figured it was time to start paying attention, he noticed a dust cloud to the south. What in the world would make a dust cloud that big? He got the answer in just a few minutes. It was a troop of cavalry. Sean kept moving, but stopped when they got closer. He heard someone yell, "Troop halt." Then two of them rode over to him. "I'm Lieutenant Carter and this is Sergeant O'Connor," said the one who looked like he was in charge. "We're making a sweep up this way because we have reports of hostiles in the area. Have you seen any hostiles, sir?"

"Hostiles, what do you mean by hostiles?" Sean asked him.

"I mean Indians. Have you seen any Indians?" the Lieutenant said.

"Why?" asked Sean, "Was I supposed to have seen any?"

About this time, the Sergeant couldn't keep himself from laughing, and let out a good laugh.

"What are you laughing at Sergeant," the Lieutenant said, "There's been nothing said that was funny. Now my good man, have you seen any hostiles, I mean Indians?"

Sean lied. "No I haven't. I've come down here from Nebraska. I saw unshod pony tracks, maybe two hundred miles north of here, but no Indians. By the way, name's O'Rourke, Sean O'Rourke."

"Well thank you for your time Mr. O'Rourke," the Lieutenant said. "We must be on our way. Let's go Sergeant."

As they were leaving, the Sergeant stayed back a little, then said to Sean. "You'll have to forgive him, my Irish friend. He's new at this. First time out. We're hoping he doesn't get us killed." Then he nodded his head, and went back to the troop.

"Hey," yelled Sean. "I forgot to ask you. How much farther is it to Texas?"

"Keep heading south," the Sergeant yelled. "You'll be there tomorrow."

Then Sean heard someone yell, "Fo-o-or-ward, Ho," and the troop left heading northeast.

"I wonder why soldiers talk that way," thought Sean. "I guess someone's got to be in charge and tell them what to do."

As Sean was moving along, not two hours after the cavalry had left, a rider came galloping his way. He was a soldier. His horse was covered in sweat and breathing hard. When he got to Sean, he stopped and asked, "How far am I behind that cavalry troop that just came through here?"

"They're two hours ahead of you," answered Sean, "You'll run that horse to death if you don't slow down some."

"It can't be helped," the rider said, "Gotta get this message to the Lieutenant. The war's started. The rebels have fired on Fort Sumter." Then he was gone.

"Well them idiots finally got it started," Sean said to himself. "I'll just wait here for that cavalry troop. They should be headed back this way. I'll go with them back to their fort and find out what's really goin' on."

The next morning, the troop arrived about mid morning. Sean asked for permission to ride with them back to the fort. "That will be fine," the Lieutenant said, "We can always use another man if we would get ambushed or something."

"Do you know anything more about what's happened," Sean asked.

"No," he answered, "All I know is that the rebels have fired on Fort Sumter, and I am to return to the fort and await further orders."

"Just where in the hell is Fort Sumter, Lieutenant?" asked Sean.

"Somewhere on the coast of South Carolina, right in the heart of secessionism," he answered.

Sean rode back to the fort next to Sergeant O'Connor. "How long have you been in the army, my mick friend" asked Sean.

"Well let's see. I joined in '46 to help fight the Mexicans, so that makes it fifteen years, doesn't it." he answered. "I joined the army not too long after I got to America. I couldn't find decent work, and my wife had just died during childbirth. Lost both of them. So what have you been up to? Those buckskins you're wearing are showin' some wear. You some kind of renegade or something?"

"I never thought of that before." said Sean. "I guess some folks would consider me a renegade. I've lived with the Cheyenne for the last five to six years. Originally from Tennessee. My family left there to get away from the war that was coming. Our little wagon train was massacred by outlaws, white men. I survived, and was found by the Cheyenne, and been there ever since. I had a wife and child too. The cholera took them."

"And how was it that you were able to survive the massacre?" asked O'Connor.

"I was out hunting for some fresh meat when they attacked," Sean answered. "There were ten of them, and we were only three families. We were trying to catch up to a wagon train that was a few days ahead of us. They killed everyone, but my Pa and the rest killed five of them. I killed the other five, three with this Sharps, and the other two with this pistol. One of them had been wounded and slipped away while I was killin' his friends. As I was buryin' everyone, these Cheyenne showed up, and had the one that got away with them. I shot him in the head with this pistol. The Cheyenne helped me bury the rest of the wagon train people, and I gave them everything except what was with my wagon. They got horses, mules, food, guns, all of it. They took me to their village, and that's where I've been till not that long ago."

"And how old were you when all this happened, my young friend?" asked the Sergeant.

"I was twelve," answered Sean.

"Mother Mary and Joseph, If what you say is true, you must be some tough customer. I suppose you're even better now with that Sharps and that pistol than you were when you were twelve?" asked O'Connor.

"Yes I am," answered Sean. "They've come in handy the last few years. I'm still alive."

"You know my friend, the army could sure use men that know how to use them weapons. You say you're from Tennessee? You wouldn't be thinking about fighting for the South, would you?" asked the Sergeant.

"No," I would never do that. You being Irish, you know what it's like to be treated as bad as a slave. When we first got our land in Tennessee, there was a slave family that came with the land. First thing my Pa did, was give him his freedom. Pa kept him on and paid him wages. Jim, that was his name. He had a wife, Betsy, and a son, Little Jim. Betsy died of pneumonia, Jim got killed in a shoot out on our place, and Little Jim went north. Haven't seen, or heard anything about him since.

"Well, young Sean," said the Sergeant, "Since you're telling your life history, tell me why there was a shootout on your place."

"My Pa and Jim were in town one day getting supplies, and four white trash guys said some insulting things to Pa, so him and Jim beat the hell out of them. They didn't like it that a black man helped whip some white men. A few days later, they got drunked up, got some more help, and came out to our place one night to burn us out and hang Pa and Jim. There were eight of them, and we killed them all. Jim got killed, and Little Jim got wounded."

"And how many of them did you kill?" asked the Sergeant.

"I killed three of them with this Walker I'm wearing," answered Sean. "My Pa killed two, and my Ma killed one. Jim killed the other two."

"And how was your life with the Cheyenne?" asked O'Connor. "Us white folks really have no idea what they are like. All you ever hear is that they're a bunch of blood thirsty savages, killin' women, children, and babies."

"That killin' stuff is a bunch of bull shit. The Cheyenne are good people, very polite They just want to live and be left alone. I had a good life," said Sean. "We moved several times a year following the buffalo herds. That was our main food source, plus the hides are used for teepees and such. The brave who took me to the Cheyenne, had a mother who had taken up with a white man. Her first husband had been killed by the Pawnee. Blue Swan was her name. She welcomed me into her lodge. The white man, Braddock was his name, taught me how to hunt and track. Well they had a daughter together. Her name was Katie. Katie became my wife when we were both fifteen. We had a daughter, Maggie, and Katie was pregnant again when the cholera took them."

"I've heard that some tribes hate other tribes," said O'Connor. "Is that true?"

"Yes, that 's true," answered Sean. "Some tribes been killin' each other for years. We had some run ins with Comanche and Pawnee when I was with the Cheyenne. Some tribes are good friends too. The Lakota, or Sioux, the Arapaho, and the Cheyenne, are very good friends. Soldiers out here need to know that. There could be thousands of them if they ever got together. Down in Texas, the Comanche and the Kiowa are good friends."

"Since you know all this," O'Connor started, "You could stay out here and scout for the army."

"No, I would never do that," said Sean, "The only Indians I would kill, would be the ones trying' to kill me. There's gettin' to be too many white folks out here anyway. The Indians will die, or get killed, or forced on a reservation soon enough without my help. If I was with the Cheyenne, I would fight the white folks too. The main Chief of the Cheyenne, Black Kettle, is a good man. He goes out of his way to avoid a fight, but he'll fight when necessary. It'll be a while before the Cheyenne are forced on a reservation."

"Sounds like you've already had a full life, my friend," said the Sergeant. "You're not yet eighteen, are you?"

"No," answered Sean, "won't be eighteen till this fall. Let's talk about something else now. Is there a town close to that fort of yours? I want to get some clothes and get out of these buckskins. They're about worn through."

"There's always a town near an army post," answered O'Connor. "There's always gotta be a place that leaches off the soldiers. Always gonna be women and liquor. If the post was out in the middle of nowhere, there would still be a sutler store."

"So what do you think the army will do with the Southern men who are in the army?" asked Sean

"I have no idea," answered O'Connor. "Most of our men are immigrants. Some of them can barely speak English. Probably joined the army like I did back in '46. Couldn't get decent work or anything, or was in trouble with the law, and joined up. We do have a few Southern men. I've never heard them say anything bad about the army, or politics or anything. We'll see what happens.

Some folks will feel an obligation to their state, whether their family had slaves or not. Could be a big mess."

"Well when we get back to your fort, and you can get yourself away," said Sean, "How about we try out a saloon in that town. I'm buyin'."

"I never turn down a free drink, my friend," O'Connor said. "It'll be a pleasure to drink with you. I'll warn you ahead of time. There's always a thief or two in an army town. Watch your money. There's also a Marshal in this town. He thinks he's a tough guy. He seems to take pleasure in busting soldiers' heads when they get a little drunk."

"Thanks for the heads up," said Sean. "We'll give no one a reason to bust our heads, but we won't take any shit either."

When they got back to the fort, Sean was surprised. It was nothing like he thought it would be. There were a few buildings and a bunch of tents. There were no tall walls surrounding the place, So why was it called a fort?

"The town's only a mile down that road," said the Sergeant. "I'll get the men and horses taken care of and make sure the Lieutenant gives a proper report for our patrol, then I'll meet you in town. Should be about two hours."

"O.K., I'll see you then," Sean said, "You might have to look twice when you see me. I'll be wearing some white man's clothes when you see me. What is your first name anyway? I'm no soldier. I don't want to be callin' you Sarge, or O'Connor."

"My name's Michael, Michael Jonathan O'Connor," he answered, "And I'll see you at the saloon in two hours."

~~~~

The general store had everything Sean needed—underwear, pants, shirts, boots, and a big black hat. Sean had to have that hat. "It'll take me a while to get used to these boots," Sean said to himself, "I've been wearing moccasins a good while." When he paid, the clerk was surprised when he saw the gold coins. "Oh my," he said, "We don't see too much of that around here. Is there anything else I can help you with?

"No," answered Sean, "But I'd appreciate it if you would throw away those buckskins for me. They're worn out anyway."

"No problem," said the clerk, "If you need anything else, come on back. Be glad to help you."

As Sean went through the door, he noticed two men setting out front. They had been there when he first went in too. Both were packing pistols and didn't look to be upstanding citizens of the community. "Afternoon," said Sean as he passed them. One of them grunted out something, but Sean didn't pay any attention.

Then Sean took his horses across the street and tied them in front of the saloon. He kept his Sharps and pistol with him. This saloon wasn't much different from the one's he'd visited up in Nebraska. There were women here, and as soon as Sean came up to the bar, one of them came up to him and said, "Buy me a drink mister?"

"O.K.," said Sean, "I'll buy you a drink. Then I want you to leave me alone, no offence intended."

"All right," she said, "But if you change your mind, I'm here, and I'm good."

She was actually very attractive thought Sean. She probably made plenty of money when the soldiers were in town. Katie hadn't been gone very long at all. Sean could not even begin to think of being with another woman. The bartender came over and gave the woman her drink. He must have known what she was drinking, or it was just tea, and Sean would pay for whiskey. It didn't matter.

The bartender asked, "Are you new around here, young man? Never seen you in here before."

"Name's O'Rourke, Sean O'Rourke. And I'm new around here. Came in to have a few drinks with my new friend, Sergeant Michael O'Connor." answered Sean.

"I'll let you know right now, friend. Mr. O'Connor can get powerful thirsty at times. Never seen the man fallin' down drunk, but he can sure put it away," the bartender said.

About that time, the Sergeant came through the door. "Let's get started, Sean," he said, "It's been a long patrol. I actually had to drink some water out there. Nice clothes. Like the hat."

"What will you have?" asked the bartender.

Sean spoke up. "Give us your best whiskey, and leave the bottle. And do you have any beer? I've never had beer."

"You've never had beer, my friend?" asked Michael.

"No, plenty of whiskey, but no beer," he answered. "When I was up North a while back, the saloons I visited were out of beer."

"Well I got beer here," said the bartender. "I'll give you a taste to see if you like it. It's not real cold, but it's good."

"Not bad," said Sean, "Give us a couple."

"You're a fine man, Sean O'Rourke," Michael said. "Let's have a toast. What should we drink to?"

"Well let's see, it's two o'clock," said Sean. "Why don't we drink to three. Then when it's three, we can have another toast and drink to four."

"O.K.," Michael said, "Let's get started."

While they were drinking, they talked about anything and everything. Sean kept asking Michael about the army. "Why do you want to know about the army, young Sean?" Michael asked, "Are you thinking about joining up?"

"Well, I'm not sure what I'll do," he answered. "This war's gonna get goin' before too long."

"I like being in the cavalry," Michael said, "I feel sorry for them foot soldiers. Always marching and walking, carryin' packs. One thing about a horse, sometimes you can get outta trouble faster than you got into it. There's no glory in seeing people get blown to hell though. Some people talk pretty brave until the shootin' starts. But mostly the army is hurry up and wait, hurry up and wait. Peace time army can drive many a man to drink. It can be so boring, there's nothing else to do. Getting shot at can drive a man to drink. I'm lucky, I don't need a reason. Well, my friend, it's time I got back to the fort. Thank you for the refreshment."

"You're most welcome," said Sean, "We'll have another drink sometime, I'm sure."

As they were about to mount their horses, Sean heard some-one say, "I'll have that money pouch of yours."

Sean turned around and it was the same two he had seen in front of the general store. The one who had done the talking, had his pistol out and pointed at Sean. The other had his hand on his pistol. "Would you move a little out of the way, Michael," Sean said, "Don't want one of these fools accidently shooting you." Michael moved as asked. "Now," said Sean, "Do either of you have any relatives in town?"

"Now just why do you want to know if we have any relatives in town," one of them asked.

"Because, you stupid fool," Sean said, "After I kill the both of you, I'll need to know if anyone else wants to die."

"Yer talking out yer ass, Mister," he said, "Now I'll have that pouch."

There was another man across the street watching, but Sean figured him just to be a spectator.

The one who had his hand on his pistol, started to draw. Sean had the Walker out before the man's pistol had even moved an inch. Sean fired, then fired again. The two shots were so close together, they seemed like one. The one who had his pistol out, fell first, then the other one. Both of them hit in the chest.

"Jesus, Joseph, and Mary," exclaimed Michael, "How did you do that? That one fella already had his gun out. Just how in the hell did you do that?"

"Well, that first fella had his gun out, but the idiot didn't have the hammer cocked. That gave me plenty of time. That other idiot was just plain slow."

Another voice came from behind them. "I'll have that pistol, mister, you're goin' down to the lock up. You just killed two men. We got laws against killin' around here." It was the Marshal.

"I don't believe so," said Sean, as he turned around.

The Marshal put his hand on his pistol. "I believe you will," he said.

"You pull on that pistol, and I'll drop you where you stand," said Sean, "Lawman, or no lawman."

"Hold on there Marshal," another voice came from across the street. It was the spectator. "I'm Captain Wallace, Texas Rangers, you pull on that man, Marshal, and he will kill you. I've never seen anyone like him before,"

"So he's fast, huh. I wonder if he can use his fists," said the Marshal. He handed his gun belt to the Ranger.

"Works for me," said Sean. "Michael, would you hold my Sharps and pistol?"

"Be glad to, Sean darlin'," Michael said. " Don't beat the Marshal too badly now."

Sean got right in his face and went to work. The Marshal must've thought he got into a buzz saw. The Marshal did get two or three swings in, but missed with them. Sean would bust him in the gut and bend him over, then go back to his face and straighten him back up. It was like he was playing with him. Then he finally gave him a tremendous right that put him down and out. Then Sean walked over to the nearest horse trough, filled his new hat with water, then came back and threw it in the Marshal's face. He came to, spitting water. "What the—" he said.

"You just got your ass whipped," Sean said. "That was a little different than you beating a few drunken soldiers, wasn't it?"

The Marshal just stayed there on the ground, saying nothing.

"You best come back to the fort with me, Sean," Michael said, "Might not be a good idea for you to stay in town tonight. We'll find you a place to stay."

"Probably a good idea," said Sean, "I don't need to kill or beat anyone else today."

As they were getting ready to leave, the Ranger spoke. "Can I have a word with you, young man?" he asked.

"O.K.," said Sean, "But I know what you want already."

"And what would that be?" he asked.

"You want me to be a Ranger. I can shoot, and I can fight. You need a man like me." said Sean.

" Nothing wrong with that, is there?" the Captain asked.

"No, not really," answered Sean, "But you Rangers spend a lot of time chasin' and killin' Indians. I got nothin' against Indians. The only ones I would kill, would be ones trying to kill me."

"These Comanche and Kiowa have killed a lot of people down here," he said.

"They most likely have," said Sean, "But I'll bet you've killed more of them than they have white folks. Besides, they were here before you, or the Mexicans, or the Spanish. The only way I'd be a Ranger, would be if I knew I was only after real outlaws, not some poor Indian who's just trying to save his way of life."

"Damn, young fella," the Ranger said. "You sound just like a college professor or something like that. Did you read all that in a newspaper or something?"

"No," Sean answered, "I lived with the Cheyenne for five or more years. Most tribes are alike. They just want to be left alone."

"Well maybe someday we'll have a detachment that just handles outlaws," the Ranger said. "Maybe you'll keep us in mind."

"I thank you for your offer," said Sean, then he and Michael left for the fort.

On the way back, Michael said, "You know, young Sean, you're awful polite for a man who can shoot and fight as well as you do. Your parents must have been good people."

"Yes, they were, my good friend," Sean said, "And so were the Cheyenne."

When they got back to the fort, Sergeant O'Connor asked the Commanding Officer of the fort, a Major Wilson, if Sean could bunk with him in his tent. He said it was O.K. if that was what

Sergeant O'Conner wanted. He could even eat at the mess hall, but would have to pay.

Sean thanked him. "Don't thank me till you've been to the mess hall," said Michael. "You may decide to move on."

Whatever it was that they had for the evening meal was a little tough, but not bad. The coffee was good and strong. "Michael," said Sean, as they were finishing the meal. "Would you mind if I hung around till we find out what's goin' on with this war?"

"That's fine by me," said Michael, "I'll ask the Major tomorrow. I don't think he'll care as long as you can pay for any meals you eat. Could be longer than you think. Word doesn't always travel fast out here. We don't have one of them telegraphs, not yet anyway. If it ends up being a while, maybe you could help teach some of these troopers how to shoot. We've got these new carbines, but some of these men had never handled any type of gun before they joined the army. They won't reach out there like your long gun, but they're accurate."

"We'll see," said Sean. "I bet the army wouldn't take kindly to a civilian showing their men how to shoot."

"You're probably right, young Sean," Michael said. "The army's funny about things like that, but maybe if you could give a demonstration, they could be convinced."

"All right," Michael," Sean said. "You talk the Major into it, and I'll see what I can do. I'm a little thirsty. Do you think the army can live without you for a little while?"

"Of course they can, my friend," Michael said, "I'll just put a corporal in charge, and we can get ourselves to town."

There were a few people in the saloon when they got to town. As soon as they got to the bar, the bartender told them the first two drinks were on the house. "Most of us folks in town never did care for that Marshal," he said. "He needed a good ass whippin'. We won't miss those two pieces a trash you shot either." Some of the girls were offering Sean some free ones. It seems the Marshal was taking a cut of their business. Since the beating, he hadn't shown his face much around town. After they finished the first two drinks, other people in the saloon were buying them drinks.

CHAPTER TWELVE

F inally, orders arrived. The Commanding Office, Major Wilson, called all of the officers, and the senior noncommissioned offers to his office. "Men, I will read you the orders we have received from the War Department."

From: District of Southeast Missouri, Brig. Gen, U.S. Grant, Commanding Officer, Headquarters - Cairo, Illinois

To: Commanding Officer, 2nd U.S. cavalry

Your Command will report to the District of Southeast Missouri Headquarters with all due haste and by any means at your disposal.

Do not engage any native hostiles unless attacked.

You may expect officer resignations and desertions from men in your command who are sympathetic to the Southern cause.

U.S. Grant, Brig. Gen. Commanding Officer

District of Southeast Missouri

"Gentlemen, are there any questions?" asked the Major. "If not, be ready to move out in two days time. We will meet the other battalions at Fort Cooper, and leave from there. Dismissed."

Only one officer resigned and there were only two desertions during the next two days. At the end of the first day, Sean and Michael decided it would be wise to visit the saloon in town one more time, at least just to say goodbye. They had their fill, and were headed back to the fort when a shot came from behind, tearing Sean's right sleeve, just below the shoulder. Before Sean could turn and draw his pistol, another shot sounded. Then it was quiet.

The Ranger, Captain Wallace, stepped from behind the general store. "That son of a bitch tried to back shoot you," he said, "Couldn't let him get away with that. I reckon the town's gonna need a new Marshal now. Figured him to try something like this. That's why I been hangin' around. I reckon you could have the job if you wanted it."

"I want to thank you, Captain," Sean said, "but I'm not interested in being any type of lawman right now. Too much gonna happen back east before too long. I reckon I'll go get myself involved in that."

"They'll probly be a whole lot goin' on out here too since all them blue boys will be goin' back east," the Captain said. "Us Rangers'll hafta take care of everything there is out here, Comanche, Kiowa, Mexican bandits, and whatever else. A lot of the men will join the Confederate Army too, and that'll cut down on help too. By the way, If you go back east, you gonna be one of them blue boys?

"If I do join," said Sean, "I'll be wearin' blue. I'm from Tennessee, but I can't abide slavery."

"I'm from Ohio myself," the Captain said, "been out here for ten years now. Consider myself just a Texan. I don't have any slaves either. I'll just stay here, and fight for my home. Good luck to you. If you don't get yerself killed, and ya get back out this way, look me up, that is unless I get myself killed."

~~~~

When they got back to the fort, Sean was informed that the Major needed to see him. "I wonder what he wants," Sean thought, "I'm not in his army just yet."

"Maybe he's gonna try to get you to sign up, young Sean," said Michael.

"Well, I best go see what he wants," Sean said, "It's a good thing we didn't get that other bottle we thought about. I wouldn't be able to stand up and listen to the man."

"Thanks for seeing me," said the Major. "I hear you have lived with the Cheyenne for several years and know your way around the Indian territories, and can communicate with other tribes. Is this true?"

"Yes it is Major," answered Sean. "I did live with the Cheyenne for several years, and I learned about pretty much everything that they know. So what can I do for you?"

"As you know," answered the Major, "We are being sent back east. We have a lot of Indian territory to get through, and I was hoping that you would scout for us. I would like to get through without any casualties. We have orders not to engage any hostiles, and fight only if attacked. You can communicate with them and tell them we are leaving for the war in the east. That will probably make them very happy."

"Yes, Major," Sean said. "Blue soldiers leaving will make them very happy. They have been waiting for this to happen. They hope you all get killed. Yes, I'll scout for you. One thing though, if somethin' happens, like if I'm talkin' with them and things don't look good, you gotta do what I say, and when I say it. Is that all right with you?"

"Yes, I'll agree to whatever keeps us from having casualties," the Major said.

"All right," Sean said, "I'll see you when we're ready to move."

"And what did the Major want, young Sean?" asked Michael.

"He wants me to scout for the army and get you through Indian territory without getting anyone killed or wounded," said Sean."

"Well that should be no problem for you," said Michael. "We'll get you into this man's army before you know it."

~~~~

Three days out, the regiment ran into a band of Kiowa. "Major," Sean said, "Go tell your boss that I'm gonna go talk to the Chief. I know him, a fella by the name of Flying Eagle. Make sure you pass the word to all of the men to keep their hands away from their carbines and pistols."

"Welcome, Sean O'Rourke," Flying Eagle said. "Why are you with all those blue soldiers?"

"Do you remember when you asked me about the war back east?" Sean asked. "Well, it's finally getting started, and I'm here to let you know that these soldiers are not here to fight you, but to go to the war back east."

"That is good news," said the Chief, "What about the Rangers? Will they leave too?"

"No," answered Sean, "But with the soldiers gone, your life will still be easier."

"Thank you, Sean O'Rourke," the Chief said. "You will always be welcome in our village."

"Any problems, Mr. O'Rourke?" asked the Major.

"No," answered Sean, "They're glad you're leaving. Now remember what I said. Make sure the men keep their hands away from their weapons."

The column left without incident, but there was plenty of grumbling among the ranks. Some of these men had been fighting the Comanche and Kiowa for a good while and didn't understand why they couldn't shoot them. Some of the Kiowa braves probably wanted to take a shot at the soldiers too.

The Commanding Officer of the Regiment, some Colonel, decided the best way to get to Cairo, would be to get to the Mississippi River, then go by river boat to Cairo. It took some time, but the journey was completed. Sean went with them, because he decided to go ahead and join up. He had asked the Major if could be in the same troop as Sergeant O'Connor, and he agreed. It was the least he could do since Sean got them safely through Indian territory.

"Now that you're one of us," O'Connor said, "we'll have to teach you how to salute, march, and about cavalry formations. After that, the boredom will set in. We'll probably set around for months and months waiting to be in some battle. It'll finally come. It'll be hurry up and wait, hurry up and wait. Then it'll be hot and heavy for a day or two. A bunch of us will be dead or wounded. The rest will set around getting bored again waiting on the next battle. There will be sickness, malaria, dysentery, and cholera. Maybe if we're lucky, we'll have a good Commanding

General, and he'll know how to use cavalry, and he'll keep us busy scouting and such."

O'Connor was close to being right about everything. All they did was drill and drill, and drill some more. Men got sick and bored. They'd heard about that battle back east, Bull Run it was called. They were eager to get their chance and show what they could do. The months rolled by with not a hint of an impending battle. One day toward the end of the year, The troop commander, Lieutenant Carter, called a special formation.

"Men, this is Captain Jones," said the Lieutenant, "He's here to tell you about a new unit that is being formed."

"Men," the Captain started, "we are forming a new group which will be called the "First Volunteer Sharpshooters of the Army of the Tennessee." We need men who can shoot and shoot accurately. You will be tested. If any man here is interested, report to my office by nine o'clock tomorrow morning. If you have your own weapons, bring them with you. Thank you. You may dismiss the men, Lieutenant."

"All right, you heard the Captain," said the Lieutenant. "Nine o'clock tomorrow morning if any of you thinks he's a shooter. Troop dismissed."

"You'll be joinin' the shooters, won't you, young Sean?" asked Michael.

"Yes, it's what I'm good at," said Sean. "A man should do what he's good at."

"Well don't be forgettin' us," Michael said.

"I won't forget you, besides you cavalry guys have horses. You can ride over and see whoever you want," said Sean.

The next morning, Sean reported to Captain Jones. "So you think you're a shooter," the Captain said.

"I've been using this Sharps since '55 and I'm pretty good with it," said Sean.

"And how old are you now, young man?" asked the Captain.

"Just turned eighteen in October," Sean said.

"Well, you sound confident to me," the Captain said, "Report to Sergeant Michaels. He's just outside the door. Oh, and a bit of advice. When you address an officer, you might think about saying sir once in a while. It doesn't mean much to me, but some of these West Pointers will fire you up if you don't."

"Thanks for the advice, sir," said Sean. "I'll try to remember, only been in the army for a few months."

"Sergeant Michaels, name's O'Rourke. I was told to report to you," said Sean.

"Just hold tight over by that tree," the Sergeant said. "Should be some more men showing up. We'll get started when they're here."

Sean went over to the tree as instructed. There were already about fifteen men there waiting too. "Name's O'Rourke, Sean O'Rourke," Sean said as he introduced himself to the others.

"I see you got a Sharps," said one of the men. "Name's George, Bill George. I'm from Illinois, where abouts you from Sean?"

"I'm originally from Tennessee," Sean answered, "but I've been out West for the last six years."

"Did you get to use that Sharps much out West?" asked Bill.

"Yep, it got me out of a few scrapes from time to time," answered Sean.

A few more men showed up, so the Sergeant told the men to fall into formation. "Men," he started, "my name is Sergeant Michaels. You can call me by my first name, Sergeant. You men think you can shoot. That's what we're gonna find out. Now we're gonna go to that field over there. The targets are at two hundred yards with ten inch circles on them. To qualify, you must put ten consecutive holes in the circle. Are there any questions?"

Sean spoke up. "Why are the targets so close?"

"Well, sharpshooter," the Sergeant said, "just how far do you think the targets should be?"

"I'd say four-five hundred yards at least," answered Sean.

"Well, sharpshooter," the Sergeant said, "we'll save you for last. Just have a seat over there in the shade. You'll get your chance."

There were twenty men, and they fired five at a time. Only one man in the first five hit his target all ten times. The others were close, but without all ten on target, they were disqualified. The second group of five did better. Three of them qualified. The third group was the same. Then came Sean's group.

"O.K., sharpshooter," the Sergeant said, "let's see how it's done."

Sean put ten shots in the circle and the group was smaller than the Sergeant's fist.

"Damn, young fella," the Sergeant said, "you sure as hell can shoot. Can you do that at five hundred yards?"

"I don't know about the grouping," Sean said, "but if I got a target at that range, I'll hit it."

"You know," said the Sergeant, "there's just one thing. Them targets weren't shootin' back at you. Do you reckon you can shoot when somethin's shootin' back at you?"

"I've been in some scrapes with some Pawnee and Comanche, and some white outlaws," Sean said, "I'm alive, they're not."

"You don't mind if we set up some targets at five hundred yards for you?" asked the Sergeant.

"No," answered Sean. "the army's got plenty of ammunition, don't they?"

"We do right now," said the Sergeant, "let's see what you can do."

"Now you understand," Sean said, "that when anyone shoots at this range, they should shoot from the prone, or a rest, right?"

"I know that, c'mon, let's see what you can do," said the Sergeant.

There were several man sized targets in different locations. One was positioned so it looked like a man half way behind a tree. Other targets were similar. Sean hit every target with what would have been a killing shot. "Damn," said the Sergeant, "I think you better come with me. We're gonna go see the Captain again."

When they got close to the Captain's office, the Sergeant told Sean to stop for a minute. "Now what's your name again?" he asked.

"O'Rourke, Sean O'Rourke," Sean answered.

"Well Sean, I'm gonna tell the Captain about your shooting ability and recommend that you should be a shooting instructor. Eventually, we expect to have a large unit. Some of them may be good, but with some of your instruction, they may be even better. Does that sound all right to you?" he asked."

"I'll do my best," answered Sean. "Maybe once the shootin' gets started, the quicker we get more of them killed, the quicker this will be over."

"Keep that attitude," said the Sergeant. "That'll help get you through all this when the bodies start mountin' up. Now let's go talk to the Captain."

"Captain," started the Sergeant, "this man is a shootin' son of a bitch. He placed killin' shots on every target we put up at five hundred yards. He's been shot at before too, so he can shoot under fire. I recommend that we use him as a shooting instructor. What do you think, sir?"

"If what you say is true, Sergeant," said the Captain, "we will use him as an instructor, at least till the shooting starts. Now what's your name, private?"

"O'Rourke, sir, Sean O'Rourke," Sean answered.

"Well O'Rourke, you're now a corporal," said the Captain.

Sean left the Captain's office not quite sure what had just happened. "So I'm a corporal now," he thought to himself, "I wonder what I gotta do to be a sergeant. I think I'll go see Michael and see what they've been doing this fine day."

"And how did it go with the sharpshooters, young Sean?" Michael asked when Sean entered his quarters.

"That's Corporal O'Rourke to you, my fine friend," said Sean.

"And what did you do to be getting promoted, Corporal O'Rourke?" Michael asked.

"All I did was show them that I can shoot," answered Sean. "They made me a shooting instructor. I gotta get my gear and move over to their quarters. Then I reckon I better get them stripes sewn on. Don't be a stranger. One of these days we'll be moving out. Let's make sure we stay in touch."

"We'll stay in touch, my fine friend," said Michael, "and by the way, Merry Christmas. It's that time of the year, you know."

"Really, is it?" asked Sean, "I haven't even thought about Christmas for the last six years. Damn, and we don't have a bottle."

"Now don't worry yourself about something that trivial," said Michael. "Michael O'Connor can find a bottle where there is none. We'll be celebrating in style."

True to his word, Michael was able to find a good bottle of whiskey. "Where'd you find it?" Sean asked.

"Let's just say some poor officer is wondering if his aid or someone took or misplaced his bottle," said Michael. "Now let's not worry ourselves about him. He had another one. Here's to us, young Sean. Let's not get ourselves killed."

"Yes," said Sean, "Let's not get ourselves killed, and Merry Christmas to you, my friend. May we see many more of them?"

CHAPTER THIRTEEN

A month passed. The unit now had fifty good men, thanks to Sean's skill. Once they improved their skills, Sean would try to explain to them how to hit moving targets.

"These targets you can hit here may be five hundred yards out, but they're not moving," Sean would say. "When we get into a shooting match, the targets will not usually stand still for you. You need to learn how far to lead a target. That'll take time. You may miss a few at first, but don't worry. I'm told we got plenty of ammunition. You need to learn how to use the wind, how to shoot uphill and downhill. You can't stay in one position yourself. If you're out by yourself, and there's no shooting going on, and you got a good target. remember, as soon you shoot, your smoke can give your position away. Sometimes, you will need to move soon as you fire, and not wait to see if you hit your target or not. This could save your life. They got sharpshooters in their army too. Some of those boys could have one of them new telescopic sights. When there's a lot of shooting going on, there'll be so much smoke, it'll be hard for someone to pick you out. It could also be a good time to move."

January rolled in and Sean thought his men were as ready as they would ever be. The weather had not been bad for this time of the year. Maybe they would be moving out soon.

Late that month, Captain Jones called a special formation. "Men," he started, "we are finally going out to see the elephant. We should be moving in less than two weeks, maybe sooner. I know all of you will do your duty. I called this formation not just to tell you that we are moving out soon, but also to tell you what I expect of you in the field. Now you men have been in the army for a while, and you should know how it works. The Generals make up the orders, and hand them down to the Colonel, the Majors, the Captains, and then down to Lieutenants. Then the orders are given to the Sergeants and the corporals who make sure the orders are carried out. Men, I want you to shoot Sergeants and Corporals. If you get a good shot at a high-ranking officer, go ahead and take it, but that won't happen on a regular basis. Some officers may decide to lead their men in attack, thinking it will inspire their men. It may inspire them all right, but chances are, they'll get themselves killed before seeing if their men got inspired or not, and they'll get killed without our help. If you can pick off the Sergeants and Corporals, and do it on a regular basis, some poor privates may decide they don't want any part of what's goin' on and skedaddle. If one skedaddles, more may follow causing wide spread panic. Once a bunch of men start running, it's damn near impossible to get them to stop. That happened to our boys at Bull Run. Some started runnin', and more took off, and they couldn't get them stopped. If they would have just stayed put and fought, maybe things would have turned out different. I assure you, this will not happen to us. I will personally shoot the first man I see going the wrong way. When we go into battle, we won't line up in some formation and march in like skirmishers. We'll fan out, pick good firing positions, and go to work. Shoot and move. Shoot and move. Staying in one place too long can get you killed. Now get your gear ready, and write your sweet hearts, wives and such. You can tell them we're moving soon, but you don't know where, which is right. You won't know. We might not know till we get there, but we're goin'. That'll be all. Dismissed."

~~~~

Sean was involved in two battles the next month. First was Fort Henry, then Fort Donelson. Both were good victories for the Union. Casualties were fairly light, and not one of the sharpshooters was even wounded. It was a good learning experience for the men. Sean personally shot fifteen men at Fort Henry, all Sergeants, and twelve men at Fort Donelson, ten Sergeants and two Corporals. Sean didn't ask the other men how they did. Most of them had never shot at anyone before, and this was hard to swallow.

The unit had no more action for about a month and a half or so. Several divisions of Grant's army were moved near a place called Pittsburgh Landing. There was a little church there called Shiloh Meeting House. The Union army had just arrived there and was getting things set up, when the rebs attacked. It was a total surprise. Sean was setting by a campfire when the shooting started. It was total chaos. They were being over run. Gray uniforms were everywhere. Sean grabbed his Sharps and shot the first gray uniform near him. Then he pulled his Walker. He couldn't kill them fast enough. They were everywhere. Fighting was hand-to-hand, men using their rifles as clubs.

Sean thought he busted the stock of his rifle when he smacked a reb in the head with it, but it was not. He changed the cylinder on the Walker and kept firing. Finally, they were able to get organized and push the rebels back. Casualties were tremendous.

Sean decided it was time to get to work with the Sharps. He found a good spot on a small knoll that still had plenty of trees left on it. In other places, the trees and vegetation had been stripped because of the intense firing. There was still plenty of firing from both sides so Sean didn't worry too much about getting spotted right away when he went to work. After ten rounds, Sean decided to move and not press his luck. When he located his next position, and was getting ready to move, he felt a sharp pain in his left arm. He looked down. A rifle ball had grazed his left upper arm. It was bleeding, but not bad. Sean got down and crawled to his next position. When he got there, he took his time, and looked for where he thought that shot had come from. He spotted him. Sean could only make out his outline, but he was in a huge oak tree that hadn't been damaged by all the firing yet. Sean took careful aim and fired. The reb fell from the tree, dead before he hit the ground. After ten more shots, Sean moved again.

Things were heating up again. The rebs would attack, get beaten back, then attack again. Sean said to himself, "How many of them are there? I can't kill them fast enough." Sean moved again. There was so much smoke in the air, it seemed he would choke to death. He found his new position, and went to work again. The firing was still intense, so finding another position was easy. He couldn't see much of anything in all the smoke, so he figured no one else could either. Sean was wrong. As he was moving, he felt a sharp burning pain in his left leg. "Son of a bitch," said

Sean. "What now?" He looked down to see blood all over his left leg just above the knee. Then he noticed blood on the back of his leg. The ball had passed through without hitting bone. Sean had a piece of cloth that he was keeping for bandages just in case the situation would arise, and wrapped it around his leg. Then he went to his position, and back to work with the Sharps.

After a few more shots, Sean discovered he was out of ammunition for the Sharps. He carefully reloaded both cylinders for the Walker, then started working his way back to where he thought the supplies would be. He finally found the supply wagons. They had been moved back because of the surprise attack. Sean found a wagon full of ammunition. There was a Captain there who said he was the Quartermaster.

"I need some ammunition for my Sharps," said Sean.

"And who might you be?" the Captain asked. "Who's your Commanding Officer? Only your Commanding Officer can request ammunition?"

"Look asshole," Sean said, "I need ammunition, and I need it now. I can't kill more rebs without ammunition, unless you think I'm gonna beat them all to death. Now give me some ammunition, now!"

"Just who do you think you're talking to?" said the Captain. "Who's your Commanding Officer.? I'm bringing charges against you."

"O.K., asshole," Sean said. "he's right here. His name is RIFLE BUTT." Sean was about to give the Captain a good clubbing with his rifle butt, when he heard a voice from behind say, "Whoa there young fella, what seems to be the problem?"

Sean turned around and there he was. General Sherman was standing there. "I need some ammunition for my Sharps so I can go kill some more rebs, General," said Sean.

"Are you one of them sharpshooters, young man?" asked the General.

"Yes, General, I am," answered Sean. "Name's O'Rourke, Corporal Sean O'Rourke."

"Well how many rebs you think you killed so far today Corporal O'Rourke?" asked the General.

"I had forty rounds for my Sharps when this started, so there's forty dead or wounded rebs out there," answered Sean. "Plus I shot several with my pistol."

"Are you that good, son?" asked the General.

"Yes sir, I am," Sean answered. "I was using this Sharps long before I was in your army."

"You think maybe it'd be a good idea if you had that leg a yours looked at?" said Sherman.

"It's quit bleedin' for now," said Sean, "I'll be O.K. I just need some ammunition."

"Well Corporal, you're a Sergeant now," Sherman said. "Captain, give the Sergeant his ammunition."

"But sir," said the Captain, "He called me an asshole and was about to brain me with his rifle butt."

"Captain, and I use that term lightly," said the General, "you are an asshole, and I might just brain you myself. Now act like an officer or I'll have you shovelin' horse shit for the rest of your career." Then the General left.

Sean got his ammunition and worked his way back up to the line. Things hadn't changed much. The rebs kept trying to push them back, but were sent packing each time. Sean found another good position and went to work. He spotted a reb Captain who looked like he knew what he was doing, so he dropped him. When the Captain fell, a Sergeant came running over to check on the

Captain, and Sean dropped him too. No one came to check on them after that.

It was evening, and the firing was slowing down some, so Sean decided it would be a good time to get his leg looked at. The hospital was over crowded. Men bled to death while waiting their turn. There were piles of arms and legs that had been amputated. The screaming was unbearable.

After what seemed like an eternity, a young soldier told Sean he would be next. "I see a ball grazed your arm, and you were hit in the leg," the soldier said. "Looks like the ball went through the leg without taking anything with it, no bone, or arteries, or vessels. I'll get you fixed up. You won't even need to see the doctor. He's about to pass out anyway. Been doing amputations and such since this mornin'."

The young soldier patched Sean up and sent him on his way. The firing had slowed to a trickle now. Sean worked his way around trying to find others in his unit. He found Captain Jones, but none of the other men. "Looks like they got a piece of you there, Corporal O'Rourke," the Captain said.

"Yes sir," Sean said, " but I gave back more than I got. That ball passed through my leg and the bleedin's stopped. I'll be ready if they come back."

"Well, tomorrow, we're goin' after them," said the Captain. "We got reinforcements coming and we're gonna shove them clear outta here. But damn, we lost a lot of men today. They sure killed more of us than we did them today."

"Have you seen any of the other men, Captain?" asked Sean.

"I've seen a few," he said. "They're just scattered all over the place. I sure hope we didn't lose many."

The reinforcements came, and the next morning, the attack started. The rebs had no intention of leaving, but being outnumbered, they had to give way. The fighting went on most of the day. The yanks kept attacking. The rebs would hold for a while, then retreat for a while, then hold, then retreat. They finally gave way. Sean started the day out O.K., but after crawling around shooting and moving, his leg began to hurt. "I best take it easy," Sean said to himself. "Don't want this leg gettin' gangrene, and gettin' chopped off. I'll just move real easy like and take longer shots."

The fighting finally stopped. Casualties were high again today, but the rebs had been whipped. The Captain decided Sean should go back to a hospital and spend a little time healing. He didn't want his best man losing a leg either. The wounded were taken by a river boat to a hospital somewhere in Kentucky. The place was crowded, but Sean had a soft bed to sleep in and no one was shooting at him. The first night, he slept ten hours straight. Sean couldn't remember ever doing that anytime in his life. When he was just gettin his eyes opened, he heard a familiar voice. "And who do you think you are to be sleeping your life away?"

Sean looked up and there was Michael staring at him. He was wearing a sling on his left shoulder. "I heard you was here, young Sean," Michael said, "so I had to get myself shot too. Wouldn't want you to be in a hospital full of strangers."

"It's good to see you, my friend," said Sean. "I hope your wound is not too serious."

"I'll be alright before you know it," Michael said, "The ball passed through, but it took a little bone with it. The doctor got all the bone chips out and I'm healing fine, so they say. When you've a mind, I got us a bottle stashed. We can have a toast to us not gettin' killed."

"Tell you what, my friend," said Sean, "After they feed us dinner today, we'll meet over by that door. I'll see you then."

~~~~

Sean thought the dinner meal was very good. He'd been eating hard tack and salt pork for a while, so anything after that would be good. Now a good drink of whiskey to wash it down. Michael and he met at the door, and went outside. there were tables and chairs set up outside for the patients who could get outside. There were even nurses who would get the men blankets or whatever they needed. Michael asked a nurse to bring them a couple of coffee cups. He didn't want it to look too obvious that they were drinking whiskey.

"And where did you get this fine whiskey, my fine friend?" asked Sean.

"Now there you go again, worryin' about trivial matters." answered Michael. "I actually took this from a reb Cavalry Captain that we captured on the first day back there. He had it in a pouch tied to his saddle. He thought we should give it back to him, but I told him that his bottle was also a prisoner, and I'd save it for a later interrogation. It's a good thing too. There's not a bottle to be found around this place."

"Well, let's get started on that toast," said Sean, "Here's to not getting killed."

"Yes, here's to not getting killed," said Michael.

They talked back and forth about small things. Then Michael asked Sean, "Well, young Sean," he started, "Is this soldierin' and fightin' anything like you thought it would be?"

"I've been in scrapes with Comanche, Pawnee, and white outlaws, but I could never even come close to imagining what we just went through," answered Sean. "Most I ever was up against was thirty Comanche. How many rebs was there anyway, thirty, forty thousand, more? It just boggles your mind to think that people can slaughter each other like that. And this war's just getting started too. Maybe we outta get the one's who started all this, put 'em in a big ring, and let 'em beat each other to death. Winner take all."

"I felt the same as you when I was fightin' the Mexicans," said Michael. "Why was I doin' it? No Mexican ever did anything to me. They probably didn't want to kill me any more than I wanted to kill them. Let's quit this kinda talk. We don't want to be cryin' in our liquor. Liquor was made to be enjoyed, not cried into."

"Yeh, you're right," Sean said, "let's move on. Have you thought about what you might do once you get out of the army?"

"No, I haven't," answered Sean, "but there is one thing that I wouldn't mind doing, and I'd probably need a partner."

"Well Michael," said Sean, "what would that be?"

"I wouldn't mind owning my own saloon," answered Michael. "It wouldn't have to be a real fancy place, but a nice place where folks would come in and feel welcome. We could have some women. If they wanted to whore, that would be up to them. As long as they're clean and nice to the customers. Anyone causing any trouble at all or giving the women a hard time, would not be welcome ever again. What do you think of that, young Sean?"

"Sounds good to me," said Sean. "let's not get killed and save our money. When this war finally gets over with, there will probably be some very thirsty people. We may as well try to help them out."

"You're a good man, young Sean," said Michael, "It's an honor to know you. I'm proud to call you my friend."

"Same here Michael, now let's see if we can finish this bottle," said Sean.

"Maybe we should save a wee bit in case we can't find another one," Michael said.

"I have faith in you, Michael," said Sean. "If there's a bottle within ten miles of this place, you'll find it."

Sean was right. Michael found another bottle before a week had gone by. "We better get some of that used up, my friend," said Sean, "they're sending me back within the week. They say my leg is healing real good, and'll be ready for me to do whatever it is that I do. And what do they say about you, Michael?"

"It'll be a little longer for me," said Michael, "they say it'll take the bones a little while longer to heal. They're doing good. They just need more time."

"I hope that next time we meet," we aren't shot up," said Sean. "If we live through this, and get that saloon, we don't want to be all crippled up, and not be able to get the drinks up to the bar for the customers."

"We'll get through this, my friend," said Michael, "we'll get through this." "Hey, I almost forgot to tell you something," said Sean. "We've been here all this time and I'm just now remembering to tell you."

"All right, all right, don't keep me in suspense," said Michael.

"The first day of the battle, I met General Sherman. That's right, I said General Sherman," exclaimed Sean.

"And why would a General of this man's army be hangin' about with, young Sean?" asked Michael.

"I had run out of ammunition for my Sharps, and I was back at a supply wagon trying to get more," explained Sean. "This Quartermaster Captain was giving me a hard time. Said my Commanding Officer had to request it. I was about to give him my rifle butt, when General Sherman just happened along and asked what was going on. I told him I needed more ammunition so I could kill more rebs. He also saw that I was wounded. Anyway, I got my ammunition, got promoted to Sergeant on the spot, and the Captain got his ass tore."

"Jesus, Joseph, and Mary," exclaimed Michael, "do you know how long it took me to make Sergeant? Twelve years, I'm tellin' you, twelve years, and you go and do it in a year or so. If you're not careful, my friend, you'll be an officer before you know it."

"I'll try to not let that happen," said Sean. "I don't really want to be responsible for anyone but myself. That's a hard enough job in itself. Got myself shot twice already."

"You'd make a good officer, my friend," said Michael. "You wouldn't put up with all the crap that goes on, ass kissin' and such. If you thought someone who outranked you gave some bad orders, or you knew something better, you wouldn't hem and haw. You'd just tell them. That's what this man's army needs. We're lucky over here. We got a couple good Generals, Grant and Sherman. They know what the hell they're doing, and if they do something wrong, they figure it out and fix it. Those poor boys back east are getting slaughtered because there's not one good General in the whole bunch. You mark my word. After we get the rebs whipped out here, they'll be sending Grant or Sherman, or both of them back east to fix things. That Lee fella, they're afraid of him. He's just a man like anyone else. He may be smart, but he's outnumbered and out gunned. We'll beat him in the end. It'd just be quicker if we had some good Generals over there."

"Damn, Michael," said Sean, "I didn't mean to get you all worked up. Let's talk about somethin' else, or let's get a drink. There's still a little of that whiskey left isn't there?"

"There's a little left," answered Michael, "we can celebrate your promotion."

"Plus they're kicking me out tomorrow," said Sean, "I probably won't have much to drink without you around, so I best enjoy what we have today."

"Once again," said Michael, "Here's to not getting killed."

"Yes, here's to not getting killed," Sean added.

~~~~

Sean got back to his unit and reported in to Captain Jones. "Glad to have you back, Sergeant. Why didn't you tell me about your meeting with General Sherman?" he asked.

"Well sir, it didn't seem important at the time. I got my ammunition, we run off the rebs, and that's what important," said Sean.

"You're right," the Captain said, "but I had a visit from General Sherman himself next day after the battle. He told me about your incident and that he promoted you to Sergeant right on the spot. He said he hoped all my men were spitfires like you. Then he said to double the ammunition for the men. One more thing, you're second in command now. Sergeant Michaels was killed the second day. I didn't know till after you went to the hospital. We also lost ten men, five killed, and five badly wounded.

We won't have more time to get more men, we're moving out shortly. I hear we'll be headed towards Chattanooga."

"Chattanooga!" said Sean, "That's great. I was born and raised about a hundred miles north of Chattanooga. When we get over that way, ask the General or whoever's in charge of the scouts, if I can go have a look see. I know that area very well. Might save a life or two."

"I will surely do that. We have an Officer's meeting this afternoon. I will let them know I have a man who knows the area," said the Captain. "I never knew you were from Tennessee. How did you end up wearin' blue?"

"Well sir," started Sean, "My parents came from Ireland and somehow ended up in Tennessee. When we first got our land, there was a slave family that went with it. The first thing my Pa did was free them and pay them wages. He said that the Irish were treated worse than slaves by the British, and he wasn't gonna be owned or own anyone else."

"Are your parents still there?" asked the Captain.

"No," answered Sean. "We left in '55 to avoid this war that we knew was coming sooner or later. My folks were killed when our small wagon train was attacked by some white outlaws. I survived, and was taken in by the Cheyenne. Later on, I met Sergeant O'Connor, and here I am."

"Sounds like you've had a full life so far," said the Captain. "Sometime when we get a chance, I'd like to hear about the Cheyenne."

"All right, sir," said Sean, "maybe after we get moving, and they sort out what and where we're goin' for sure. If we are headed toward Chattanooga, we'll have plenty of time to talk. I'll go check on the men, sir. Make sure they're doing their soldierly duties, and such."

"Thanks Sergeant," said the Captain, "See you in the morning."

CHAPTER FOURTEEN

T he Captain was right. They would be heading toward Chattanooga. After morning formation, the Captain told them to be ready to move out in an hour. They marched for days and days. There was no harassment from the rebs at all. When they came to a place that Sean knew was only about five miles from his old home, they stopped and set up camp.

"Captain," said Sean, "this is where you should turn me loose to do some scouting. My old home is only five miles from here."

"All right, I'll get with the General and let him know," said the Captain. "I'll be back shortly."

"General Sherman," the Captain started, "That man in my unit who's from this area, says we're only five miles from his old home. May I suggest that we let him scout a bit for us."

"Of course," said the General, "what's his name anyway?"

"Sergeant O'Rourke, sir" answered the Captain.

"Oh, that spitfire of yours," Sherman said, "well, get him a horse and turn him loose. We could use some good intelligence for a change."

"Yes sir," said the Captain.

A half hour later, the Captain returned to the unit with a horse for Sean. "Well get out there and see what you can see," said the Captain. "You'll be out there by yourself. Don't be gettin' yourself captured. Try not to be seen too much. I'd say the rebs know we're coming, but if some of the civilians would see you and recognize you, they might not think too kindly of you wearin' blue. Stay off the roads when you can. If you can't get back till tomorrow, don't worry about. Be careful, and good luck."

"Captain," started Sean, "I doubt if any folks would recognize me from a distance. We left here when I was twelve. I've changed some. Be back when I can."

In about an hour, Sean was looking at his old home. It was looking a little run down. the barns needed some repair, and it looked like the fields hadn't been worked for a year or two. No one was around. Then he skirted the town. Not many people browsing, and no rebs. After watching the town for a good while, he swung out, making a wide circle, maybe five miles out from the town. There was a reb camp to the east of town. Sean estimated it to be about battalion strength, and the camp didn't look permanent like. They were probably just stopping for the night. He saw a few scouts out, but was not spotted. It also looked like a very large force had passed through maybe the day before. "It's time to head back," Sean said to himself.

He got back to his camp in two and a half hours. It had gotten dark, but there was a full moon so Sean rode on. As he neared the camp, some trigger happy sentry took a shot at him. He missed. Sean got off his horse, snuck around him, and then scared the crap out of him. "Next time," said Sean, "don't be so quick to shoot. I mighta been General Grant."

Sean reported his findings to General Sherman. "Sergeant," Sherman started, "how 'bout gettin' a little rest, then goin' back out and keeping an eye on them for us. I figure same as you. That outfit's just there for the night. We can't catch up to them tonight, but you can watch them and make sure we're both right. Either way, we'll be moving first light whether you get back by then or not. That'll be all Sergeant, and thank you."

"Yes sir," said Sean, "I'll get a couple hours sleep and head back out."

Two hours later, Sean was mounted, and on his way. He stayed off the roads and kept his wits about him. The rebs probably knew where the yanks were, and maybe had their own scouts out just in case the yanks would try to catch them that night. The full moon made it easy to move. It also reminded him of the time over six years ago when the night riders came to their place.

When he neared the reb encampment, he spotted the pickets, but no scouts spotted as of yet. Sean moved back to where the camp was just barely visible, dismounted, tied his horse, and just tried to spot any scouts that might be out. He took a slug of water, then ate some hardtack. Still no scouts spotted. About an hour before daylight, movement began in the camp. No breakfast fires were started. They just packed up, and began moving toward Chattanooga.

Sean started thinking now about Sarah. "I wonder if she's even around here anymore," he said to himself, "I have time to slip over that way before the troops get this far. I believe I will." He was at the plantation in no time. It was almost daylight now. Sean spotted an older woman, probably a house slave, and called to her. She gave a strange look when she first saw the blue uniform, then she looked happy. "Yes, suh," she said, "what can I do fo you, Yankee soldier?"

"My name is Sean O'Rourke," Sean started, "Sarah and I grew up together. Is she still here?"

"Yes suh," she answered, "but she be sleepin'."

"Would you please wake her up, and tell her Sean O'Rourke is here to see her?" Sean asked, "I'm sure you won't get into trouble for waking her up."

"All right, Mr. Sean," she answered, "I go wakes her up and tell her you here."

"Sean O'Rourke," Sarah shouted, "are you sure that's his name?"

Yes ma'am, I is," she answered.

"Well fetch my robe, quickly now," Sarah said. Then she ran downstairs and out the front door.

"Sean, oh Sean," she said, "Is it really you, after all these years? I have thought of you a lot these last few years." Then she grabbed him and hugged him.

"Yes, it's me," answered Sean. "I was beginning to think we'd never see each other again, and now here I am."

"I see you're wearing the blue," Sarah said, "I always figured that if a war did get started, you'd end up in blue. So why are you here in this area?"

"I'm doin' some scouting," he answered, "There's gonna be a big battle probably over towards Chattanooga. The rebs are moving that way. I really feel bad about this, but I gotta get back to my unit. After this battle, I should get a little rest time. May I come and see you?"

"Yes, you may," answered Sarah. "Now don't go getting yourself killed. We have a lot of catching up to do." Then Sarah pulled him to her, and kissed him full on the mouth.

"I'll be back," said Sean, "May take a few weeks or so, but I'll be back." Then he pulled her to him and kissed her again.

When he left, it looked like Sarah was crying. "Get your head on straight," Sean said to himself. "You'll be back to see her before you know it."

~~~~

He met the troops after they had just started moving. He made his report, then got back to his unit. They marched for several more days, then caught up to the rebs. The Battle at Chattanooga was another good Union victory. Casualties weren't terrible, and none of the sharpshooters were killed. Sean and the Captain had made sure they had plenty of ammunition this time, so there were many dead and wounded Sergeants and Corporals. Sean even took some prisoners. One of them asked Sean, "Hey yank, what's yer name and where ya from?" He made a strange face when Sean told him. "I heard a you," he said, "yer that guy whose family killed all those night riders bout six or so years ago, aren't ya? I'm from bout thutty miles down the road and we heard bout it back then."

"Yep, that was my family," said Sean. "There was eight of them."

"How many'd you kill, yank?" he asked.

"I killed three of them," answered Sean, "with this Colt Walker I still carry."

"Damn, yank, how old was ya? Couldn't been more'n twelve," the reb said, "You must be a rough customer."

"No," said Sean, "just staying alive. You boys want some coffee? I'll get us some."

"Hell yes, yank," the reb said, "haven't had no coffee for quit a spell now."

"Well let's get over to my place and have some coffee, then I gotta get you to wherever they're keeping the prisoners," Sean said, "Before I forget to tell you, I'm pretty good with this Walker, and I can hit a man at over five hundred yards with this Sharps, so don't even think about leavin'."

"We believe ya, yank," the one reb said, "I got 'nother question. Are you the yank who's been killin' all our Sergeants and Corporals?"

"I've done my share," answered Sean, "Why'd you ask that?"

"Tell ya why, yank," said the reb, "Yer gettin' a reputation. All our sharpshooters are lookin' fer ya. Some a our boys quit wearin' their stripes."

Captain Jones came walking by. "What have you got goin' on here, Sergeant?" asked the Captain.

"Just doin' a little interrogatin', Captain," Sean answered, "we're about done."

"All right, report back to me after you get the prisoners to the holding area," the Captain said.

Sean delivered the prisoners and reported back to the Captain. "What can I do for you, sir," asked Sean.

"Did you find out anything during your interrogation of the prisoners?" asked the Captain.

"I did, sir," Sean answered, "but it's probably nothing we didn't expect sooner or later anyway."

"And what would that be, Sergeant?" he asked.

"Just that a lot of those rebs have quit wearing their stripes," said Sean, "They're tired of us pickin' them off, and their sharp-shooters are tryin' real hard to get us."

"Well," the Captain started, "that is something that was expected anyway. You've been around a while now and been in some engagements. You can pretty much tell who the Sergeants are anyway."

"Yes, I can," said Sean. "Will there be anything else?"

"Yes, Sergeant," the Captain said, "we'll be pulling back to a rest area tomorrow. Not too far from the main body, but somewhere we won't be shot at. Notify the men."

"Captain, do you have any idea how long we will be there?" Sean asked.

"I'd say a week at least, but I'm hoping for two," he answered.

"Since we're gonna be out of action for a while," started Sean, "do you think it would be possible for me to slip away some and visit an old friend from my old home town?"

"She's not a reb spy, is she?" asked the Captain.

"How do you know it's a she?" asked Sean.

"Because, Sergeant," started the Captain, "I saw that face of yours light up as soon as I said we were pulling back. I like women too. I haven't seen my wife since forever. Who is she anyway?"

"She was my childhood sweetheart," answered Sean, "I got my first kiss from her when we were both twelve. My family left not long after that, and I haven't seen or heard from her since."

"Well, Sergeant, I personally don't see anything wrong with this, but I'll ask the General to make sure it's O.K." said the Captain. "I don't foresee a problem. He already likes you."

~~~~

The rest area was less than ten miles from Sean's old home. Sean was granted a ten day furlough. Captain Jones checked with General Sherman to make sure it was all right for Sean to visit his old sweetheart, even though she was a Southern girl. The Captain even got him a horse to use. "I'll be back in ten days," Sean told the Captain. "If I see any rebs or anything goin' on that needs reported, I'll get back pretty darn quick. I wanna thank you, Captain, for gettin' me this furlough. I hope you get to see your wife before too much longer."

When Sean arrived at the plantation, Sarah was sitting on the front porch. As soon as she knew who it was, she ran to him. After he dismounted, they grabbed each other and hugged. Then she looked into his eyes and then kissed him. "You are here again," Sarah said, "I have been thinking of nothing but you ever since your visit."

"I was wondering," said Sean, "What will you father think about you kissing a Yankee in his front yard?"

"I'm not sure," she said, "why don't we go find out." Then she took him by the hand and they went into the house looking for her father. They found him in his study.

"Papa, this is Sean O'Rourke," she started, "you remember the O'Rourke's, don't you?"

"Looks like a Yankee to me. What are you doin' here, yank?" George said. "I'm just kiddin', son. I know who you are and I know why you wear that uniform. That don't bother me. If Sarah likes you, it's all right with me. You bein' here's not gonna change the outcome of this war anyway. You two go on and enjoy each other's company. Go on now."

Sarah took Sean out back. There was bench under a big oak tree, and they sat there, just staring at each other for a while. Finally, Sean asked her, "What has been going on in your life these last years? Where's that brother of yours?"

"Well, that brother of mine still hates your guts," she started. "One of the last things he said before he left home, was that he was gonna shoot you someday. He joined the Confederate Army right after they fired on Fort Sumter. He got kicked out of the army. They said he was crazy and couldn't be tolerated. I believe he shot some prisoners. Last we heard, he was in Missouri with that Quantrill outfit. I hear they don't follow regular rules like the army does. Me, well, I was married for a little while. My father kind of arranged it. He was a nice man. A little older than me. I thought I could learn to love him, but I just never really fell in love with him. He joined the Confederate Army and was killed at Bull Run. I've been a widow for a year or so now. Grandpa died two years after your family left. Papa had an accident the next year, and broke his hip. He wanted to join the Confederate Army too, but they wouldn't take him because of his hip. He was upset about it for a while, then decided it was for the best. He still has Charlie, that horse your father broke for him when your family first got here. He was afraid the army would take him, but when they found out his age, they didn't. Well, I've been talking. Now you tell me all about your life."

"It's a long story," said Sean, "are you sure you want to hear it?"

"Yes, Sean, I want to hear everything," she said.

"All right," he started, "We got out to Missouri to catch a wagon train. We had missed the last train by a few days, but there were two other families ready to go too, so we headed out and figured we could catch the train in a week or so. On the fourth day, I was out from the wagon train hunting, when some outlaws attacked. I killed five men that day. My Pa and Ma and all the others were killed, but they killed five outlaws before they were killed. Some Cheyenne braves happened along, and I went to their village and ended up staying with them for over five years. I stayed with a Cheyenne woman who had a white husband. He taught me to hunt and track and everything. They had a daughter, Katie was her name. We got married when we were fifteen. She was beautiful. We had a daughter, Maggie. Katie was pregnant again when the cholera took them. We lost many people then. The white man and I were gone when the cholera took everyone. After that, I went off to be by myself for a while. I met a Sergeant in the Cavalry and we became good friends. After Fort Sumter was fired on, his unit was ordered back east. I scouted for them to get through Indian territory. Then I joined the army, and here I am."

"You've had a full life, haven't you," said Sarah. "Not very many people in this world have done that much or had that much happen to them. Now, why don't we quit talking about ourselves for a while." Then she moved closer to Sean, wrapped her arms around his neck, and began kissing him.

"Do you know that you are a beautiful woman, Sarah," said Sean. "You are truly beautiful."

"Well thank you, Sean," she said. "I always thought I was pretty, but I never thought of myself as beautiful."

" Well Sarah," Sean said, "You are. You are beautiful. A man would have to be dead for five years to not know that."

They kissed and pawed at each other for a good while. It was evident to both of them that they were getting very aroused. After a few more minutes, Sarah said, "Let's go over to the horse barn.

There's a room with a bed in it that the overseer used to use when we had an overseer. It hasn't been used in years. Papa has them keep it neat and clean. Why, I don't know. Let's go." Then she grabbed Sean's hand and led him there.

"Would you like to undress me, Sean?" Sarah asked.

Before she had finished asking, he had already started.

Four hours later, they emerged from the horse barn. "Are you sure your father will not be upset about us?" Sean asked her.

"You were there when he told us to go and enjoy each other, weren't you?" she said. "And isn't that what we have been doing?"

"Yes, it is," answered Sean, "I believe we both have been enjoying each other very well."

"I would like to do this on a regular basis." Sarah said. "How much furlough time did you get?"

"Ten days, ten wonderful days," said Sean. "Will I be able to stay here?"

"Yes you will," she answered. "I intend to sleep with you every night you are here. Papa will not mind. We will sleep out here so the noise we make will not keep anyone else awake. Let's get something to eat. I'm hungry after all that."

"That sounds good, we'll need to keep our strength up," said Sean. "I've got a question for you. If it's none of my business, just let me know."

"All right, Sean," she said, "What is it?"

"Sarah, I've known you for a long time," said Sean, "but I have never seen your mother, and I don't recall you ever talking about her. Is there something I shouldn't know?"

"My mother has some problems," she started. "Right after I was born, Papa said she became very withdrawn. She didn't want to breast feed me. She didn't want anything to do with Papa either. They have separate bedrooms. I was nursed by one of the house slaves. She just stays by herself about all the time. Sometimes, when we have guests, Papa has a doctor come out and give her something so she can come out and act normal. Papa has had a lady friend in town for years, and I don't mean one of the whores. He can spend as much time with her as he wants. Mama, wouldn't know, or wouldn't care either. We may not see her the whole time you're here. Now, can we eat?"

"O.K.," I didn't mean to stir up any old wounds," said Sean.

After they ate, they went out walking and talking. "You told me you were with the Cheyenne?" Sarah said. "What was it really like. You know most white folks think Indians are just a bunch of blood thirsty savages, don't you?"

"Yes, I know what most white folks think," answered Sean, "but the Cheyenne are some of the nicest people I have ever met. They are so polite."

"Well tell me how their life is out there," said Sarah.

"It's a hard life, but a good life," started Sean. "They live by following the buffalo herds. That's the main food source. Everything from the buffalo is used for something. Nothing is wasted. Hides make the teepees, and clothing, and blankets, and robes. The bones are used for tools, and needles, and such. Some of the organs are used for water containers. When the herds move, so do they. A lot of warmer weather is spent getting ready for winter. When they go to a winter camp, they stay till spring. The men are always hunting. Buffalo is the main food, but much of that is dried for the winter. They hunt deer, antelope, elk, and other animals all year round. The women work constantly, gathering wood, roots, nuts, berries, and other food. They do all the cooking. Some tribes don't get along with other tribes, and they raid each other from time to time. We had some trouble with the Comanche and the Pawnee when I was there. I learned to speak Cheyenne, and I also learned their sign language so I could speak to other tribes. Everyone works together to help each other out. It was a good life."

"Tell me about your wife," said Sarah. "Did you all live together in the same teepee before you got married?"

"Yes, we all lived in the same lodge," started Sean. "Her father's name was John Braddock, and he liked to be called just Braddock. Blue Swan was her mother's name. Blue Swan was a very attractive woman. Her first husband was killed in a raid by the Pawnee, and about a year later, she took up with Braddock. He was a mountain man. Blue Swan had a son by her first husband. His name was Black Wolf. He was the brave that took me to the Cheyenne. Katie was Braddock's and Blue Swan's daughter. Katie taught me the Cheyenne language and sign. Whenever I wasn't out with Braddock hunting, I was with Katie. We fell in love from the start. We were only fifteen, when we got married. I talked to Braddock about it. I was concerned because most white folks don't get married that young. Anyway, we got married. They gave us our own lodge when we got married. We were so much in love. Little Maggie, my daughter came along, and we were in heaven. The next winter, Katie was pregnant again. The next spring, Braddock and I decided we wanted to go to a town to get the women something nice and would be gone for about a week. The cholera came right after we left. My Katie and Maggie were the first ones to die. It killed at least one person from every lodge. I told you a lot of this stuff already. Sorry, I didn't mean to rattle on."

"I'm glad you can tell be about your life," Sarah said. "The Cheyenne must be very good people to take you in like that. I'm sorry about Katie and Maggie. You must have loved them very much. Now, can you tell me about this war stuff? My husband was killed. I don't know how he died or anything. They just sent word that he had been killed. It was an honorable death, they said."

"I really don't want to talk about such things right now," Sean said.

"Please, just this once, and I'll never ask you again," Sarah said.

"All right, here goes. There is no glory in any of this," Sean started. "People get blown to hell. Heads, arms, and legs get torn off. Guts hang out. Do you know what I do Sarah? I kill people. That's what I do. I'm very good at it. I figure the more I kill, the quicker this war will be over. I've killed so many, I've quit counting. Now, can we please talk about something else, say for instance, how about your life before you were married. I know you didn't just sit around and miss me."

"Sean, my sweetheart, I will never bring this up again," she said. "And yes, I did just sit around and miss you, at least for a little while. There's really not much else to tell. I tried to get Papa to send me to school in Chattanooga, but he wouldn't hear of it. My brother was away causing trouble somewhere. I really missed Grandpa. He would take me places and do things. Papa was always too busy for anything."

"Well tell me about your husband," said Sean. "Was he from around here? Was his family well to do? Did your father like him?"

"Well, his family has a plantation about twenty miles from here. It's about half as big as ours. My father met his family at some meeting, and Papa and his father thought it would be a good idea for us to court. I said he was older than me. Well, he was twenty-one. He courted me almost a year before he proposed. He was a kind gentle man, very polite, fairly good-looking. I thought I could love him, but I just couldn't. He wasn't a very good lover, but he tried. I guess when the war started, he had to run off and prove what a man he was. We had been living at his father's plantation. When he was killed, I came back home. I don't think my father ever really liked him. I figure he just thought I would be well taken care of, and would have the life I was accustomed to. I never got along with his parents either. They mistreated their slaves, and talked down to even the regular white folks. We didn't miss each other when I left."

"Have you ever thought what life would be for you without slaves?" asked Sean.

"No, not until this war started anyway," she answered. "I've always been waited on hand and foot. It would be a big change not to have slaves."

"Well there's people who have house servants that get paid a wage," said Sean. "If you didn't have slaves, maybe your father could pay someone wages. You know that eventually, the North is gonna win this war, don't you, and they'll be no more slaves?"

"You're probably right," she answered. "I've heard that some of the other plantations are having trouble with runaways. Maybe because they're mistreated. I don't know. Having no slaves would be a big change of life for a lot of folks. I do believe that I could take care of myself and a family if it came right down to it, without slaves. I can cook, and I can sew, and I think I know how to keep a man interested."

"You sure as hell know that," said Sean.

That night, they made love all night long. They finally fell asleep around daylight, and then slept till noon. When they awoke, they started again where they left off. After a couple of hours, they decided it was time to eat. "We better get something to eat." Sarah said. "I fully intend to wear you out while I have you, so you will need your strength."

After eating, Sean asked Sarah if there were any other clothes that he might be able to wear while he was there. "I wouldn't want to get myself shot wearing this blue uniform. Some reb could happen by."

"I'll see what I can find," said Sarah. "My brother's not quite as tall as you, but between his clothes, and Papa's, we'll find you something to wear. I don't want you getting shot either. I can see that you've already been shot a few times. It hurt, didn't it?"

"Well, none of them hurt at first," said Sean. "The pain came a little later. Those holes on my left side, well, they're from a Comanche arrow. It went in the front, and stuck out the back. What hurt, was when Braddock broke off one end, and pulled it out the other side. That scar on my left arm was just a graze from a bullet. Those on my left leg are where a ball passed clean through. Didn't hurt at first. Started hurting a little later. My friend, Michael O'Connor, he's the sergeant I told you about. Well, we were in the hospital at the same time. He got shot through the shoulder. The ball passed through, but some bones got chipped. He was healing O.K., but they thought he needed some more time. He was still there when I left. I haven't seen him since. I hope he's all right. We talked about goin' together and owning a saloon some day. Michael likes his whiskey, but he's no drunk, and he's a fine man. Every time we got together, we would have a toast. We would always drink to not getting killed."

"Would you like to have a drink now?" Sarah asked, "Papa always has some good bourbon. We could drink a toast too."

"What would we toast?" Sean asked.

"We would have a toast to us, my dearest," Sarah said. "I've only ever had a few drinks, mostly champagne, but I have tasted Papa's bourbon, and I kind of like it, so let's get it, and drink to us."

"Wow, that bourbon is a little stronger than I remembered," said Sarah as she was trying to keep from choking.

"Just sip it. Enjoy the flavor and the feeling you get when it goes down," said Sean. "People who just throw down shots, can't be really enjoying it. They just want to get drunk. Good whiskey is a gift. It shouldn't be abused."

"Gees, Sean," Sarah said, "you're getting philosophic on me. You must take your whiskey seriously."

"Yes, I do," said Sean. "Like I said, it's meant to be enjoyed, not abused."

"Well let's enjoy having our toast. Now, what shall we say, sweetheart?" said Sarah.

"How about this," answered Sean. "May our passion never cease."

"Yes, may our passion never cease," added Sarah. Then she wrapped her arms around him and began kissing him. They went to the horse barn again, and didn't emerge for another two hours.

"Sean, you said something about you and your friend maybe having a saloon some day," Sarah said. "Were you serious about that, or were you just talking?"

"Michael and I were serious about it," started Sean. "We figure there will be a lot of thirsty people after this war, and someone should help them out. Neither one of us is going to get killed. We might get banged up some, but we won't get killed. I won't allow it."

"It's good that you have that attitude. That will probably really help you get through this war," said Sarah, "It could last a good while longer."

"It probably will," said Sean. "The Union needs to get some better Generals over east. They need someone who's not afraid of Bobby Lee. Soon as Grant or Sherman get done over here, they'll go over there and finish up."

"Well, just where do you think you'd like to have your saloon?" she asked.

"Michael and I have never talked about where," answered Sean, "but I'm assuming it will be out West somewhere. When the war's over, I figure there will be a lot more people headin' west. They'll want to get away from everything that went on over here and start a new life. I just hope they don't try to settle on Indian land. They'll be fightin' again out there."

"What do you think you'll be doing with yourself?" Sean asked Sarah.

"I figure on being with you," Sarah answered.

"Is that right?" asked Sean. "And what would you be doin' with me?"

"Well, you're going to marry me, Sean O'Rourke," Sarah answered. "A wife should be with her husband."

"And when will this marriage take place?" asked Sean.

"As soon as this war is over, and you come back to me," she answered.

"I better damn well make sure I don't get killed then," said Sean.

"Yes, you better make damn well sure," she said. Then she wrapped her arms around him and began kissing him.

~~~~

Sean didn't believe that anyone could have a furlough as good as this. They were so happy together. They walked for hours at a time and talked about anything and everything. The days went by, and the war seemed so far away, On the eighth day of his furlough, they decided to go riding. "I can ride old Charlie," said Sarah. "He doesn't know he's supposed to be an old horse."

"I'm taking my pistol with me," said Sean.

"Why would you need your pistol?" asked Sarah. "We won't go off the plantation."

"Look, woman of mine, there's soldiers from either side, not really that far away," answered Sean. "You never know what you might run into. It's best to be ready, just in case."

"All right," said Sarah, "you know more about what might be out there than I do."

The plantation was huge. They had ridden for hours, so they decided to stop at a small stream and give the horses a drink and a little rest. "Does your Papa know you're not riding side saddle?" asked Sean.

"That saddle you saw in the barn is not mine," she answered, "Papa got that for Momma years ago, before she had her troubles."

"How deep is that stream?" asked Sean.

"It's plenty deep enough if you're thinking what I'm thinking," said Sarah.

Before Sean could get a word out, Sarah was running toward the stream, throwing off her clothes as she went. Sean wasted no time. After about an hour, they were laying on the bank, letting the sun dry them. After some more passion, they decided they should get dressed and ride some more.

They hadn't ridden for a half hour, when Sean saw two riders in the distance, coming toward them. When they got a little closer, they could see the gray uniforms. "Sarah," Sean started, "When I tell you, stop your horse and dismount. With your left hand, pull the horse to your left, so he is between you and the riders."

"What's going on?" Sarah asked, "If they are Confederate soldiers, I'll just tell them that you're my cousin, and you're on leave, recovering from being shot three times. If they don't believe me, we'll show them the scars."

"Sarah," Sean said, "quit talking now, and do what I told you, right now."

Sarah stopped the horse, and did what she had been told to do. Sean did the same. When the riders got closer, the one on the left, pulled out a pistol, and pointed it at Sean. The other one had a rifle pointed at Sean too.

"We'll have those horses," the one with the pistol said. "And we'll have your wallet too. Hand it over, fella. We'll be takin' the woman."

They had their weapons pointed at Sean, but they couldn't keep their eyes off of Sarah. Sean stepped from behind his horse, pulled the Walker, and shot both of them out of the saddle.

"What just happened here?" asked Sarah. "Those two were Confederate soldiers, weren't they?"

"No, Sarah," answered Sean. "They were not. They were deserters. See all that stuff they have strapped to their horses. They've been out looting."

"Does this stuff happen a lot?" asked Sarah.

"I'd say so," answered Sean. "Probably more than either side would be willing to admit."

"You mean Yankees desert too?" she asked.

"I suppose they do," answered Sean, "but there hasn't been any from any unit I have been in yet. Don't mean there won't be though."

"I see what you meant when you said you were good at killing," Sarah said.

"I'll do whatever it takes to stay alive," said Sean. "Those two would have killed us sooner or later. We best get some shovels and get these two underground. We don't need any dead bodies out here attracting attention. We'll throw some brush over the dirt too, so the graves don't look too obvious. We'll throw their loot in the stream, and give their horses a swat. We're not that far from the house now. You go get some shovels and I'll stay here just in case someone else happens along. If you run into your father, and he asks you what the shooting was about, just tell him that I shot a snake. He doesn't need to know this."

Sarah returned, and let him know that she had not seen her father. The ground was fairly soft so the digging was fairly easy. "You're pretty good with that shovel for a Southern belle," said Sean. "Are you any good with a plow?"

"Hey, sweetheart, I told you I could take care of myself," Sarah answered. "I expect that I could handle a plow and the mule pullin' it."

"Woman, you're getting me worked up again," said Sean. "Let's hurry up and get these guys in the ground and get back."

"You're too easy, sweetheart," Sarah said, "let's do hurry."

The rest of Sean's furlough seemed to fly by. When it was time for him to leave, it seemed like one of the hardest things he had ever done. "I don't think I could ever get you kissed enough," said Sean. "I hope you feel the same."

"I do, sweetheart," Sarah said, "Now get back out there and get this war over, and get back to me."

"Before I leave," started Sean, "there's one more thing we should talk about."

"What is it?" asked Sarah.

"I'm not trying to scare you, my love," answered Sean, "but does your father have any guns in the house? We ran into those two deserters already. You never know who may show up around here. Don't trust too many people, and don't wander off by yourself."

"Papa has a Colt revolver and a shotgun he keeps in his study," she said, " and I know how to use them. Don't worry, I'll keep myself safe for you."

"We can try writing each other, but there's gonna be fightin' all over the place, and who knows if any letters we write will make it, but we'll try. I love you, Sarah."

"I love you too, Sean O'Rourke," replied Sarah.

Then Sean bent down from his horse and gave her one last kiss, and then was on his way.

CHAPTER FIFTEEN

When Sean reported back in to Captain Jones, the Captain could tell that Sean had a good furlough. "You didn't get married while you were gone, did you Sergeant?" asked the Captain.

"No sir, I didn't," answered Sean, "But she informed me that we were getting married as soon as this war's over."

"So you didn't see any rebs the whole time, comin' or goin', or while you were there?" asked the Captain. "We get reports once in a while on a few reb stragglers in the area."

"I didn't see any stragglers, but we ran into some reb deserters," said Sean. "I had to kill them. Sarah was with me when it happened. She took it very well."

"Sounds like you'll be gettin' a good woman," the Captain said.

"She is a very good woman," said Sean. "Now that I'm back, I need to make sure that I have my mind on my work. I don't want to be thinkin' about her at the wrong time and get myself killed."

"That would be a good idea Sergeant," the Captain said. "Cause we're getting ready to move out again. Gonna be another battle before too long. This time I think we'll be headed toward

Nashville. We haven't recruited any more men, but we still have a good unit. We can still hurt them badly."

The Captain was right. The next battle took place at a town called Murfreesboro. It was a Confederate victory. It was one of the few victories that Confederates had on the western front during the whole war. There was another battle a couple months later at some place that Sean didn't know the name. Neither side claimed victory. Then in December, there was a battle at Hartsville. It was another Confederate victory, but only because some of their troops had worn Yankee uniforms. Sean was very glad that he missed that battle. There was also a battle at Jackson that December. Sean was there, and it was another union victory.

1863 rolled around, and it seemed like it was just one battle after another. The union kept winning, but the rebs kept fighting. Sean had quit counting the number of men he had killed a long time ago. "How many more men am I gonna have to kill to get this over with?" Sean started saying to himself almost every time he squeezed the trigger. The sharpshooters had fared well. They had several men wounded, not seriously, and none killed.

Sean had not received one letter from Sarah, so he assumed that she hadn't received any of his. "It's been over a year now since my furlough," he thought to himself. "Maybe sooner or later we'll head back toward Chattanooga, and I can slip over and see her."

"You lucked out, Sergeant," said the Captain after a battle at a place called Hoover's Gap. "The rebs have attacked Chattanooga, and we gotta get there and help the boys who're defending the city before they get run out. We should be by your old home place again. We'll be moving shortly."

lawless states before the war even started. Things could be worse after this war is over. As Federal Judge, I have the authority to appoint Federal Marshals. I will need men like you. Sergeant O'Rourke, if we live through this war, after it's over, I want you to look me up. I want you to be a Federal Marshal. What would you think about that?"

"Colonel, I would not mind being a Federal Marshal," said Sean, "There is one thing that I won't do though. I will not hunt or kill any Indians, unless those Indians are trying to kill me. Would that be a problem?"

"No," answered the Colonel, "when the war is over, troops will be sent back out to handle them, if the need would arise."

"Just one more question, Colonel," said Sean, "where is my mick friend Sgt. O'Connor?"

"He's here with the Cavalry," the Colonel said. "He'll be on patrol in the morning. That's what he told me. When they get back, he intends to look you up. He says you two are gonna own a saloon after the war."

"Yes sir," replied Sean, "we intend to just that. We figure there will be a lot of thirsty people after the war, and we intend to help them out. If I do become a Federal Marshal, I'll need a place to call home. There's no reason it couldn't be a saloon."

"Well, I wish you the best, and I hope you look me up after the war," said the Colonel. "I would bet a month's pay that your Sergeant friend will have a bottle so you two can have a toast. What was it he said? Oh yeh, here's to not getting killed."

The next day, after he returned from patrol, Michael stopped by to see his friend. "I don't know what to say that would help anything," said Michael. "You've had too many losses in your life for a man so young."

"I'm just glad to see you, my friend," said Sean. "We'll have to sit down some time and figure out where we're gonna have that saloon. That Colonel you talked to the other day, well he's a Federal Judge in St. Louis, and he wants me to be a Federal Marshal after the war. I told him I would, as long as I didn't have to kill any Indians. Now all we gotta do, is not get killed."

"You're right, young Sean," said Michael. Then he pulled out a bottle. "It's time to toast again, my friend. Here's to not getting killed."

"Yes, here's to not getting killed," added Sean. "You just never know where either one of us will be when this war is over. If you can't find me, just get ahold of Judge David Simmons in St. Louis. You'll be easy to find. If I know you, you'll still be in the army."

"You may be right, my friend," Michael said, "But I'll probably have twenty years in. I may call it quits after that. I still say that you'll be an officer before this is over with."

"Well, if they would happen to make me an officer," said Sean, "I would be commissioned, right? If I was commissioned, I could resign any time I damn well wanted to, right?"

"I'm not sure," but I think you're right," answered Michael. "Officers can resign their commission whenever they want. It's not like when you're enlisted. If you enlist for three years, then you're in for three years. Don't be tellin' me you're thinkin' about getting a commission just so you can get away from all this?"

"No," answered Sean, "I wouldn't do that, but I would probably piss off the wrong person and be asked to resign my commission."

"I don't think that would happen, my young friend," said Michael. "General Sherman likes you. You're one hell of a killer. They need men like you to help get this war over with. You'd have to piss off Abe Lincoln himself to get yourself thrown out of the army. That's not gonna happen. I know it, and you know it."

"That's probably true, Michael." said Sean, "next time we get together, let's try to figure out where we're gonna have our saloon."

"Sounds good," replied Michael. "Here's to not getting killed."

"Here's to not getting killed." added Sean.

CHAPTER SIXTEEN

T he second battle of Chattanooga was a Union victory, but it was hard fought, and casualties were high. Sean had a hard time getting his mind on his work. Sarah was in his thoughts, and as hard as he tried, he could not get her out. He was on a ridge, overlooking the battle, and picking his targets, when he got a strange feeling. He stopped firing for a few minutes to see if it was just his imagination. Then he heard a voice. "Drop that rifle, yank. I never miss at this range." Sean was in the prone position, and he figured the reb didn't know he had the Walker. He dropped his Sharps as instructed, and waited for the reb to speak again.

"Now turn over and let me see your face, yank," the reb said. "I bet yer the one been killin' all our sergeants and corporals."

Sean turned over as instructed, and as he was turning over, he drew the Walker and fired. The reb was thrown backwards. The ball had struck him in his right shoulder. Sean ran over to him and took his pistol.

"How the hell did you do that, yank?" the reb said. "I had you covered."

"First off, " Sean started, "You never had your hammer cocked. Second, you were too busy talking."

"Just what are you saying, yank?" asked the reb.

"Look, if you're gonna shoot someone, just shoot them," answered Sean. "Don't talk about it. No one ever got talked to death, unless it was some poor dumb slob who had a mother-in-law pissed at him. Looks like the ball went through. Hold still and I'll put a bandage on it for you."

"Thanks, yank," the reb said, "I never woulda dreamed a yank would be a patchin' me up after shootin' me."

"You're a Major aren't you, reb?" asked Sean. "Why would they have an officer out tryin' to find me?"

"Well, yank," answered the reb, "we're runnin' out of sergeants and corporals. Seems you kill em even if they aren't wearin' stripes. Name's O'Brien. I'm from Georgia. How bout you, yank. where you from?"

"Name's O'Rourke," Sean answered, "I'm from Tennessee."

"You're from Tennessee, and you're wearin' blue. Why's that, yank?" asked the Major.

"We never had no slaves." said Sean. "Can't see anyone keepin' slaves."

"Me or my family never had slaves either, yank," the Major said. "Just figured I had to go along with Georgia."

"We're a bunch a dumb asses, aren't we Major," said Sean. "Out here killin' each other for no good reason. Let's go get some coffee. They can kill each other without us for a spell."

"Sounds good, yank," said the Major. "Haven't had any real coffee for a good spell. Stuff we've been drinkin' been made from chicory or peanuts. Gotta get used to it."

~~~~

"You cook good coffee, yank," the Major said. "What's your first name, and are your folks from Ireland?"

"I'm Sean," he answered, "and my folks came over from Ireland. They ended up in Tennessee, and that's where I was born."

"My mother came from Ireland, but my father was a full-blooded Cherokee," said the Major. "We had a hard life sometime. Nobody where we were livin' cared for Injuns much."

"That's why you was able to sneak up on me, reb," said Sean. "Plus I had my mind on other things. What's you given name?"

"Jonathan, Jonathan O'Brien," answered the Major, "When my mother married my father, she kept her name."

"So your father was Cherokee, huh," said Sean. "I spent over five years with the Cheyenne after my folks were killed. It was a good life."

"If I'm not bein' too nosey, how'd your folks get killed, Sean?" asked Jonathan.

"We left Tennessee back in '55 to get away from the war we knew was coming." answered Sean. "When we got out to Missouri, a wagon train had left a few days before. My folks and two other families thought we could catch the train in a week or so, so we took off. Four days later, we were attacked by some white out-laws, ten of them. They killed everyone but me. I was out hunting. My Pa and the others killed five of them. I killed the rest. The Cheyenne happened along and took me in. Stayed with them for over five years. I lived with a Cheyenne woman who had a white husband. He used to be a mountain man and he taught me how to hunt and track. They had a daughter. She became my wife later.

We had a daughter, and she was pregnant again when the cholera took them."

"Who taught you to shoot?" asked Jonathan.

"My Pa at first, but it's somethin' that I'm just really good at," answered Sean.

"So how'd you end up wearin' blue?" Jonathan asked.

"After my wife and daughter died, I was out by myself trying to think, when I ran into a troop of Cavalry," answered Sean. "I made friends with a Sergeant. When they fired on Sumter, that regiment was ordered back east. I was asked to scout for them to get through Indian territory. I joined the army on the way east. And here I am."

"You said a while back that I was able to sneak up on you cause you had your mind on other things," said Jonathan. "What was that about?"

"Well. all this talkin' is makin' me feel better, so I'll tell you," said Sean. "We left Tennessee when I was twelve. I had a sweetheart then. After the first battle of Chattanooga, we got back together. We were gonna get married after the war. Not long ago, her, and her parents were killed by some dirty rotten Yankee deserters. I was out scoutin', and happened by when some of it was goin' on. There were four of them. I killed three of them rotten bastards. Blew their damn brains out. My girl or her father had killed one of them before I got there."

"Damn, Sean, I feel for you," said Jonathan. "That'd probably make me one crazy son of a bitch."

"Thanks, Jonathan," said Sean, "I needed someone to talk to. Now let's get you to the hospital and have that shoulder looked at. After they clean you up, I'll figure out what to do with you."

"What do you mean, Sean?" asked Jonathan.

"Well, maybe I'll see if you can escape," answered Sean. "Those prison camps are some pretty god awful places. You'd probably rather get shot and killed than die in one of those camps. Sound O.K. to you?"

"Sounds O.K. to me," Jonathan said, "but how are you gonna get away with that?"

"How long have you been in the army?" asked Sean. "One of the first things you should have learned is that all you gotta do is act like you know what you're doin', and hardly anyone will question it."

"That's true, Sean," said the Major, "Yer army must be just like ours."

It didn't take long at the hospital to get the Major patched up. Sean was right. The ball had passed through, and hadn't taken anything important with it. The surgeons were all quite busy, but one of the medics was able to take care of Jonathan. The medics were quite good at what they did. At times, they did almost everything except for the amputations, and probing for bullets that were near main arteries or organs. As they were leaving the hospital, some Colonel who Sean had never seen before came up to him and asked, "What are you gonna do with the reb Major, Sergeant?"

"I'm taking him back to my area to be interrogated, sir," answered Sean. "He's been shot in the shoulder, and it also clipped a lung. He's already got some infection. We need to interrogate him before he gets sick and dies on us."

"And just why do you need to interrogate a Major, Sergeant?" the Colonel asked.

"Because, Colonel, this Major is in charge of the reb sharpshooters," answered Sean, "and my unit is the sharpshooters."

"Excellent, Sergeant, excellent, keep up the good work." said the Colonel as he left.

"You're some piece of work," Jonathan said, "that Colonel probably would have believed anything you said."

"What'd I tell you?" replied Sean. "All you gotta do is act like you know what you're doing. Now after I turn you loose here in a bit, if someone asks about you, I'll tell them you died, started coughing up gobs of blood and such. Now let's get back up on that ridge over there. I'll hold my rifle on you like you was a prisoner."

The battle was still raging as they neared the top of the ridge, but it had moved some as the yanks were pushing the rebs back. "Now you just stay here and lay low for a while," said Sean. "I'll be moving over to where they're shootin'. You should be able to slip back to your own lines if you're careful. Bein' part Cherokee should help you with that."

"Thanks, Sean," said Jonathan, "I hope we don't ever hafta look down our sights at each other again. Maybe we'll run into each other after this mess is over with. Could be sooner than we might think. After Vicksburg and Gettysburg, it'll all be goin' yer way. Take care of yourself. You're a good man, yank. Never thought I'd be sayin' that."

"You're a good man too, reb," said Sean. "Now don't be gettin' yourself captured. Now I better git."

Sean got himself back into the battle. He hoped Jonathan would slip away without any trouble. Every time he squeezed the trigger, he said to himself, "How many more do I have to kill to get this over with?" The firing on both sides showed no signs of slowing down. Sean reached into his ammunition pouch and discovered it was empty. "Where's your head, mister?" he said to himself. "You always keep track of your ammunition. You're starting to slip some. Well, go get yourself some more ammunition, before another reb slips up on you while you're feeling sorry for yourself."

Sean worked his way back to the supply wagons, and was ready to head back out, when the division commander spotted him. "Is that you, Sergeant O'Rourke?" he asked.

"Yes, General, I'm Sergeant O'Rourke," Sean answered.

"Sergeant, Captain Jones has been seriously wounded," the Colonel started. "Even if he lives, his military career will be over. He's already been shipped out to a good hospital. You are now Captain O'Rourke."

"Are you sure you can do that, I mean can you really make me a Captain?" asked Sean.

"I'm a damn General, son," he answered. "I can do any damn thing I please. That's what General Sherman said anyway. Just how old are you, son?"

"I'll be 19 come October, sir," answered Sean.

"Well, I can't be sure, but I'd say you were the youngest Captain in the whole Union Army." the General said. "Now go take care of your men."

"Yes sir," replied Sean, and then he headed back toward the battle.

As he was working his way back, a troop of cavalry passed him. Who was at the head of the column? None other than Michael O'Rourke. He noticed Sean right off. "I'll be looking you up as soon as we get done here, young Sean," Michael said. "We'll be needin' to have another toast."

The battle finally ended. Pickets were stationed, and positions were fortified for the night. When the sharpshooters all got to their area, Sean informed them about Captain Jones, and that he was now their Captain. The men had no objections. They knew Sean to be a good leader, and he would make sure their needs were covered. Then Sean asked them, "I need to know which two of you are the most senior men here. The men kind of just looked at each other, then talked among themselves. Then one of them came forward. "We are sir, I'm Downs, and that one over there is Smith," he said, "I've been here maybe a month more'n him."

"Well," said Sean, "you are now Sergeant Downs, and he's Corporal Smith."

"But what if I don't wanna be no Sergeant?" asked Downs.

"I didn't hear anyone ask you, soldier," answered Sean. "Now you make sure the men get more ammunition, and get fed, then get all the sleep they can. I do not know what's happening tomorrow. Maybe the rebs will counterattack. Make sure we're ready."

Michael found his way to Sean's area right before dark. "And how are you this day, my young friend?" asked Sean.

"Your young friend is now a Captain," said Sean. "The Captain is fine, but Sean needs that toast. I hope you have something for us."

"You should know me by now," Michael said. "I can find it where there is none. Now that you're an officer, you'll be needin' this on a more regular basis. You'll be the one writin' the letters for the one's who get killed and wounded. Wouldn't want that job for no amount of money. I told you that you were gonna end up bein' an officer."

"I just hope that Captain Jones lives and he's not stuck in a chair the rest of his life," said Sean. "I didn't get to see him before he was sent out. He was a good man."

"I'm sure he was and still is," added Michael, "now we'll have our toast. Here's to not getting killed."

"Yes, here's to not getting killed," added Sean. "Let's have one more. You just never know when we'll see each other again. I've heard that Sherman wants to go after Atlanta, and the rebs want to keep us fightin' up here in Tennessee."

"Well now that you're an officer," started Michael. "you may get to know some of this stuff before the rest of us lowly enlisted men. Just kidding, my friend. Now let's take that drink. I gotta be gettin' back and make sure my new young Lieutenant is doin' his duties. I hate breakin' in a new man. Here's to us,"

"Yes, here's to us," added Sean. They had their drinks, then said their goodbyes. Michael went back to his unit, and Sean went into his tent and fell fast asleep.

Next morning when Sean got up, he was amazed at how well he had slept. "I guess being a Captain's not much different from what I've been doing already," he said to himself. "I thought I'd be up all night worryin' about it."

CHAPTER SEVENTEEN

T he war kept grinding on, one battle after another. The South kept losing. "How in the hell can they keep going?" Sean thought after each battle. The scuttlebutt ended up being correct. The rebs wanted to keep the yanks up in Tennessee to keep them away from Atlanta. Atlanta was a major rail center for the South, and if it was taken, it would be a major disaster. Sherman wanted Atlanta, so he took part of his army and headed that way, and left part of his army to fight in Tennessee. Sean and his unit went with Sherman.

A lot of Sherman's men were armed with the new Spenser repeating rifles, seven shots without reloading. Sean didn't see how anything could stop them now. He was right. There were a series of battles, but the outcome was evident before they even started. Then they reached Atlanta. It became a siege. Sean's men had it pretty easy when the siege started. They basically took themselves advantageous positions, and waited for someone to get careless and expose themselves just long enough for a clean shot. Artillery barrages on the reb positions seemed endless.

One morning during Officer's Call, after the siege had been going on for a few days, General Sherman asked Sean to meet with him in his quarters. Sean reported to him as requested.

"Captain O'Rourke, my aide, Major Woods was badly wounded two days ago." the General said. "I need a new aide. I want you to be my aide, Captain. You've been one hell of a soldier, and a damn good officer. I need you."

"What about the sharpshooters, General?" Sean asked. "Will we get another officer for them?"

"That's why I like you, O'Rourke," Sherman said. "You care about your men. Yes, we'll get them another officer. Is there a man in the unit who you would consider promoting?"

Yes sir," answered Sean. "Sergeant Downs would do just fine. Will we make him a Captain like they did me?"

"No," Sherman answered, "We'll just make him a Lieutenant. We made you a Captain because you had a world of experience. So, O'Rourke, you'll be my aide?"

"Yes General," answered Sean, "I'd be proud to be your aide."

"Good," said the General, "you are now a Major."

~~~~

The next day, after Officer's Call, Sean noticed that one of the other officers was carrying a newspaper. He could make out part of the headline. It read, "Cheyenne Defeated at Sand Creek". After the meeting, Sean asked the officer if he could borrow his paper just long enough to read the article. The officer let Sean read the article. "The Cheyenne, under their Chief, Black Kettle, were defeated at Sand Creek by a unit of Colorado Volunteers." Then it went on to say what a great victory it was and how many of the hostiles had been killed. Sean returned the paper, then tried to find out if anyone would be able to tell him what really happened, and would there be a casualty list for the hostiles? There were always reporters who followed the army around. Maybe one of them would know. The first reporter, Sean asked, didn't know anything other than what he had read in that same paper. The second reporter said that he heard that the Colorado Volunteers had massacred a bunch of women and children, and that Black Kettle had raised a white or an American flag and the volunteers just ignored it. He'd also heard that most of the braves were out hunting when this happened. He also suggested that Sean check with General Sherman's Adjutant. Maybe he would know something or could find out.

Sherman's Adjutant was a full bird Colonel. Sean tracked him down and requested permission to speak with him. "Yes, Major," the Colonel said, "what is it I can help you with?"

"Colonel," started Sean, "I read a newspaper article about a fight with the Cheyenne at a place called Sand Creek. I was wondering if you knew, or could find out anything about it. Would the military keep a casualty list on the Cheyenne?"

"Just why in the hell would anyone care about a damn casualty list for some damn Cheyenne savages?" asked the Colonel.

"Look, Colonel," said Sean. "I asked you nicely. Can you help me or not?"

"Get the hell outta my office, Major." the Colonel replied. "I couldn't care less about some damn red savages. Now get outta here before I have you arrested."

Sean was about half way across the Colonel's desk, ready to grab him, when he heard a familiar voice. "All right, O'Rourke," General Sherman said, "just what in the hell is goin' on here?"

The Adjutant jumped up and started to speak, but Sherman cut him off. "I didn't ask you, Colonel," Sherman said, "I asked O'Rourke here. Now what's goin' on, son?"

"General, I just read a newspaper article about a battle at a place called Sand Creek between the Cheyenne, and some Colorado Volunteers," started Sean. "I was asking the Colonel if he knew anything or could find out anything. Would there be a Cheyenne casualty list? You see, General, I spent over five years with these same Cheyenne. Black Kettle was our main Chief. I lived with a Cheyenne woman and her white husband. Their daughter became my wife. My wife and daughter were taken by the cholera, but my mother-in-law was still alive last I knew. That's why I would like to know about Sand Creek, sir."

"Sounds like a reasonable request to me," said Sherman. "Colonel, you see what you can find out for this man. That's an order. O'Rourke, let's you and me go outside here for a minute."

"Major," the General began, "you can't go around whippin' your superior officers just because they may be jackasses, even though they may be. Do we understand each other?"

"Yes, General," answered Sean, "I'll do my best to control my actions."

~~~~

Two days later, The Adjutant sent a note to Sean. Apparently, he didn't want to see Sean face to face. The note was as follows: As per your request, no existing casualty list for Cheyenne. Casualties, 100–150, mostly women and children, Official Investigation in progress. At least that was something thought Sean. "I'll probably never know if Blue Swan or Braddock are still alive," he said to himself.

Every once in a while, the rebs would send an artillery barrage at some of the Yankee positions, probably just to let them know they were not quite ready to give up. One day, right after one of these barrages, something happened to Sean that had never happened so far during the war. He got a letter. A young soldier brought it to him proudly. "Look Major, that letter's followed you all over the place." he said. "It was written when you were still a Sergeant. Glad you finally got it." Then he was on his way.

The letter was from Sarah. It was postmarked three weeks before she was killed. "Should I read this or not?" Sean thought. "It took me forever to get may head back on straight after she was killed. Will reading this letter make me crazy?"

After a several hour debate with himself, Sean decided to read the letter. He sat down next to a cook fire, laid his Sharps across his lap, and opened the letter. It began:

My Dearest Sean,
Apparently our letters have not reached each other. I miss you terribly. I cannot wait for you to hold me in your arms again and love me.

Sean was so mesmerized by the letter, that he failed to hear the incoming barrage. An exploding shell landed not far in front of Sean, and sent him flying through the air. He was thrown about fifteen feet and then slammed into a huge oak tree. He was ten feet off the ground when he fell downward. His head smacked into a huge rock when he landed.

Sean had been unconscious for several hours when he finally came to at the hospital. "Where's my letter, where's my letter?" he kept saying. A young soldier came over to him and asked if he could help him in any way. "I had a letter," said Sean. "I had a letter with me when the barrage started. Where is it?"

"There was no letter with you when you were brought here," said the soldier. "It was probably burned in the explosion. There was a Lieutenant here that said he knew you, and asked me to tell you that your Sharps and your Walker were totally destroyed. He said the Sharps looked like the rim of a wagon wheel, and they could only find a few pieces of the Walker."

"Well, are you gonna tell me what's goin' on with me now," asked Sean.

"Yes, Major, I will," the soldier said. "I'm the one who took care of you. Your upper left arm is broken. It was a clean break and should heal well. You took several shrapnel wounds to both legs. No bones broken, but some bones were chipped a little. You took a good smack on your skull. Probably got a concussion."

"How bout my privates?" Sean asked. "Do I still have my privates?"

"Yes, Major," the soldier answered. "everything down there should still be in good working order. It'll take a while, but you'll heal up. Gonna keep you outta the fight for a while. You'll be gettin' sent to a nice hospital somewhere. You'll be sleepin' in a nice soft bed, maybe even have female nurses. I forget how to act around women, but I'd be willin' to give it a try."

"I thank you for all you've done for me, soldier," said Sean. "I hope you keep yourself safe till this is over."

That afternoon, Sean had a visit from General Sherman. "Why is it that I can't keep an aide?" said the General. "Is it so bad to work for me that my aides go get themselves wounded to get out of it. Just kiddin', son. You'll heal up good and be back before you know it."

"General," Sean started, "it was my fault this time. I got careless, and it cost me. That will be the last time I ever get careless about anything."

"Major," replied the General, "I heard about that letter of yours. Only one in over a year, and written before the tragedy. That would distract the most ablest of men. Now you get yourself healed up, and get back here. That's an order."

As the General was making his exit, Michael arrived for a visit. "What's this I hear about you bein' a Major now?" he asked. "And then goin' and gettin' yourself wounded just to get out of here. You might miss the grand finale. Atlanta can't last much longer, and Grant is keepin' up the pressure back east. We'll be havin' our saloon before you know it."

"I hope you're right, my friend," replied Sean. "I don't see how the rebs can keep it up much longer. Did you bring us something to toast with?"

"There you go again. Worryin' about trivial matters." said Michael. "Of course I have something for another toast. So, here's to not getting killed."

"Yes, here's to not gettin' killed," added Sean. "They'll be sending me to some nice hospital somewhere, maybe as early as tomorrow. I figure that once Atlanta falls, Sherman is gonna take off for Savannah. If that does happen, I might just miss the grand finale."

"Well don't you worry yourself, young Sean," Michael said. "You've been around for too much already. Look at it this way. You didn't get to see the very beginnin', so it shouldn't matter if you don't see the very end."

"Sound wisdom, Michael, sound wisdom," replied Sean. "Now don't forget. Once this is over, you can reach me by gettin' ahold of that Federal Judge in St Louis. You be careful, my friend."

As they were saying their goodbyes, a young medic came over to Sean. "Major," he started, "you'll be shipping out first thing in the morning. I hear you'll be going clear up to some hospital in Pennsylvania. Sounds like General Sherman wants to make sure you get the best care. Are you O.K. right now, or do you need something for the pain?"

"Thank you, soldier," said Sean, "the pain's not bad. I would take a shot or two of whiskey if that would be available."

"I believe that would be possible." Replied the medic. "We use it a lot when we're low on drugs. Be right back."

Sean sipped the whiskey, and enjoyed every last drop. Then he fell into a deep sleep. The next thing he knew, he was on a wagon ambulance being transported to a train station. The train ride was long and not that comfortable. They had to change lines several times before the final destination.

When they finally arrived at the hospital, Sean thought he was in some plush hotel. It was so clean. There were women nurses, and several doctors. There was no blood anywhere to be seen. This wasn't like the hospitals by the battlefields. After admiring the place for a while, Sean asked one of the nurses, "What kind of place is this? It's clean and nice, and no blood everywhere, and no one screaming in pain."

"I'm not sure what the name for a place like this is," she said, "but patients come here to recover from their wounds. Most of the surgeries have been done before any of the patients get here. They're here to get rehabilitated, either for going back to their unit, or going home if their injuries are too severe. Have I helped you out, Major?"

"Yes, you have, ma'am," answered Sean. "I'm very fortunate to be here. My wounds are nothing compared to the others I see here. I shouldn't be here long at all."

"Well if you need anything, Major, my name is Annie," she said. "Just call my name, and I'll be there soon as I can."

"Thanks, Annie," said Sean, "I shouldn't need to bother you too much. Think I'll get some sleep now."

When Sean awoke, there was a man standing beside his bed. He was using a pair of crutches, and most of his left leg was missing. "Do you play poker?" he asked Sean.

"Well I never have, but I'd be willin' to learn," answered Sean.

"Good, name's Bill Clay," he said. "I'll teach you soon as yer allowed to get around some. Got a brand new deck a cards, and can't get anyone to play."

"I'm Sean O'Rourke," said Sean. "Glad to meet you. I always thought I wanted to learn to play poker. A friend of mine and I are plannin' on ownin' a saloon after the war. I figure if a man owns a saloon, he should know how to play poker."

"Yer right there, Sean," Bill said. "A good game a cards will always help sell a few drinks, but not to me. When I play poker, I play to win. I don't need my mind all fuzzied up by any whiskey or beer. I do like my whiskey and beer, just not when I'm gamblin'. I'm gonna hobble myself outside for a bit. They got some nice chairs and tables out there. Check on you in a few days."

After a few days, they let Sean roam around some, as long as he didn't stay on his feet too long. It worked out well, because Bill had him outside in the nice chairs learning to play poker. Sean learned fast. They didn't have any money to play with, so Annie got them an assortment of buttons. They used them as if they were poker chips. This size was worth this much, and so on. They played stud and draw.

"Now that you know the basics," said Bill, "you need to learn how to bet properly. How to bluff, and when to fold. Some men are easy to read, some are not. Take's time and practice. Some people cheat. Some are good at it. Some are not. You'll learn what to look for. Don't ever trust a man who doesn't keep his hands above the table. Some will try to deal from the bottom of the deck. Some will use marked cards. Others work in pairs, maybe at the table, or somewhere near, so they can see your hand and signal their partner. A lot of men use women for this. Most gamblers carry a gun or a knife somewhere on them. I always liked a small piece strapped to my left shoulder, under my coat, so I could pull it easily since my hands are always above the table. That's a lot faster than reachin' for a piece that's down on your belt. Don't ever take your eyes off the table. Some men will try to swap cards when you're playing stud. Say you looked at their hand and they had a black ten. Was it a spade or a club? Most folks wouldn't remember, they'd just remember black. Well I hope you learned something, Sean. I hear they're sending me back home in a week or so. I hope my wife doesn't miss my leg as much as I do. The real important stuff still works, though."

"I've enjoyed your company Bill," said Sean. "I hope it's O.K. for you when you get home. I'm sure your wife will still love you just the same."

"Thanks, Sean," Bill said, "I hope that saloon of yours works out too. If you get back out there to the shootin', keep yourself safe."

That was the last Sean saw of Bill. He was sent home a little earlier than expected. Sean made friends with some of the other patients, but none of them wanted to play poker. He hadn't worried about any news of the war for some time. He knew that Atlanta had probably been taken, but was Sherman about to take Savannah?

CHAPTER EIGHTEEN

T ime went by and Sean got better. His arm was healed, and there was no pain in his legs. His cracked skull wasn't causing any headaches, so it must've healed too. He figured they would be sending him back before too long, but where to? Finally, his orders came. They said:

From: U.S. Army, Chief of Staff
To: Major Sean O'Rourke

Sir: You are to report to U.S. Army Headquarters, Washington D.C. for further assignment. Use any means at your disposal for your transport.
Major General Halleck, Army Chief of Staff

Sean boarded a train that same day, and was in Washington D.C. the next. He immediately reported in. He was assigned quarters, and told that they would find him when his assignment was made. Until then, he was pretty much on his own. The next day, it was announced that Sherman had taken Savannah.

Days and days went by, and still no assignment. "I don't understand," thought Sean, "the killins' not over yet and they got me here doing nothing. I just don't understand." Again, he went to headquarters and asked if there was an assignment for him yet. There were several cavalry units that were stationed in and around Washington, so Sean went around to each one just to check and see if maybe his old friend had been reassigned and was up here. He was not. Then Sean got to thinking. "I'm getting bored out of my mind," he thought. "Maybe I'll see if they'll let me do some work with the horses. Might keep me out of trouble."

The next day, Sean went to the Regimental Commander of the cavalry unit that was nearest his quarters. He figured this way, he would be easier to find if an assignment did come for him. Sean explained his situation to the Commander. "Are you crazy, Major?" the Commander asked, "You're an officer. Officers don't shoe horses. What was it you did before you were assigned here?"

"Sir," Sean answered, "I was an aide to General Sherman. Before that, I was with the Volunteer Sharpshooters."

"You're not the one who was shootin' all the Sergeants and Corporals, were you Major?" he asked.

"I was one of them, sir." Sean answered.

"We heard about you all the way over here." the Commander said. "We had sharpshooters over here, but none of them got a reputation like you did over there. We heard the rebs put a price on your head."

"I don't know about the price, sir," said Sean, "but they were sure after us."

"How many times you been shot or wounded?" he asked Sean.

"The first time, I was shot in the arm and the leg." answered Sean. "This last time, I got a broken arm, shrapnel in both legs, and my skull cracked."

"Do you know what I think, Major?" the Commander asked. "I think General Sherman is lookin' out for you. Maybe he figures that you've been banged up enough, and he's keepin' you out of the fight for a spell."

"I guess that would be possible," said Sean. "I reckon I killed my share of rebs too. So, sir, would you care if I worked on your horses? My father was a blacksmith, and taught me everything there was to know about it. I can take off this jacket so no one will see those major insignias. I'll start tomorrow, if it's all right with you. If I'm not here by 6am, it's because an assignment came for me."

"All right, Major," replied the Commander, "see you tomorrow."

~~~~

It didn't take Sean very long to get comfortable with the horses. The army had certain ways of doing things, but they weren't much different than what Sean was taught by his father. The other men were amazed when they found out that Sean was a Major. They just couldn't understand why an officer would want to be bent over all day long, holding up horse legs, and nailing on shoes. Officers just don't do that.

A month went by, and still no assignment. There was a siege at Petersburg, and Sherman had taken Columbia S.C. The end was very near. Sean was happy with the horses. He learned which ones were knot heads, and which ones were gentle. By the time he had worked with them a few times, most of the knot heads were now gentle.

Time passed, and Sean quit going to headquarters and asking about an assignment. Finally, it happened. Sean was just finishing up the Commander's horse when some young Lieutenant came running by. "Lee's surrendered. Lee's surrendered. The war's over. The war's over." People everywhere were yelling and running around. Sean knew it wasn't quite over yet because those rebs down in Carolina hadn't surrendered yet, but surely they wouldn't hold out much longer.

Sean made up his mind what to do right then. He went back to headquarters, and asked to speak to the Chief of Staff. He was not there, so another General asked Sean if he could help him.

"General," Sean started, "I am Major Sean O'Rourke, formerly an aide to General Sherman, and formerly with the Volunteer Sharpshooters."

"Yes," the General said, "what is it I can do for you?"

"Sir," answered Sean, "effective today, I am resigning my commission. I have waited for 3 or 4 months for an assignment, and now the war is almost over. I am not needed, so I am resigning. I have it in writing. It was an honor to serve." Then Sean gave a salute, an about face, and walked away.

CHAPTER NINETEEN

S ean went to the paymaster and got all his pay. Then he went to his quarters and packed up his meager belongings, and went to the train station. It was a total madhouse there, but Sean was able to catch the first train headed west. He was bound for St. Louis, but needed to stop in Cairo. He still had money in a bank there. He had placed it there when his first unit was stationed in Cairo back in '61 when they were sent east, from Texas, at the start of hostilities. There would be several stops and changes on the way, but he would get there sooner or later. He was in no hurry.

When Sean finally arrived in St. Louis, he checked into a nice downtown hotel, and then went looking for what he thought would be the nicest saloon in town. It didn't take long. The saloon was called "The Palace", and it looked like one from the outside. When he stepped inside, it was beautiful. Beautiful pictures were on the walls, some were of naked ladies. It had fancy chandeliers, fancy bar, padded chairs and bar stools. The list could go on and on. It was late morning, and there were only a few men at the bar. Sean just stood and took it all in. A man came over to him and asked if he could help him with something.

"I'd like to speak to the manager or the owner," responded Sean, "if he's available."

"And what would your business be with him?" asked the man.

"That would be between him and me," answered Sean.

"I'm afraid you'll have to leave, sir," the man said. Then he grabbed Sean's arm and tried to lead him to the door.

"Take your hands off me, sir," Sean said. "That is, if you wish to remain standing."

The man reared back and took a swing at Sean with his right arm, but Sean side stepped him and he missed. As he was getting ready for another swing, Sean caught him with a right hook to the gut and bent him over. Before Sean could strike again, there was a voice from behind. "I'm the owner here, name's Sam Draper," he said, "Would you mind tellin' me what's goin' on here?"

"No," answered Sean, "I wouldn't mind tellin' you. I came in here and asked to speak to the owner or manager, and this boy of yours tried to escort me out the door. If this is some of your help, you need a change."

"Go over and set down, Tom," said Sam, "I'll see what this fella wants. Start talkin', mister."

"Name's Sean O'Rourke," said Sean, "My friend and I are intendin' to have our own saloon out West shortly. I really admire your place. By the way it looks, it seems that you've turned a dollar or two over the years. I would like to learn the business some, so we don't make total fools out of ourselves, and lose our shirts right off. I could work for you for a while too. Do you know a Federal Judge named Simmons?"

"Yes I do," answered Sam. "He's frequented my establishment a few times. He's a good man. How do you know him?"

"I met him in Tennessee in '63, and he asked me to be a Federal Marshal when we got back from the war. I resigned my commission right when Lee surrendered. He'll probably be along before too long."

"If Dave Simmons wants you," said Sam, "you must be O.K. I can already see you know how to handle yourself. How about working as a bouncer in the evenings. We don't usually have any trouble, but every once in a while, someone gets too drunk, or gets mad about losing at cards, or wants to get nasty with the girls. Can you start tomorrow?"

"Just give me a time," answered Sean, "and I'll be here."

"Meet me here at 7am and I'll take you to breakfast," said Sam. "I'll start fillin' you in on the place, and how I like to run it."

Sean spent the rest of that day sight seeing. Then he took a meal at a fancy looking restaurant, had a drink at a not too fancy saloon, and the retired to his hotel room. At 7am he met Sam for breakfast. "First thing we need to do is get you some clothes," said Sam. "Do you have anything besides your uniforms?"

"No, not anymore," answered Sean. "I've had nothing but uniforms since '61."

"We'll take care of that," said Sam. "There's a nice store just down from my place. They'll fix you up. You're a nice lookin' man. My girls are gonna want to have their way with you, so we don't want you lookin' too pretty."

"How many girls do you have, Sam?" asked Sean.

"I have ten girls," answered Sam. "Five of them are just for getting the men to drink more. I don't pay them a wage. They keep track of drinks, and I give them a cut. They do very well. The other five are soiled doves. I am not their pimp. They use rooms upstairs, but I make enough money off the drinks, so I don't charge for the rooms. They're clean girls too. I have a doctor keep tabs on them, and the girls do a good job making sure none of their customers have a problem. When you come back this evening, you'll see why I do so well. My girls are absolutely beautiful. I don't care if my people fraternize. As long as it doesn't interfere with work."

"How do you handle the liquor end of things, Sam?" asked Sean.

"I have a very good salesman. He can get me anything I want, and he doesn't rip me on prices," said Sam. "He comes in once a week, takes an inventory, we go over it, and the order is placed. I trust him. He's my bother-in-law. Over the years, I've had trouble with bartenders skimming from me. I've learned to keep an eye on them. You can't really count how many beers are in a keg, so you need to make sure the bartender doesn't pocket a nickel here and there. A few nickels add up. Same with whiskey. Some comes in already bottled. Some comes in barrels and has got to be bottled here. How many shots are in a barrel? Some could get spilled or misplaced. You get the idea. Are you taking all this in, Sean?"

"Yes, I am." Sean answered. "I just need to know how you want trouble taken care of. I can be polite, or I can be very firm and forceful."

"Most of the time, polite will do," answered Sam. "Sometimes, force must be used. Every once in a while, someone will pull a knife or a gun. If that happens, take them out the quickest way possible. Don't shoot anyone if you don't need to. If you see someone cheating at cards, I need to be told. I take care of that myself."

"I do not have a pistol at this time, Sam," said Sean. "It was destroyed just outside Atlanta when I was wounded last time. I had been using my own personal weapons until then. I was issued a service revolver after that, but had to return it when I resigned. I need to find a good gunsmith. I have several items I want him to make for me before I take that Marshal's position."

"It sounds to me like you know weaponry, Sean," said Sam. "We'll lend you a pistol until you can get your own. I'll see you at 6pm. Don't forget the clothes."

"Thank you, Sam," said Sean, "I'll see you at 6 and I'll have some nice clothes."

~~~~

The first thing Sean did was find a local bank and open an account. He didn't want to be carrying around too much money. He still had most of the money he got when his folks were killed, and most of his army pay. Then he went to the clothing store. "I need some nice clothes," said Sean, "but I don't want to look like a banker, or like I'm goin' to a wedding or a funeral."

"We'll fix you right up, sir," the clerk said.

After about an hour, they had Sean all fixed up. "Come back in two or three hours, and we'll have the alterations finished." the clerk said.

Sean also bought two sets of clothes that would be suitable for out on the trail, plus a big black hat.

After a noon lunch, Sean found a barbershop, got a shave, and had his hair trimmed. Then he asked the barber if he knew of a reliable gunsmith in town. "The best gunsmith I know is just the next street over," the barber said. "Got a big sign. Can't miss it." Sean thanked him, paid him, and gave him a tip.

Sean found the gunsmith with no problem. He was a middle aged man, tall, and looked very strong. "Name's Sean O'Rourke," said Sean. "I need a Henry rifle. Then I need some things that maybe you can make for me. Have you heard about Sharps rifles and some pistols being converted to metallic cartridges?"

"Yes, I know about such conversions," he said, "I've done a few. I'm Walter, Walter Black. Now just what do you need?"

"Well Walter, first, I need a new Sharps," started Sean. "I need the biggest cartridge you can handle. Then I need two pistols, at least .44 caliber, and then a smaller caliber pistol if possible."

"Just what do you intend to do with all the firepower?" Walter asked.

"I'm takin' a job as Federal Marshal shortly," answered Sean. "I intend to not get killed for lack of shootin' back."

"Well, all of that should help you with that," Walter said. "Which one would you need first?"

"I need myself a pistol first," answered Sean. "I've been without for a little while, and I feel naked without one."

"O.K., here's what I would recommend," said Walter. "For the two .44's, we'll go with Remington. The cylinders are easy to change out. You could get some extra cylinders made up too. For the smaller one, if I were you, I'd stay with a .44. We'll just take an army .44, and cut the barrel down. Are you intending to keep it in a shoulder holster?"

"Yes, I am," answered Sean.

"It should work well for you," said Walter, "plus you still got the large caliber. Now the Sharps, I can handle up to .45-120. Is all this agreeable to you?"

Yes," answered Sean, "but I forgot another item. I need a shotgun, sawed off some, and 10 or 12 gauge."

"Not a problem, Sean," said Walter. "I'll get started tomorrow. You know this won't be cheap, don't you?"

"Yes, I do," answered Sean. "I'll be needin' plenty of ammunition for all this stuff too. Once I get out there, I'll be gettin' with you from time to time so you can have a good supply for me. From what I hear about where I'm headed, I'll need plenty of ammunition."

"If you're goin' where I think you're goin', you will need all the ammo you can get." said Walter. "Check back with me in a week or so. I may have the Henry in by then."

"Thanks, Walter," replied Sean, "I'll check back in a week."

~~~~

Sean arrived at The Palace a little before six. Sam took him around an introduced him to the other help. Sam was right. His girls were absolutely beautiful. "A man would have to be dead at least five years to not know that," Sean said to himself. He knew it would be hard to remember all the girls' names, but it seemed as though most of them wanted to get to know him better.

His first night was not too eventful. There was one drunk who got a little loud, but he got up and left on his own. At closing time, the place was almost empty, so there was no one to help out the door. As Sean was just out the door, and headed toward his hotel, one of the girls, Suzie, grabbed his arm and tried to talk him into spending the night with her. "I thank you for the offer," said Sean, "But I don't think it proper for us to spend the night together on my first day here. Maybe tomorrow night."

"I'll have you then," Suzie said. "You will like what you see and get."

"I already like what I see," said Sean. "I figure I'll like what I get too. You'll like what you get too! Tomorrow night then." Then Sean went to his hotel and spent the night wondering why he was by himself.

Sean's second night was Friday. When he arrived at 6pm, the place had only a few people. By 8pm, it was almost full. "Just wait till tomorrow night," said Sam. "The place will be completely full, the bar, the tables, and people will be standing. You got your work cut out for you. It's harder to spot things when we get that full." Sam was right. About 9, he thought he spotted a card cheat, but there were so many people, he couldn't be sure. After about a half hour, he knew he had spotted one. The card player was three tables away from the bar, facing it, and there was a man at the bar giving him signals. Sean went a little closer to the man at the table, so he could see if he was armed. He was. Then he slipped up to the bar and ordered a drink as if he were a customer. The man at the bar had a pistol on his left side and a knife in his right boot. Then Sean found Sam and told him about the two.

"The card player is three tables away from the bar facing it." started Sean. "He has a small pistol in his right coat pocket. His partner is at the bar, across from the beer taps. He has a pistol on his left side, and a knife in his right boot."

"O.K., Sean," said Sam, "you take care of the one at the bar, and I'll take care of the one at the table. Get the one at the bar first."

"All right," said Sean, "but you be careful. Either one of these guys could have another pistol or knife tucked away."

The place was so crowded, it was easy for Sean to work his way toward the man at the bar. The man was facing toward the tables, and his jacket was wide open. When Sean got close enough, he stumbled, as if he had tripped over something, and fell into the one at the bar. As he was doing his fake fall, with his right hand, Sean reached into the man's jacket and grabbed the pistol with his right hand. At the same instance, he used his left hand and grabbed the knife. Then, before the man knew what had happened, Sean cracked him over the head with his own pistol.

When Sam saw that the one of the bar was down, he worked his way to the table where the card cheat was setting. He started talking to the men at the table, tellin' them that he was the owner and hoped that they were enjoying themselves. He worked his way around the table to each man, there were four of them, and shook their hands. When he got to the card cheat, he pulled a small pistol, and placed it on the cheat's forehead. "Real slow like, sir," Sam said, "you reach into your right pocket and get that pistol, butt first, and hand it to me. I warn you, sir. I never miss at this range." The cheat did as instructed. "Now, sir," began Sam, "your money stays at the table, and you and your friend are leaving town. If I see you in this place, or cross your path in this town, I will kill you. Do you understand?"

Sean threw some water on the man he had knocked out, and he was up now. The man never even knew what had happened. Both men started toward the door. A path was made to insure they got out quickly. Sean's eyes never left the two. When they were almost out the door, Sam turned his back on them for just a second. When he did, the card player turned, and had another small pistol in his left hand. Before the card player had turned enough to fire, Sean had his pistol out and was firing. The bullet struck the card player in the side of his head, and blood and brains went all over his partner. The partner then started to turn toward Sean. Sean saw his hand move toward a pocket. Sean did not hesitate. He fired again, hitting the man dead center in the chest. Sean went over and checked the man's pocket. There was a small derringer inside.

There was total silence in the place for what seemed to be fifteen minutes. Finally, someone said, "Holy shit, did you all see that? Damn, that man can shoot. Holy shit! Have you ever seen the like?"

Sam was in disbelief too. "Damn," Sam said, "you been here two days and you saved my life. Tomorrow, you check out of that hotel you're in, and move in here. I have plenty of rooms for my special guests, and you sure are special. Now we need to get the town Marshal, and let him know what happened. His name is Mike Kiley."

The Marshal arrived, and Sam and Sean told him what had happened. "Don't look like there'll be any problems," said the Marshal, "Hell, ya got over 200 witnesses. I'll send someone over to get those two outta here. Now what's your name young fella?"

"I'm O'Rourke, Sean O'Rourke, pleased to meet you Marshal," said Sean.

"I heard something about you becomin' a Federal Marshal," said the Marshal. "Is that true?"

"Yes, it is," answered Sean. "Soon as Dave Simmons gets back from the army."

"I know the Judge. He's a good man," said Mike. "You wouldn't consider being a deputy here till he gets back, would you?"

"No," answered Sean, "but I thank you for the offer. If you ever need help while I'm still here, don't hesitate to ask. I'll be glad to help."

All anyone talked about the rest of the evening was the shooting. The women seemed to be impressed by it too. Sean had six different offers before closing time, but tonight was reserved for Suzie. After closing, they went back to her place. "I've only got one question before we start, lover." she said.

"What is it, Suzie?" asked Sean.

"What do you like for breakfast?" Suzie said.

The next morning, before breakfast was even started, Suzie was all over him. "I think I'll keep you all to myself," she said. "The other girls want you too, but you're just too good to let go."

"I'm young yet," responded Sean, "there's still enough of me to go around. Now can we eat? I need to get my strength up."

"Ham and eggs, lover?" Suzie asked.

"I'm sure anything you make will be fine," said Sean.

They finally got breakfast eaten, and were saying their good-byes, when Suzie started pulling off his clothes. "Hey," said Sean, "I just bought that shirt. Don't tear it."

"Don't you worry, lover," said Suzie, I can get you another one."

Sean finally made it out the door with all his clothes intact. Today he would check out of his hotel, and move into The Palace. After checking out, he took his meager belongings, and went to The Palace. "I have three suites that you can choose from." said Sam, " They're all upstairs, all the same size, and have the same accommodations. One of them is on the end."

If it's all right with you, Sam," said Sean, "I'll have the one on the end."

"That'll be fine," said Sam, "How was Suzie last night?"

"Sam, that woman tried to wear me out," answered Sean. "I didn't think I was gonna get out of there today."

"Well don't wear yourself out too quickly, my young friend," said Sam. "The other girls are after you too. Don't forget, there's ten of them, and only one of you."

Sam was right, there were ten of them. Next came Janie, then Betty, then Audrey, then Lilly, then Annie, then Debbie, then Rosie, then Tabby, then Mary, then back to Suzie. Between Debbie and Rosie, Sean remembered to check with the gunsmith.

"The henry's here," said Walter, "came in yesterday."

"Is there a place where we can go shoot, so I can see how it does?" asked Sean. "And not upset anyone with the shooting."

"Sure," answered Walter, "I got a place just outside of town where I go to test fire all the time. I can go with you right now, if you want."

"Yeh, let's go," said Sean.

On the way there, Walter spoke. "I heard about that shootin' the other night," said Walter. "Folks said it was somthin' to see. They say you're a hell of a shot."

"Well, Walter," said Sean, "I do shoot very well, but seeing someone get killed is not something anyone should want to see."

"That's right, young fella," replied Walter. "You're gonna be a damn good lawman."

They arrived at the place and set up some targets for Sean, around one hundred yards out. "Did you ever shoot one of these?" asked Walter.

"No," answered Sean, "I carried a Sharps and had a Colt Walker during the war. Some of Sherman's men had Spencers, but I never got to shoot one of them either. I was awful busy with my Sharps."

"Well let's see what you can do with this henry," said Walter. "It won't have no recoil at all compared to a Sharps."

Sean loaded up fifteen rounds then started firing. Five rounds at three different targets. On each target, the grouping was no more than three inches. "Damn, son," said Walter, "you sure as hell can shoot. What was it you did in the war?"

"I was a sharpshooter," answered Sean.

"You sure as hell were," said Walter, "I never seen shootin' like that before. If I ever get into a scrape, I hope you're on my side. Well, let's get on back, unless you wanna shoot some more."

"No," said Sean, "I know what this henry can do."

When they go back to the shop, Sean paid Walter for the henry and said he'd check with him in a week or so to see if anything else might be done. "That Sharps'll probably be done by then," said Walter. "That's gonna be some fine rifle. Probably be able to drop a buffalo at eight, maybe nine hundred yards the way you can shoot."

~~~~

The next two months were quiet at The Palace. Business was quite good, but there were no problems whatsoever. Sam figured that word must have spread about the shooting, and how good the young man was. Maybe some of the customers came just to see Sean. The Sharps was finished during this time, and Walter and Sean had taken it out to test fire. "Damn," said Walter, "are you sure you can handle that recoil?"

"Not a problem," answered Sean, "I won't be firing shots one right after the other with this thing. Every shot will be slow and accurate. But you know, you could be right. I might be able to drop a buffalo at eight or nine hundred yards with this thing. You did good work. I thank you."

"You're most welcome," said Walter, "I hope it helps keep you alive. We'll get together in a couple weeks. I could have the pistols done by then, shotgun too."

"I'll be needin' some holsters, Walter," said Sean. "Do you handle them too?"

"I can get you whatever you want, just tell me," said Walter.

"O.K., I need a shoulder holster for the smaller pistol, left shoulder," said Sean. "Then I'll need a holster that goes on my left side so I can cross draw with my right hand. Then I'll need one for a regular right hand draw. Rig the gun belt so I can put a couple extra cylinders for the Remingtons on it."

"I'll say one thing for you there, Sean," said Walter. "You won't get killed for lack of shootin' back."

"Those are my feelins' too," replied Sean.

Walter had all the weapons done in the time last mentioned. They took them out to test fire. Walter was amazed again. He never dreamed that anyone could shoot that fast and that accurate. Sean was totally pleased with Walter's work. He actually paid him more than the price he quoted. Now all he needed was for Judge Simmons to get back to St. Louis.

It was still quiet at The Palace. That is, except for Sean. The women would give him no rest. Some of them wanted to have threesomes, but Sean wanted no part of that.

CHAPTER TWENTY

T wo weeks later, Judge Simmons returned to St. Louis. Sean was going to let him have a full week before he went to see him. He figured he'd want a little time alone with his family after where he had just been, but after five days, the Judge made an appearance at The Palace. "I hear you have my new Marshal working here," the Judge said to Sam. "I heard about that shooting all the way over in Washington. I knew it had to be my man. Is he here?"

"He's upstairs in his room, Judge," said Sam. "I'll go get him. Good to see you, Dave."

"Good to be back, Sam," he replied.

~~~~

"You got a visitor downstairs, Sean," Sam said as he was knocking on his door. "Get your clothes on and get down here. Judge Simmons is here."

"Be right down," said Sean. "Suzie, you go back to sleep. I got business downstairs. Be back shortly."

Sean threw his clothes on as fast as he could and went downstairs to meet the Judge. "Are you ready to go to work, young man?" asked the Judge.

"Yes sir, your Honor," answered Sean. "Got all my gear ready to go."

"Come to my office tomorrow around 8am, and we'll get you started," Dave said. "I'm glad you're here."

"See you at 8, your Honor," said Sean.

~~~~

"You'll be leavin' us soon, my friend," Sam said. "I'm glad I know you. You're gonna have your hands full tellin' all the girls goodbye. If you see Dave tomorrow at 8, he's gonna want you on your way soon as you get out his office. You should start tellin' the girls goodbye today, so you'll have time for all of them."

"Well, Suzie is already in my room," started Sean, "so I'll start with her. Let's see. It's 11am now. That'll be plenty of time. I can get some goodbyes in before going to work today, and finish up after. I should be done before I go see the Judge in the mornin'. If I'm goin' where I think I'm goin', I can sleep some on the train."

Sean got all his goodbyes said and reported to the Judge. "First thing we gotta do, is get you sworn in," said the Judge. Sean was sworn in and they got right down to business. "You understand that you are a Federal Marshal. You answer to no one but me, or one of my superiors. Your territory is anywhere in the United States, ex-Confederate States included, and all our territories, and the Indian Nations. Where I am sending you, there is hardly any law, very few jails, no judges, no courts. You will be by yourself. How you do things, is up to you. I am sending you after the most wanted criminals. These are not men who go to Sunday school picnics. They kill just to be killing. They rape. They steal. They rob. They burn. These men will not surrender peacefully. If you do capture someone, what you do is up to you. As I said, there are very few jails, no courts or judges out there. It's doubtful that any of them could be taken alive anyway. You will be paid $50 a month, plus expenses. You can keep any reward if you want. You will begin along the Kansas, Missouri border. There were a lot of border gangs there even before the war. Some of them left for Texas, but some are still in the area. We will stay in touch by telegraph when possible, by whatever other means when there is no telegraph. Do you have any questions?"

"No, your Honor," answered Sean.

"Very well, then," the Judge said. "We'll go over this stack of wanted posters here. Most of these posters have no pictures of the outlaws. Some of them have drawings that are supposed to be accurate. First on my list is a George Anderson. He rode with Quantrill and Bloody Bill during the war, and he hasn't slowed down one bit since the war ended."

"I know that son of a bitch, your honor," said Sean.

"How do you know him?" asked the Judge.

"Do you remember back in Tennessee, when I brought in those dead deserters?" asked Sean. "Well, that woman that they killed and raped, that was his sister. I used to beat up George when we were in school. He joined the Confederate Army when the war started, but they kicked him out. Said he was crazy. His sister told me he was shooting prisoners. Then he joined Quantrill. She told me the last thing he said when he left home was that he was gonna shoot me some day. I'll get him for you."

"That's good," said the Judge. "Next we have the Haney brothers. There's three of them, Tom, Bill, and George. They're wanted for multiple murders, multiple rapes, armed robbery. You name it, they did it."

"After that," continued the Judge, "we have Billy Samuels and Ezra Hawk. They work together. Both wanted for multiple murders and rapes, cattle rustling, horse stealing, and armed robbery. I can go on and on, but you know how to read. Just remember, we want the worst ones first. Now I want you on a train to Kansas City today. Get yourself some horses there, and get started. Best of luck to you." Then the Judge extended his hand to Sean for a firm handshake, and Sean was on his way.

Sean got back to The Palace, packed his gear, and went downstairs to leave. Sam had a buckboard, and was taking Sean to the train station. It was a sight to see. Ten women all trying to kiss Sean goodbye, all at the same time. The town would probably never see anything like that again.

Sean slept almost the whole train ride. When he arrived in Kansas City, he hired a man with a buckboard to take him to a reliable livery stable. "You're loaded fer bear, aren't you, young fella," said the man after seeing all the weaponry.

"I need it for my job," responded Sean.

"And what job is that?" he asked.

"Federal Marshal," answered Sean.

"It's about damn time," the man said. "There's been no law to speak of out here for who knows how long, maybe never. You got your work cut out for you, young fella."

Sean was dropped off at the livery, and the man wished him good luck. "Who's the boss here?" asked Sean.

"I am, name's Charlie, Charlie Watson. What can I do for you, young fella?" Charlie asked.

"I need a good packhorse, and a good ridin' horse," responded Sean. "My Pa was a blacksmith and a horse trainer. I learned all he knew, so don't try to skin me."

"I wouldn't do that," Charlie said. "With all that iron you're packin', and supplies, you'll need some good horses. You can look'em all over, and I'll give you my price. What is it you do, young fella?"

"Federal Marshal." answered Sean.

"I thought mebbe you was some type a law, or a very serious person when it comes to firearms. I didn't see no badge."

"It's in my pocket," said Sean. "I guess this is as good as time as any to put it on." Sean put the badge on his shirt, right over his heart. "That'll make someone a nice target he thought to himself. I reckon I can take it right off when the situation arises. A lawman, with or without a badge, is still a lawman."

Sean looked over the horses and made his choices. "I'll take that big sorrel gelding, and that bay mare," Sean said.

"I'll tell you right now, mister." Charlie said. "That sorrel is a fine lookin' horse, but he's not been rode much. Fella I got him from couldn't handle him. That mare'll make ya a fine packhorse. How bout fifty dollars for both?"

"That'll be fine," replied Sean. "Got any saddles and some rifle scabbards?"

"I got plenty a saddles out back, go look and take yer pick," Charlie said.

Sean picked out a good saddle, and offered Charlie ten dollars for it, and Charlie accepted. "I'm goin' to a general store and get some more supplies," said Sean. "I'll be right back."

Sean made his purchases, returned to the livery, packed up and headed out. He had the henry and the Sharps both in scabbards on his riding horse, and the shotgun was strapped to the top of the supplies on the packhorse. He sweet talked the sorrel a bit, told him who was in charge, and told him there wouldn't be any trouble. As he was leaving, he asked Charlie, "You ever heard of a man named George Anderson?"

"Hell yes," answered Charlie, "everybody around here has heard of that son of a bitch. Hangs out mostly in eastern Kansas, and holes up sometimes in the Nations. I've heard of him being in Texas, and even Mexico. He's a bad one. I believe he'd kill his own mother if he didn't like what she fixed for dinner. Good luck with that bastard."

"Thanks Charlie," said Sean. "I'll get that son of a bitch sooner or later." Then Sean rode out of town heading west, southwest into Kansas.

After he got out of sight of the town, Sean didn't see anyone for the next two days. On the third day he passed a couple of wagons of homesteaders. Sean talked to them a bit. They told him that they had enough of outlaws, Indians, and nasty weather, and were going back to Pennsylvania.

On the fourth day, he came to a small town, if you could call it that. There were four small buildings, not much more than shacks. One of them looked to be a saloon. There were four horses tied out front. Whoever owned them, hadn't taken care of them. Their hooves were in terrible shape, and the ribs were showing on all four of them. Sean tied his horses and went in. The bar was nothing more than a board laying across two barrels, and there were three very rough looking tables with some rough chairs. Four men were inside besides the bartender. Two were standing at the bar, and the other two were at a table. "Anyone in here know the whereabouts of George Anderson?" asked Sean.

One of the men at the bar spoke. "Who the hell wants to know?" Sean faced the man. "Well lookey here, Roscoe, we got us a lawman. Look at that badge. I never have killed me a lawman, have you Roscoe?"

The other man at the table answered. "No Joe, I never killed me a lawman neither. I think mebbe we should."

They both started to stand and draw, but before they had even touched their pistols, Sean put holes in both their chests. "Now does anyone else in here know the whereabouts of George Anderson?" asked Sean.

One of the men at the bar spoke. "You never give them two a chance lawman. How bout puttin' that shooter back in that holster and try me."

Sean left his pistol in his hand and pointed at the man at the bar. Then he cocked the hammer. "I'll ask one more time. Does anyone here know the whereabouts of George Anderson?"

"You wouldn't shoot a man just like that, lawman," the man said. Then he reached for his pistol. Sean let him get his hand on it before he shot him in the face.

"Now, are these friends of yours?" Sean asked the last man.

"They were till you killed 'em," he answered.

"I want their names and I want them now," said Sean.

"That's Roscoe Bailey and Joe Hill at the table, and this one here is Al Tucker," he answered.

"And what would be your name?" asked Sean.

"It's Doug Martin," he answered.

"Are you wanted for anything, Doug?" asked Sean.

"I rode with Quantrill during the war, but I haven't done nothin' since," he answered

"All right, Doug," said Sean. "I'll leave you alone, but you're gonna do something for me. You're gonna put the word out there that there's a new lawman around, and he don't take no shit from nobody. Make sure that word gets to George Anderson. Tell him my name's O'Rourke. He'll know who I am."

"Yes, Marshal, I will," he said. Then he got on his horse and headed south.

"Bartender, is your whiskey any good, or is it some home-made crap?" asked Sean.

"It's good stuff, believe it or not. Came from Kentucky." he replied.

"Gimme a glass then," said Sean.

"What about these dead bodies, Marshal?" the bartender asked.

"If I was you," answered Sean, "I'd sell the horses and guns, take the money from their pockets, pay someone a few bucks to bury them, then keep the rest. Sound O.K.?"

"Sounds good Marshal," he replied. "I also heard that Anderson is holed up in the Nations. Haven't heard where down there."

Sean drank his whiskey, got out a pencil and some paper, and wrote down the names of the men he had just shot. He'd check the posters later to see if any of them were wanted. Then he paid for his drink and left. He came to a small steam after about another hour, and stopped to water the horses. While he was there, he checked the posters. All three of those men were wanted for armed robbery and cattle rustling. A $100 reward had been offered for each of them. "I'll just go ahead and camp here for the night," Sean said to himself. "Good water here, and a couple of trees for cover in case I need them."

For supper, Sean made himself some biscuits and beans and coffee. At dark, he hobbled the horses and tied them to the trees. He made sure his fire was out, grabbed his blanket, and went to sleep. About midnight, the horses were a little restless, and it woke him. He stayed low and looked in every direction. Then he spotted someone hiding behind one of the horses. "Come on out," Sean said. "I don't wanna have to shoot you."

A young boy, maybe thirteen, stepped out from behind the horse. He was Indian. "What tribe are you, boy?" Sean asked. "And why you tryin' to steal my horses?"

"I am Osage," answered the boy. "My family is hungry. I would steal your horses and sell them for money to buy food. We never have enough food on the reservation. Agents always cheat us."

"Well son, let's get some sleep, and I'll give you breakfast, and we'll talk in the mornin'," said Sean.

"How do you know I won't try to steal from you again?" the boy asked.

"Because you don't want me to hunt you down and shoot you, do you?" answered Sean.

"I'll talk with you in the morning," the boy said. Then Sean gave him a blanket and told him to go to sleep.

Next morning, Sean gave him breakfast, the handed him forty dollars. "You give this to your folks and tell them to buy as much food as that'll buy, O.K."

"I will, white man," the boy said. "Why are you out here alone, what is it you do.?"

"I am a Federal Marshal, and I'm out here tryin' to track down some bad outlaws," answered Sean. "Have you ever heard of a man named George Anderson?"

"I have," answered the boy, "he stays on our tribe's land sometimes. I think it is after he kills someone, or robs someone. I think he was there last week. He has ten or more men he rides with. They are all bad men."

"Well, I thank you son," said Sean. "Now don't forget to give that money to your folks."

"What is your name, white man?" the boy asked.

"O'Rourke, Sean O'Rourke," answered Sean.

"I am John Littletree, I will make sure my people know your name." the boy said.

"You be careful next time you try to steal someone's horses," said Sean. "If you get caught, they'll either shoot you or hang you, boy or no boy. Is there a town close to here?"

"Yes, there is a small town not too far away," the boy answered.

"Tell you what we're gonna do," said Sean. You're goin' with me. We'll take that forty dollars and get some food, and then we'll go see your folks. Sound O.K.?"

"Yes, but some of those people won't like seeing an Indian in their town," replied John. "They will wonder why I am off the reservation."

"Don't you worry about that," said Sean, "I'll take care of any problems. Now get up behind me on this horse."

When they got to the town, Sean went right to the general store. "You stay with the horses," Sean said, "and I'll be right out. Just let out a yell if anyone bothers you." Sean hadn't been in the store for five minutes, when John let out a yell. Sean set down some of the supplies, and went out the door.

There were two rough looking men, rough handling the boy. Sean took out his pistol and cracked one of the men's skull with the butt of it. Then he pointed it right at the other man's face. "Let go of the boy, or I'll fix it so you mother won't recognize you," said Sean.

The man then saw Sean's badge. "Wearin' that badge don't give you the right to interfere with folks," he said. "Take that gun outta my face, and I'll give you a good beatin'."

Sean put the pistol back in his holster, and got right in the man's face. "Come on, you son of a bitch," yelled Sean. "Gimme that beatin'."

The man reared back with his right arm to take a swing at Sean, but as he was raring back, Sean hit him in the nose with a left jab. Blood went flying everywhere."

"You broke my nose, you bastard. You broke my damn nose," the man yelled. "I'll break you in two for that."

"Come on, you wind bag," replied Sean, "Come on and break me in two."

The man reared his right arm back again to take a swing. Sean let him take the swing, but side stepped him, and then Sean gave him a right in the gut, bending him over. Then Sean gave him a right uppercut that sent him flat on his back. About this time, the one that Sean had pistol-whipped was coming to, and was coming toward Sean. Sean turned around and caught him with a right hook that sent him sideways. As the man was falling sideways, Sean gave him a tremendous right to the jaw. Sean heard the jaw-bone snap. Both men were down and unconscious. There were a few spectators, but none of them offered to help the two men.

"Well, John," said Sean, "I'll finish gettin' them supplies now." When Sean finished buying the supplies, he realized that he had too much for the packhorse to carry. "We'll go down to the livery, and I'll get us another horse to help carry all this stuff. I can sell that horse later."

There wasn't much of a selection at the livery, but Sean bought an older bay gelding. "He'll be alright," said Sean, "probably got five, maybe six good years left in him." Sean only paid ten dollars for him.

They headed south and were just out of town when the boy asked Sean. "Where did you learn to fight like that? I have seen fights before, but not like that."

"My Pa taught me when I was very young," answered Sean. "He always said a man should be able to take care of himself. Don't go lookin' for trouble, but don't run from it either."

"I will tell my family all that you have done for me," said John. "We will be there in three hours."

~~~~

When they got to the village, Sean was surprised. The people lived in cabins or small shacks. John took Sean to his home. John's mother and father ran out the door of the small cabin and proceeded to give John a good scolding. When they were finally done yelling at John, John spoke up and told them all that had happened, including the part about trying to steal Sean's horse. Then, his parents gave some more harsh words. Then they thanked Sean for bringing their son home.

"I'm Sean O'Rourke. I got you some supplies on that bay gelding there," said Sean. "Should help you out for a while. John was tellin' me that the agent here is a cheat. Is that true?"

"Yes it is," answered his father. "He's getting rich by cheatin' us, and no one can or will do anything about it. Please excuse me. I am sorry for being rude. It is not polite when you do not introduce yourself when you are meeting someone for the first time. I am also called John Littletree and my wife is Martha."

"I'll go have a talk with that agent before I leave," said Sean. "I think I can persuade him to be a little more honest."

"From what my son has told us, you can be a very good persuader," said John.

"Well. I want something from you in return," said Sean.

"What is it I can do for you?" asked John.

"Your son told me that an outlaw named George Anderson and his gang hideout on this reservation at times," said Sean. "I'd like for you or someone here to tell me where you think their hideout may be."

"This Anderson and his gang are very bad men," started John. "We have our own police force here, but they do not mess with them because they have too many men and too many guns. I will help you find their hideout. We'll get started right after we have a meal."

As they were preparing to head out, Sean asked John. "Do you have a rifle that you can bring just in case we get into trouble?"

"I have this '63 Springfield," John answered. "It's beat up some, but it's accurate."

"Tell you what John," Sean said. "I'll let you carry my henry and some extra ammunition." Then Sean handed the henry to John. He could tell by the look on John's face that he was totally amazed."

"I have heard of rifles like this," John said, "but I have never seen one. I have heard that it holds fifteen bullets. Is that true?"

"Yes it is," answered Sean. Then Sean showed John how to load and work the lever.

Three hours later, they found the hideout. It was down in a valley beside a small stream. There were plenty of trees for cover. There were two small cabins, a shelter and a corral for horses. There was no one there. They waited a while, then went down to the cabins. The sign showed that they had been gone around a week. "Probably back up in Kansas now," said Sean.

"Well, now you know where they hide," said John. "Maybe you can set a trap for him another time."

"Tell you what I'm gonna do, John," Sean said. "I'm gonna burn everything down. Then I'm gonna leave Anderson a note telling him that I did it. I want that son of a bitch to know who did it. It'll make him crazy lookin' over his shoulder all the time expectin' to see someone. He's been gettin' away with everything all this time. He's not used to someone coming after him."

When the fires were finally out, Sean put notes all over the place for Anderson to see. Some notes, he put in pouches, so if it rained on them, they wouldn't get ruined. Then they went back to John's place.

"I'll be leavin' now," Sean said. "I thank you for your help. I'll stop off and have a word with that agent too. You keep that bay gelding. Only cost me ten bucks anyway. If you ever need my help, I can be reached through Judge David Simmons in St. Louis. He's my boss and a Federal Judge. I keep in contact with him when I can. He would find me if you needed me."

"You are a good man, Mr. O'Rourke," John said as he shook his hand. "Good luck with your job."

~~~~

Sean found the agent without any trouble. He was a middle aged man, short fat and bald. "Just what are you doin' here on this reservation?" he asked Sean.

"I hear you've been cheating folks on their rations" Sean said. "Come to see for myself."

"I am not a cheat," he said. "Those red devils will say anything."

"Well let's just see," said Sean. "Do you weigh out flour, sugar, and things like that?"

"Yes, I do," he answered.

"Well let's just check them scales," said Sean. "My pistol weighs exactly three and a half pounds when it's loaded. Let's see what this scale says." Sean laid one of his pistols on the scale. "Funny," Sean said, "I better put my pistol on a diet. Seems it's gained over half a pound."

"Look, mister," the agent said, "I don't answer to you. Just who the hell are you anyway?"

"Name's Marshal Sean O'Rourke," answered Sean. "That's who the hell I am. Now I'll tell you one thing right now, mister. You better get these scales fixed. If I hear that you're still cheating folks after today, I'll come back here and pistol whip you till you can't stand. Do you understand me, mister?"

The agent couldn't talk, he was shaking so badly. "I'll take all that shakin' to mean a yes," Sean said. Then Sean was on his way back up into Kansas.

CHAPTER TWENTY-ONE

S ean rode north for two days without seeing a living soul. Then on the morning of the third day, he came upon an elderly man and his wife. They had a buckboard fully loaded with furniture and trunks and all their household goods. "Mornin'," said Sean, "where you headed?"

"Anywhere, but where we just come from," the man answered. "Is that a real badge on you, mister?"

"Yes it is," answered Sean. "Names' O'Rourke, Marshal Sean O'Rourke. What's goin' on where you just come from?"

"Bout five days ago, this band of outlaws showed up and just took over the town," he answered. "They killed ole Sam, the saloon owner, and Tom. He run the general store. They been doin' whatever they please ever since they been there. Some folks tried to sneak outa town, but they killed 'em. We were lucky. We snuck out this mornin' before daylight. I figure we got away cause they were all drunk."

"Would you happen to know any of their names?" Sean asked.

"Hell yes," the man answered. "There's the three Haney brothers, Billy Samuels, Ezra Hawk, and a man they call Snake

Eyes. They didn't seem to care if we knew their names or not. Are you goin' in after 'em?"

"Yes," Sean answered, "they were wanted for plenty of other murders and crimes before they came to your town."

"Well I hope you know how to use all them guns you're carryin', cause you're gonna need them," the man said.

"How far is this town of yours?" asked Sean.

"You'll be there in an hour," he answered. Then he worked the reins, and got his wagon moving again.

When Sean neared the town, he spotted an elderly man back behind a barn, probably the livery stable. The man saw Sean, and motioned for him to ride up easy. "I seen that badge of yours," the man said. "I'm Fred White, I run this livery stable. Are you goin' in after them outlaws?"

"Yes Fred, I am," answered Sean. "Name's O'Rourke, Marshal Sean O'Rourke. Do you know where they are right now, Fred?"

"I know where three of them are," Fred answered. "The three Haney brothers are in the saloon. Billy Samuels and Ezra Hawk rode outta here not a half hour ago. I don't know where the one they call Snake Eyes is. There's some whore who lives across the street from the Saloon. Mebbe he's at her place."

"I thank you, Fred," said Sean. "Now you stay clear of downtown for a spell. If you see any other folks, tell them the same. There's probably gonna be some shootin' here in just a little bit. I'm gonna leave my horses here behind your barn." Then Sean checked all three of his pistols to make sure they were fully loaded, then he got the shotgun, and some extra shells, off the packhorse.

Sean worked his way downtown. No one was out moving around. The swinging doors of the saloon were in the center of the building. On each side of the door, were double windows. Sean worked his way to the saloon. He crawled below the windows on the left side, then stood up before he got to the door. The Haney's were inside all right. One was setting at a table not far from the bar with a glass of whiskey in his left hand, and he was facing the door. His right hand was under the table. The other two were at opposite ends of the bar. Both had a glass of whiskey in front of them, and both had tied down pistols. Both were leaning on the bar.

Sean cocked both hammers of the 10 gauge, and went through the door. He stopped about ten feet from the one at the table, and pointed the shotgun at his chest. "I can kill you Haneys right here," Sean said, "or I can take you somewhere to hang. Shootin' you right now would be a lot easier."

None of the Haneys said a word. The two at the bar started turning around. Sean could see that they were starting to draw. Sean fired the first barrel from the shotgun into the one at the table, then the second barrel, he fired into the one at the left end of the bar. The Haney on the right had his hand on his pistol now and was pulling it from it's holster. Sean made a cross draw and had his pistol out and firing before the Haney brother had his pistol up far enough to fire. The bullet struck the Haney between the eyes. There was blood everywhere. The Haney that was setting at the table was practically torn in two. The one at the left end of the bar was a bloody pulp. There was bone and brains all over the bar, and on the mirror behind the bar, from the one that Sean had shot with his pistol. Sean still had his pistol in his hand, when he heard someone yell from out in the street. "I don't know who you are, mister," he said. "but I'm gonna kill you."

"That must be Snake Eyes," thought Sean. Snake Eyes was out in the middle of the street and already had his pistol in his hand. Without saying a word, Sean walked out the door with his pistol raised, and before Snake Eyes could react, Sean put a bullet in his forehead.

Fred from the livery and some of the other town's people come out to see what had just happened. "You took care of them sons a bitches," said Fred.

"Yep," said Sean, "they won't kill anyone else now. Fred, would you bring me my horses? I gotta get goin' after them other two. Should catch up to them this afternoon some time. You folks'll have to clean up this mess." Fred brought the horses and as he was leaving, the town's people wished him well. "Who was that guy?" one of the people asked.

"That was Marshal Sean O'Rourke," answered Fred. "He's a killer all right, but for what's he's gotta do, he's gotta be a killer. Yes sir, he's a killer, a killer for the common good."

~~~~

Two hours before sunset, Sean caught up to Billy Samuels and Ezra Hawk. They were down in a small valley, next to a small stream, and were setting up camp for the night. They had no idea that Sean was around. Sean tied his horses behind a small hill so they wouldn't be seen. Then he grabbed the Sharps, and worked his way to the top of the small hill. Sean was maybe one hundred and fifty yards from their camp and had a perfect view of everything. The wind was at his back, which is what he wanted. He wanted his voice to carry when he yelled at them from his position.

The outlaw's horses were unsaddled, and were tied loosely so they could graze and take water. The outlaws were about a hundred feet from their horses. Both men were sitting by a campfire drinking coffee, when Sean let out a yell. "This is Marshal Sean O'Rourke," said Sean. "I can kill you right now, or I can take you somewhere to hang. Shootin's easier."

Both men were startled for a second. "Where is he?" said Ezra.

"Hell," said Billy, "he's up on that little hill there. Hell, he's too far way. He can't hit us from there. Let's git to them horses."

Sean already had one of them in his sights. When they turned to run for the horses, Sean squeezed the trigger. The bullet hit Billy right between the shoulder blades knocking him forward on his face. Ezra kept running and grabbed one of the horses and mounted him bare back. Then he took off at a dead run. Sean had already reloaded the Sharps, and had Ezra in his sights. As soon as Ezra cleared the trees, he would fire. At close to four hundred yards, Ezra cleared the trees and Sean fired. The bullet hit him dead center in his back and threw him from the horse.

Sean collected his horses and went to make sure the outlaws were dead. They were. Then he rounded up Ezra's horse, and then decided that since the outlaws had already set up a camp, he might as well use it. The next morning after some coffee and biscuits, Sean tied the outlaws to their horses and headed north, northwest. Sean had heard that there was a new town somewhere in that direction. Maybe they had a telegraph too.

Sean was right. He came upon a town in the early afternoon. When he neared the town, the first thing he saw was the livery stable. There were several buildings. It looked like a town that was trying to grow. As he neared the livery, he saw a young boy out front shoveling horse manure. "Hey son," said Sean, "is there any law in this town?"

The boy seemed startled at first, then said, "We kinda got a part time town Marshal, at least when he's not drunk or with the whores. Are those men really dead?"

"Yes, son, they better be, cause they'll be gettin' buried," answered Sean.

"The Marshal's office is just up the street on the left. If he's not in there, he'll probably be across the street in the saloon. It's the only saloon in town. What'd these men do?" asked the boy.

"Son, this is a small town," Sean started. "In a few minutes after I talk to the Marshal. I'm sure everyone in this town will know." Sean eased on up the street to the Marshal's office, as expected, curious people started filling the street to see what was happening. When he got to the office, he dismounted and tied the horses to the hitching rail.

The Marshal was standing in his doorway looking things over. He was a tall thin man, wore a big black hat, maybe thirty, and had his colt tied down. "All right mister," the Marshal said, "Who are you, and who are they?"

"Name's O'Rourke, I'm a federal Marshal and one of them is Billy Samuels and the other one is Ezra Hawk. Both of them were wanted for murder, horse stealing, and cattle rustling," Sean answered.

"They both been shot in the back, and those are some big holes in them," the Marshal said. "Why are they shot in the back?"

"Well that's really pretty simple," answered Sean. "They were running away from me and I couldn't get them to turn around. Sharps'll make a hole like that too."

"That Hawk fella's got kin around here and they won't take kindly to you killin' their kin," the Marshal said. "Oh shit, here comes one of them now."

"All right, what back shootin' son of a bitch killed my cousin?" he said. "Where is he? I'm gonna blow his damn head off." He was a big bull of a man, well over six feet tall, maybe thirty, and well over two hundred pounds. He looked like he hadn't taken a bath in over a year. He wasn't drunk, but the smell of whiskey was on his breath. He packed a tied down colt.

"Name's O'Rourke," Sean said, "you got a problem, you take it up with me."

"Well I'm Simon Hawk, and I'm gonna kill you, back shooter. I'm gonna kill you right now." he said.

"Well just hold on there a minute. Are you ready to die?" asked Sean.

"Yer the one's gonna die, back shooter," Simon yelled.

"O.K., you dumb peckerwood," said Sean. "are there any more of you stupid sons a bitches in town today who wanna died for your cousin?"

Three more men stepped out of the crowd. Two of them said, "We're with him and we aim to kill you." The two of them were carrying Colts. The third man said, "Mister, right now, I don't have my gun, but when they get done, I'll make sure the buzzards pick your bones."

Sean looked at the town Marshal, then said, "well this is your town, get these people outta the way, so one of these pecker-woods don't accidentally shoot them. The Marshal did as told.

Then Sean said, "O.K., you three that are packing, you get over there in the middle of the street, and you with no gun, you stand over by the Marshal.

"Hey back shooter," Simon yelled, "ya got enough iron there to back shoot the whole town."

Sean was packing his normal amount of weaponry. A .44 on his left hip for his cross draw. A .44 on his right hip for a straight draw, and the short .44 strapped to his left shoulder. "Don't worry yourself, dead man," said Sean. "One's all I'll need today."

Sean had just finished talking when Simon started to draw. Before anyone knew what was happening, there were three dead men laying in the street, holes in their chests, blood everywhere, and Sean just standing there with the smoking pistol in his right hand. The three shots and been fired so fast, they sounded like only one. Not one of the three had even touched leather.

"Jesus Christ," the town Marshal said. "how in the hell can anyone shoot like that? We never even seen you draw. Holy shit! How did you do that?"

Sean then approached the last of the kin who hadn't been armed and said, "Now, Mister, do you reckon there's any more of your kin willing to die today? If so, you go fetch them and we'll get this over with today. I don't intend to be looking over my shoulder cause you peckerwoods wanna start a feud."

The man was shaking. You could see the fear in his eyes. "Lawman," he said, "you'll have no trouble from me, and I'll sure as hell tell my kin what they'd be up against if any of them feel like dyin'. Now I reckon I better take all them home to get buried."

"Hey, O'Rourke," said the town Marshal, "What am I gonna do with this other fella?"

"If I was you, and no one claims the body, I'd sell his horse, guns, and whatever else is on him. That should get him buried and then some," said Sean. "What you do with the rest is up to you. Now where's that young fella from the livery?"

"I'm here, Marshal," he said, "you want me to look after your horses?

"Yes, son I do," replied Sean. "Marshal, is there a telegraph in this town, and just what is your name? We can't be saying Marshal this and Marshal that all the time."

"Name's Ike Coleton," he said, "and yes, we have a telegraph."

Sean went to the telegraph office, and wrote a message for Judge Simmons. It went as follows:

> Judge David Simmons, Federal Courthouse, St. Louis, Missouri.
> Haney Brothers <stop> Ezra Hawk <stop> Billy Samuels <stop> Roscoe Bailey <stop>
> Joe Hill <stop> Snake Eyes <stop> all dead <stop> will pursue Anderson <stop>
> O'Rourke

"Now send this for me," said Sean, "I'll be in town a day or two so find me if there's a reply."

Then Sean figured he'd try out the saloon for a while. The sign said "Maggie's Place." Sean had never been in a saloon that was owned by a woman, at least he figured Maggie was the owner. The inside of the saloon was actually very nice, very clean. There were nice tables and chairs, a nice bar with a fancy mirror on the wall behind it. On one of the walls was a huge painting of naked lady. She was a red haired beauty, very buxom, and an hour glass figure that could give even the youngest man a heart attack. She was laying on a couch, on her right side, with her head propped up with her right arm. Her long red hair hung straight down, not hiding any part of her body except the sides of her face. The curvatures of her body were breath taking. Her left arm was just under her breasts, cupping them, but not touching them. Her left leg was down a little, just covering her most private parts. An older, bald headed man, stood behind the bar. "Welcome sir, name's Tom," he said. "What'll you have? Take a seat and I'll bring it to you."

"Thanks," said Sean, "have you got any good bourbon?"

"Yes sir, we do, best there is, straight from Kentucky. You won't find any cheap liquor in Maggie's Place," he said.

"Bring me a bottle and glass Tom," Sean said. Then Sean took a seat at a corner table so he could keep his back to the wall. The place was empty now. Probably because most folks had been outside for the shooting and were still outside talking about it.

Tom brought over the bottle and glass. Sean thanked him then asked, "Is that Maggie's painting on the wall over there?"

"Sure is sir," Tom said, "and I'm telling you, that picture doesn't do her justice. You'll see for yourself shortly."

"Tom, do me a favor, will you?" Sean asked.

"Anything sir," Tom answered.

"Could you quit calling me sir, name's Sean, Sean O'Rourke."

"O.K., Sean it is." Tom replied.

Sean had just filled his glass, when Ike walked in and came to his table. "Mind if I set down for a spell," Ike said. "That shootin' made me thirsty."

"No, pull up a chair," replied Sean. "Hey Tom, another glass please."

"If you don't mind, Sean, I'll set with my back to the wall too," Ike said. "We don't have too much trouble here and I'm really only part time law, but I still like to see what's goin' on, especially after today."

"Sound wisdom," said Sean, sound wisdom."

"Those Hawks you just killed. Well they got a spread only about two miles from town," started Ike. "The whole damn clan lives there. They can be a mean bunch. They don't cause much trouble here, but I'd say they do somewheres else. Seems like their cow and pony herds get bigger all the time when nobody's else's does, especially after a hard winter or a drought. As far as I know, there's no posters on any of the other Hawks, but I'm saying you should just be ready. I don't think any of them would face you, but you don't have eyes in the back of your head. If something starts, I'll back you up."

"Thanks for the offer, Ike," said Sean. "I appreciate it. I'll be in town tonight and tomorrow. That should give any of the Hawks time to think about dying. Now let's enjoy this good bourbon. Good liquor is a gift. It's here to be enjoyed and not abused. There's been too many good men who's got themselves killed by abusing this gift."

"Whoa there Sean," Ike said, "you're not gonna start preachin' at me, are you?"

"No," Sean said, "Sorry, I didn't mean it like that. I like my liquor and I like my women. I just don't like the abuse of either."

"Well," Ike started, "I have my problems with the bottle. It started after my wife died about three years ago. I'm doin' better now and I've never been drunk when I was needed for lawman duty. I'll have just one more, and I'll get back to work."

CHAPTER TWENTY-TWO

B y this time, more men were filtering into the saloon. The place was about half full by now. Just as Sean was getting up to leave, a red haired beauty was starting down the stairs to the saloon below. The place was totally silent and all turned their heads to look at Maggie. That was her, from the painting. Tom was right. That painting didn't do her justice. She wore a light blue colored dress, no bustle and it fit her very snugly, showing every curve of her body. It was low cut in the front, exposing a fair amount of her ample bosom. She was maybe five and a half feet tall. She went straight over to Sean's table.

"Hello, Mr. O'Rourke," she said. "I'm Maggie, and welcome to my place."

"How did you know my name, Maggie?" Sean asked.

"Because one of my girls saw the shooting, and came in here and described you to me," Maggie answered.

"How did she describe me?" asked Sean.

"She said you were six feet one or two, dark hair, hair long in the back, full moustache, medium to slender build, small waist, muscular, big hands, chiseled chin, handsome face, and a nice butt," Maggie answered.

"Sounds to me like she had me undressed," Sean replied.

"We'll do that later," said Maggie. "For right now, if there's anything else you need, just let me know. I have rooms upstairs, we have a kitchen, and I have five girls who work for me."

Sean couldn't keep his eyes off Maggie. "Are you liking what you see, Mr. O'Rourke?" she asked him.

"Maggie, a man would have to be dead for ten years to not like what he sees when he's looking at you," Sean answered.

"I think you and I will enjoy each other very much later today, Mr. O'Rourke," Maggie said.

Before Sean could another word out, Someone started yelling in the street.

"Lawman, get your hide out here. I'm Ethan Hawk. I can't take you in no gunfight, so I'm gonna beat you like you never been beat before. Now get out here," he said.

Sean stood up from the table and said, "Please excuse me Maggie, I'll be back shortly. Don't go away."

Sean went out into the street to meet Ethan Hawk. He was a big man, bigger than the other Hawks. He apparently hadn't taken a bath for a good while because he smelled bad. Sean figured they sent him because he was the biggest and meanest Hawk.

Ike came up to Sean. "I didn't see anyone around hiding so they could back shoot you. I looked all over," he said.

"Thanks Ike," replied Sean, "would you please hold my guns for a spell? I believe this gentleman and I have business to take care of. Mr. Hawk, let's get started."

They both squared off in the street. "I'm gonna rip your arms off and beat you to death with them, lawman," said Ethan.

"Do you dance as good as you talk, Mr. Hawk?" asked Sean.

Just then, Hawk lunged at Sean, and took a big swing with his right hand and missed. Sean countered with a left jab and caught Hawk square on the nose. Blood went everywhere. Hawk fell back cursing, wiping off blood. Before he could recuperate, Sean was on him. A left hook to the ribs doubled him over and then a right uppercut sent him flat on his back. While he was down, Sean didn't let up. He sat on his chest and gave him several punches to his face. First a right to the jaw, then a left, then another right, then another left. Then for good measure, he gave Hawk a few shots to the ribs. Then Sean stood up and said, "Would anyone else like to dance? If not, let's get this man some medical attention." Then Sean turned to Ike and asked, "Have you got a jail in this town?"

"Yes, we got one cell," answered Ike.

"Well, when he gets patched up, I want him locked up for attempted assault on a Federal Marshal," Sean said. "He gets out when I'm ready to leave town. He and I will have a nice long talk before I leave."

Sean decided it was time to get back to Maggie's place. As he was heading that way, a young man ran up to him and handed him a telegram. It read as follow:

From: Judge David Simmons Federal Courthouse St. Louis Missouri

O'Rourke <stop> good work <stop> good luck finding Anderson <stop>
Friend Michael O'Connor asking for your location <stop>

"That's good news," Sean thought to himself. "Michael made it through the rest of the war. We should be seeing each other before too long."

Sean went to the telegraph office and sent a telegram to Judge Simmons telling him that Michael could track him down in Abilene, Kansas. Sean had a good feeling that he would be coming here to Abilene often to be with Maggie.

Then Sean went back to Maggie's place. Maggie was there hoping he would return. "I need to eat," said Sean. "I'm gonna need all my strength for what's gonna happen with us."

"I timed it just right," Maggie said. "I had them put a steak on for you about ten minutes ago."

"Maggie," said Sean, "Can I ask you something?"

"Sure," she answered, "What is it?"

"Who painted that picture of you?" Sean asked.

"My husband, a couple years ago," she answered. "He was a good artist, but he thought he was a better poker player. He got himself shot in New Orleans by someone who thought he was cheating. I don't know if he was a cheat or not. I took our money and started this place. They keep saying this town is gonna grow. There's some guy named McCoy, and he's supposed to get the railroad here, and he's gonna build huge cattle pens so the cattle drives will come here to ship. If this happens, this town will really grow. Now you hurry up and eat. I have plans for you."

~~~~

When Sean was finished eating, Maggie took him straight to her room. "My weapons go with me," said Sean. "You won't need them for what we're gonna do," replied Maggie. Once they were in Maggie's room, they were all over each other, and clothes were flying everywhere. They did not come out for two days. Maggie had some food sent up once on the second day. On the afternoon of the second day, while still engaged, Sean couldn't keep from looking into Maggie's eyes. "What is it, lover?" she asked, "Why do you keep staring into my eyes?"

"Because they are so blue and beautiful," answered Sean. "I have been with very beautiful women, Maggie, but you are just so beautiful, it hurts. Just how can anyone be as beautiful as you?"

"You, my lover, are a superbly handsome man yourself," she said. "Now no more talking, and let's get back to business."

On the third day, they actually left Maggie's room and came downstairs to eat. Then they went back upstairs for the rest of the day.

The next morning, they were awakened by the sound of gunshots. Sean ran to the window and opened it. Two riders were galloping out of town. Someone yelled, "they've robbed the General Store. Ike's been shot. Ike's been shot."

"Maggie," said Sean, "I need to get up on the roof. Show me how to get there." Then he grabbed his Sharps.

"You're naked, my lover," Maggie said.

"That won't affect my shooting," Sean replied.

"Well I'm going with you," said Maggie.

"Well, at least put my shirt over you," said Sean, "and grab a few of those shells."

Maggie took him up to the roof. The riders were way out of town now. "Hurry up and shoot, hurry up and shoot," said Maggie. "They're getting out of range."

"Don't you worry, sweetheart," Sean said. "I'm pretty good with this thing."

One rider was a little ahead of the other and they were moving fast. "Just how in the hell is he going to hit them at this range?" thought Maggie. "They've got to be over six hundred yards away now."

Sean checked his sights, took a quick check of the wind, and began his squeeze on the trigger. The big Sharps let out a roar. Sean had taken a bead on the lead rider. The bullet struck him square in the back, passed through, and struck the horse in the back of the head. The horse and rider went down hard. The second horse tripped over the down horse and it's rider went flying through the air. Sean watched for a few seconds. Nothing moved but the second horse, but it couldn't get up.

"Let's go get dressed, and then I'll go check the damages," said Sean.

In the street, people were amazed. How could a man shoot like that. Someone decided to measure the distance. "Eight hunnerd and ten yards, eight hunnerd and ten. Just how in the hell can someone shoot like that?" he said.

Sean got dressed and came downstairs and the first thing he did was check on Ike. Ike was O.K. He'd been hit in the right leg and the bullet had gone straight through. Then Sean got his horse and rode out to where the outlaws were laying. Some of the town's people went along. Maggie did not go. She did not want to see any dead men up close. When they got to where the men were, Sean could see that the second rider had broken his neck. Sean then took one of his pistols, and shot the crippled horse. Both of it's front legs had been broken. "Anybody know these two?" asked

Sean. No one did. "Well bury them horses. They never did anything to me. I don't care what you do with them two fellas."

The rest of that day, and most of the next, Maggie and Sean
were in her room. Finally, Sean decided that he better get back to
work, and find George Anderson. "I've gotta get back to work
Maggie," Sean said. "First thing I gotta do is go have a talk with
Ethan Hawk. Then I'll be back for a proper goodbye."

~~~~

Sean went to the jail. Ike was setting inside with his wounded leg
propped up. "Let's get this man outta jail now," said Sean, "that is,
right after we have ourselves a talk."

"Hawk," Sean started, "do you know what I do? I kill people.
That's what I do, and I'm very good at it. I don't ever want to hear
the name Hawk outside of this town, or see it on a wanted poster.
If anybody I know, tells me that you're causing any kind of trouble, I know where you live. I'll come back and kill all of you. Can
you understand that?"

"This'll never be over, lawman," Ethan said. "There's more of
us than there is of you. We'll get you killed one day. We'll get you."

"You got women and kids out there too, Hawk?" said Sean.
"You go home and ask them if they want to be orphans and wid-
ows. Now you're free to go. Get outa my sight."

Hawk didn't say another word. He went out the door, over to
the livery, got his horse, and rode out of town.

"You take care of yourself, Ike," said Sean. "Maybe someday
this might be a full time job for you."

"I don't know," said Ike, "this gettin' shot stuff doesn't set too
well with me. I could be gone next time you come back."

"Well whatever you do," Sean replied, "the best of luck to you."

Then Sean went back to Maggie for a proper goodbye. "I'll be comin' back to see you every time I get a chance," said Sean. "In fact, I'll make sure I have plenty of chances. There's a friend of mine comin' here sometime, a Michael O'Connor. We were good friends in the army. We always said we would have a saloon together if we lived through the war. Well, we both made it. If that McCoy fella does what he said and gets the railroad here and those cattle pens, maybe someday, you'll get so big, you'll need some partners."

"Yes, maybe I will need some partners if that happens," said Maggie. "Now you hurry up and get your work done and get back to me. I will be looking for you every day."

"I will be back, you can count on that," Sean said. Then he kissed her and was gone.

There was a tear on Maggie's cheek. She wiped it off, then went back to work. "He'll be back, I know he'll be back," Maggie said to herself.

~~~~

Sean had not been gone for fifteen minutes when the telegraph operator came running into Ike's office. "Important telegram for that Federal Marshal," he began, "Bad doins down in the Nations. You better read this too Ike."

"That telegram is for Marshal O'Rourke, not me," Ike responded. "Now go get that boy from the livery, tell him to take my horse, and get this to the Marshal. The operator did as instructed, and the boy was on his way in no time.

Sean had been heading north, then was going to turn west, then south. He was just hoping to pick up any information anywhere he could about Anderson. When he had gotten out of sight of town, he sensed he was being followed. He couldn't see anyone yet, so he took his horses and tied them to some scrub brush by the trail, then laid down in some high grass and waited.

As soon as the young boy spotted Sean's horses, he started yelling at the top of his lungs. "Marshal, Marshal, important telegram. Ike sent me after you."

"All right son," Sean said. "Calm down now and give me that telegram. You didn't read it did you son?"

"No sir," the boy answered. "I can't read." Then he handed the telegram to Sean. The telegram was from Judge Simmons. It began,

> Anderson gang of fifteen to twenty men in the Nations <stop> Several tribal police and others killed <stop> Information came from John Littletree <stop> Littletree badly wounded <stop> Littletree place being watched <stop> Deputize anyone you see fit <stop> Michael O'Conner to arrive Abilene within the week <stop> God speed <stop>
> Judge Simmons

"Young fella, you get back on that horse, and gallop back into town," Sean started. "Tell Ike I'll be needin' to have some words with him before I take off for the Nations. I'll be wantin' to buy any repeatin' rifles that anyone has in town, and all available ammunition. Get goin' now, I'll be right behind you."

~~~~

When Sean got back to town, he went straight to Ike's office. Ike was at his desk with his leg propped up. "Did that boy tell you what I'm needin'?" Sean asked.

"Yep he did," Ike answered. "You should check at the General Store first. They don't usually have a whole lot of guns, but sometimes they do some tradin'. I have seen some beat up Spencers in there from time to time, but never a Henry. I see a few men at Maggie's place from time to time carryin' Spencers, but they're mostly just passin' through. There's not much here to keep people interested in stayin'. If that McCoy fella does what he says, this place will be boomin'. I'll be long gone before then. I'll be leavin' soon as my leg's good enough to ride. Maybe goin' to California."

"Ike, I'm sorry to hear that you're leavin'," Sean started. "Bein' a lawman is not a job too many men would want. You are right though. If that McCoy fella gets goin', this place will boom, and they'll need plenty of law. Now I'm goin' over to the store, then Maggie's place. I'll need to see you again before I head to the Nations."

~~~~

They did have a Spencer at the General Store. The stock was beat up some and the barrel had some rust on it, but the bore was clean and the action was smooth. They also had fifty rounds of ammunition for it. Sean purchased it, then took it out and tied it on his packhorse. Then he went to Maggie's place.

It was early in the day, so there were not too many people in the place, but there was one man at the bar. He looked familiar to

Sean, but more important than that, he had a Henry rifle right
next to him leaning against the bar.

Sean eased his way up to the man, staying behind him. "Excuse me there stranger," he started, "could I have a word with
you? Name's O'Rourke, Marshal Sean O'Rourke."

"Yank, is that you?" the Stranger said. "You didn't come in
here to shoot me again did you?" Then he turned around and Sean
recognized him right off. It was Jonathan O'Brien, the reb Major
that he had shot, patched up, then turned loose at Chattanooga.

"Yep it's me reb," said Sean. "Just what brings you to this
place and I see you made it through the war."

"I made it through the war alright, but just barely," he
started. "things were bad for us. Always short of men and food
and supplies. I got shot up again about a month before Lee surrendered and was in a hospital for a good while. While I was in the
hospital my folks died of the fever. I came here just to see this
place before it gets too big. I'm headin' down to the Nations to see
if I can find any of my Pa's kin."

"I'm headin' to the Nations myself," Sean began. "The
Anderson bunch is down there and there's been several killed, in-
cluding tribal police. I was goin' to see if I could purchase that
Henry. Just where did you get it anyway?"

"Believe it or not,"Jonathan answered, "I got it from the yank
who shot me last time. He'd hit me twice and thought he had me
killed. When he came up to check on me, I seen that he didn't
have his hammer cocked, so I whipped out my pistol and shot the
man. I had the Henry in my hands when they took me to the hospital. Someone kept trying to take it from me, but I assured them
that if they tried, they would be in the hospital too. I even had it
with me when they were taking the slugs out. That doctor was

sure I was plain crazy. Now, I won't sell you this Henry, but I'll be glad to give you a hand. I figure you saved my life back there in Tennessee."

"Raise your right hand, and I'll swear you in as a Deputy Federal Marshal," said Sean. After the swearing in, Sean told Jonathan to get his gear ready and if he needed anything, get to the General Store, and tell them to charge it to him. They'd be leaving right after he talked to Maggie and Ike, and he'd get the bill paid before they left.

~~~~

Maggie was upstairs asleep when Sean knocked on her door. "Maggie, it's me Sean. I need to talk to you," Sean said.

"Come on in. Why are you back already," Maggie started. "You just left not that long ago."

"A telegram came right after I left," answered Sean. "The Anderson bunch is down in the Nations. Goin' after them. I want you to be very careful while I'm gone. I don't want anyone using you to get to me, namely the Hawks, or the Anderson bunch."

"You're my man, aren't you?" Maggie said. "I'll make it a point to keep safe for my man. I may wear snug fitting dresses, but I know how to hide a pistol, and there's always two shotguns behind the bar. Now, you are my man, aren't you?"

"Yes Maggie, I'm you're man as long as you want me," answered Sean. Then he kissed her. Before they could get involved, Sean told Maggie that his friend Michael would arrive within the week. "You'll know who he is without any description, and I want you to do something for me," said Sean.

"Anything for you, my man," said Maggie.

"I want you to take on Michael as a bartender. If money is a problem, I can pay his wages. In fact, I can make him a deputy and the government can pay him. I just want him here near you in case there would be any trouble. Michael is a very good man and can take care of just about anything. Now I'm gonna kiss you a good one so it will last a while." After a long and passionate kiss, Sean asked her why she was sleeping so late in the day.

"I was trying to get some extra rest because I figure we'll be busy tonight," she answered. "All anyone is talking about is the shootings we've had here the last few days. You are very popular, man of mine. Now give me another kiss and hurry back to me."

Sean gave her another kiss and then went to Ike's office. "Ike," started Sean, "a good friend of mine will be here within the week, and I need you to give him this note I'm gonna write. His name is Michael O'Connor. You'll know who he is. He'll be the big Irishman lookin' for me. Now promise me you'll get this note I'm gonna write to him."

"Sure," Ike began, "I'll make sure he gets the note. If he's gonna be here within the week, I'll still be here waitin' on this leg a mine to heal."

Sean pulled out some paper and pencil and began writing.

My Good friend Michael,

Glad you are here. It will be good to see you again when I get back. I will be down in the Nations after the Anderson bunch. I got you a job tending bar at Maggie's Place. She's my woman, and I need you to look after her while I'm gone. I had a run in with some local trash there named the Hawks. I had to kill some of them and beat the hell out of another one. They've sworn to get me. I don't know if they would or not, but everyone knows that Maggie is my woman, and I don't want them or anyone using her to get to me. Ike Coleton, the town Marshal got shot in the leg a while back and says he'll be leavin' soon as his leg is good enough to ride. When he goes, there'll be no law there. Consider yourself a Deputy Federal Marshal. I'll have Ike swear you in when you arrive. Whatever happens, look after Maggie. I got another Deputy with me, He's a reb I shot at Chattanooga. It's a long story. Tell you when I get back, and we will toast again "To not getting killed."

Your Good Friend,
Sean

Here ends The Sean O'Rourke Series, Book 1, *A Killer For The Common Good*. Continue reading for a preview of The Sean O'Rourke Series, Book 2, *A Killer For The Common Good—Lawman*.

The Sean O'Rourke Series

Book 2

A Killer For The Common Good— Lawman

by

Michael E. Cook

CHAPTER 1

Sean handed the note he had written for Michael, to Ike, and told him one more time, "Make sure he gets this note. I have told Michael what's going on and I want you to swear him in as a Deputy Federal Marshal. I know that is not legal, but I won't be here to do it, so I'm giving you the authority. Ike, you are now a Deputy Federal Marshal. Consider yourself sworn in."

"Hey, I never said I would do this," said Ike, "I'm leaving afore too long anyway."

"Don't worry about it Ike," started Sean. "Things will not be different for you. Just swear Michael in when he gets here, and as soon as your legs heals, go ahead and resign and take off. Tell him I'll get him a badge later when I get back, unless you got a badge laying around that says Deputy on it."

"Actually, I do have a Deputy's badge," responded Ike. "I'll give it to him and if he wears it, it's up to him.'

"Thanks Ike, I'll be goin' now. Best of luck to you, and tell Michael I'll be back as soon as I can," said Sean.

"Don't go gettin' yerself killed," said Ike. "You are very out-numbered this time."

~ ~ ~ ~

Sean went to the General Store where Jonathan was waiting. "Got all you need?" asked Sean. "Do I owe anything?"

"No, I'm well supplied," answered Jonathan. "Let's get movin'."

They took off at a trot heading south. After maybe a mile out of town, Sean asked Jonathan, "What do you like to be called? Do you want to be called Jon, Jonathan, or maybe even reb."

"Well, most folks call me Jonny. Where did you think they got the name Jonny Reb? Just kiddin' there yank. Call me Jon and I'll call you Sean if that suits you," said Jonathan.

"It's a good thing you got a sense a humor, there Jon," said Sean. "You'll need it where we're goin'. You got plenty of ammunition for that Henry?"

"Believe it or not, that yank had over two hundred rounds on him when I took his rifle," answered Sean. "Never knew there was that many bullets for just one man. I've fired it several times, and it's a honey."

"That's good," said Sean. "Now what's that pistol you got in that flap holster?"

"It's just an army colt, cap and ball," said Jon, "but it's in good shape."

"Well if we don't get ourselves killed shortly, I'll get you a new pistol. One of those new conversions to metal cartridges. I got a gunsmith in St. Louis who can do conversions. I carry three of them, plus my Sharps, a henry, and a ten gauge. I bought that spencer for a friend of mine down in the nations. He was badly wounded by the Anderson bunch. I hope he's still alive when we get there."

"I reckon you don't want to get killed for lack of shootin' back, do you?" asked Jon.

"No, I do not," answered Sean. "This is a rough bunch we're after. Are you ever gonna ask me what this job pays?"

"I wasn't worried about it," said Jon, "but since you brought it up, tell me."

"I'm the Marshal, and I get fifty a month," said Sean. "You're a deputy, so you'll get forty. Plus, we can collect any reward money offered. You cannot make that much money anywhere, but it's a dangerous business. I'm savin' my money for a good saloon. If we don't get killed, you can think about spending your share."

~~~~

In a few days, they arrived in the Nations. They had not seen a living soul on the entire trip. As they moved deeper and deeper into the Nations, they still saw no one, but almost every house or shack or barn of any kind had been burned or shot to pieces.

"Who does this Anderson fella think he is, Sherman marchin' to the sea?" exclaimed Jon as they neared another burned house.

"I told you this was a rough bunch," said Sean. "When I was down here a while back, he wasn't here, but I found his hideout and burned it to the ground. I left notes all over the place so he'd know who did it. That man's hated me since we were boys back in Tennessee. He joined the reb army at the beginning, but got kicked out for shooting prisoners. Then he joined Quantrill. After the war, he didn't slow down one bit. He might be goin' around killin' and burnin' to find out if anyone gave me a hand when I was here."

"Well did anyone help you when you were here?" asked Jon.

"Yes, a man named John Littletree, said Sean. "I came to know him because his son tried to steal my horse one day, but that's another story. Telegram from the Judge said his place is maybe being watched. We'll be there shortly. When we get closer, I'll slip over that way and have look-see, then we'll figure out how to move. I hope you're good at slippin' up on folks."

"Don't forget," exclaimed Jon, "I'm half Cherokee. Remember, I slipped up on you, and I've learned a lot more since then. You shot me when I was too busy talkin' and didn't have my hammer cocked. I shot the yank who shot me when he didn't have his hammer cocked. I don't intend to get shot again."

~~~~

When they neared the small village where John Littletree lived, they dismounted, and tied the horses in a small thicket of trees. Jon stayed while Sean slipped in to see what, if anything was going on. As he got closer, he spotted some horses. There were two of them hobbled about five hundred yards north of the village, and two more were hobbled about four hundred yards to the south. Sean had his spyglass and was careful to make sure it didn't glare in the sunlight. About two hundred yards from the horses to the north, he spotted two men. One appeared to be sleeping while the other was keeping watch. To the south, there were also two men. One of them appeared to be sleeping also. Sean could see their rifles, but could not make out what they were. He worked his way back to where Jon was.

"Well, there's four of them watching the place," started Sean. "When it's closer to dark, we'll get closer and I'll show you where they are. After dark, we'll slip up on them. Try to take one of them alive if you can. If you can't, try to not fire any shots if possible. Don't hesitate. I don't wanna bury you yet. I assume you have a good knife, right?"

"Yep," answered Jon, "I got a good knife and it's sharp enough to shave with."

~~~~

The small village was down in a small valley with woods on the north and south sides. The woods were not thick as they had probably been harvested for the building of the village. Right before dark, they made their approach and Sean showed Jon the layout and the location of the men watching. "I'll take the two on the north side, and you get the two on the south side," Sean began. "Remember, try to take at least one alive if possible, and no shooting unless there's no other way. If I were you, I wouldn't use that Henry for a club. They're good shootin' rifles, but they weren't made for cracking someone's skull."

"I'll get it done," responded Jon, "now let's get movin'."

~~~~

Both men started their move. There was a half moon, so there was some light, so they'd have to be very careful. Sean moved like a cat. His years with the Cheyenne taught him well. He moved to within ten yards of the two men and they had no idea he was around. Jon had moved well too and was close to his two. On the north side, one of the men was still sleeping. He was snoring something awful. The other man keeping watch, was chewing on a piece of jerky. With all that noise from the snoring, Sean crept up behind the one who was awake and cracked the back of his head with the butt of his Sharps. The man asleep woke up at the sound of the crack and started yelling, "What the—" Before he could finish, Sean cracked his head with the Sharps also.

It was very quiet that night, and the sound really traveled. Jon had heard the crack when Sean had hit the first man, and then heard the second man start to talk, and then the crack when Sean hit him. The man awake on Jon's side had heard it also. He had his rifle up and was going to shoot when Jon came from behind and stuck his knife upward, just under his ribs on his right side and practically gutted him. The man was thrashing some, and it woke up the second man. Before he could do anything, Jon had his pistol stuck on the man's forehead. "I wouldn't move if I were you, I never miss at this range," said Jon. The man must not have believed that Jon would shoot him, and reached for a pistol that was laying beside him. As soon as his hand touched it, Jon squeezed the trigger and the man's head practically exploded. Then there was total quiet.

Lamps were being lit down in the village. People were coming outside to see if they could see what had happened. Sean waited a good fifteen minutes, then let out a yell. "Are you still with me Jon?"

Jon answered back, "I am, but these two are not, had no choice."

"Let's get their horses and take them down to the village," said Sean. "I got my two tied and gagged."

~~~~

When they got down to the village, young John Littletree was standing in front of his family's cabin. "Hey young man," said Sean, "is your Pa healing up alright?"

"Yes he is," answered young John. "We have been waiting for you and are glad you are here."

"Glad to be here," said Sean. "This here is my Deputy, also named Jon, Jon O'Brien. I want you to round up any elders you can find or any of your tribal police and bring them here. I'll go check on your Pa while you're gone."

Young John did as instructed, and Sean went inside to see his friend. Jon stayed out and kept watch. "I see you're getting better, my friend," said Sean. "I hope you'll be up shortly. What we're gonna do here may get rough. I brought you a repeatin' rifle also, a spencer, seven shots without reloading, and fifty rounds."

"It is good to see you, my friend and I thank you for the rifle," John said. "I hope to be better before it gets too rough. Our people have put up with those outlaws for too long, and we will not do it anymore. They have killed too many, and now they will bleed."

"My new deputy and I just took care of four of them," said Sean. "Two are dead, and two are tied up outside. I figured to see what your tribal police wants to do with them after I try to get them to talk."

"I'll tell you right now, my friend," said John. "We will do it the white man's way. We will hang them."

"That's alright by me," said Sean. "I do hope we get some information out of them first." Sean heard some talking outside and he knew the police or some elders were outside. "I'm goin' out to talk with your people, John," said Sean, "be back in when we're done."

Sean went back outside, and there were four men standing beside young John. John introduced them as tribal police. One spoke. "I am Tom Redshirt," he started. " I became the Chief of Police after these men killed our Chief, Sam Eagle. "We will hang these men in the morning. If you want to question them, do it before then. I will look for a good tree right now."

"Alright," said Sean, "see you in the morning. Jon, see if you can get any information outta those two, like where's Anderson, how many more are there, name's and such. Try to make them think we'll go easy on them if they talk."

~~~~

Jon pulled the two from their horses and tied them to a hitching rail and began questioning them. They must have been loyal to Anderson, because Jon couldn't get anything out of them. He stopped after a good while. He thought about doing some nasty things to them, but decided it didn't matter. They were going to hang in the morning anyway.

Sean came back out after talking with John for a while. "Well, any information?" he asked.

"Nothin'," answered Jon. "I guess they don't believe in snitchin' even if they know they're gonna die."

"Well anyway, you and I will take turns keeping watch, two hours at a time," started Sean. "Won't be long and they'll know something's wrong when those men are missing or don't show up back at their camp. I'll take first watch. You bed down over by that big oak so you won't be far away if something happens."

~~~~

Nothing happened that night. Right at daylight, the tribal police came and put the two outlaws on some horses with their hands tied behind their backs. They moved to the far end of town. There was another huge oak tree with a big limb that looked like it was perfect for the job. John and Sean stayed by John Littletree's cabin. They wanted to let the tribal police take care of things.

Just as Tom Redshirt was about to swat the horses on the rump, Sean heard the thump as a bullet struck Tom in the back, then tear through his body. Then he heard the shot. When the blood splattered from his body, the horses bolted, and the two outlaws were hanged. "Take cover," Sean yelled. "They got a man up there somewhere and he knows how to shoot."

To continue reading, look for The Sean O'Rourke Series, Book 2, *A Killer For The Common Good—Lawman* at your favorite online retailer starting in Spring, 2015.

ABOUT THE AUTHOR

Michael E. Cook was born in 1951 in South Central Ohio. After High School graduation, he served four years in the U.S. Marine Corps and saw service in Vietnam. After military service, Mike attended and graduated from Ohio University, Athens, Ohio, majoring in Psychology. While attending the university, he met his wife of 38 years. After working in maintenance for a short period, he worked as a brakeman, and then a locomotive engineer on the B & O Railroad of the Chessie System. When his division was shut down, Mike became Plant Manager at a snack food production facility and stayed there for almost thirty-one years, retiring in early 2014. He now resides on his mini-farm in Southwest Central Ohio with his wife. They have two children and two grandchildren. Mike's goal is to write Westerns that can be entertaining and believable.